R.B. YOUNG

Crimes of Disrespect

First published by Bard Owl Books 2020

Copyright © 2020 by R.B. Young

All rights reserved. No part of this publication may be reproduced, stored or transmitted in any form or by any means, electronic, mechanical, photocopying, recording, scanning, or otherwise without written permission from the publisher. It is illegal to copy this book, post it to a website, or distribute it by any other means without permission.

This novel is entirely a work of fiction. The names, characters and incidents portrayed in it are the work of the author's imagination. Any resemblance to actual persons, living or dead, events or localities is entirely coincidental.

R.B. Young asserts the moral right to be identified as the author of this work.

Second edition

ISBN: 978-1-7772533-1-8

This book was professionally typeset on Reedsy. Find out more at reedsy.com

To Audrey and Joe, for life, love, and guidance;
And to Jeanine, for support, love, and encouragement

When people do not respect us, we are sharply offended; yet deep down in his private heart no man much respects himself.

— Mark Twain

Chapter 1

September 2006

Coyote River First Nation

Sharing the river is dangerous. Though Pamela Renard knows a J-stroke from a draw or a pry, boulders and fallen pines narrow the water, and rapids buffet her canoe and its twin as if they were elm leaves. Six paddles swirl and splash. The two crews labour to keep their vessels parallel—that's the point of the exercise—but a submerged rock halts Pamela's craft cold. The force jolts her over the bow. She tumbles into cold wet, and pain hits the back of her head like a hammered spike. Screams gurgle from above the silver surface. Some must be coming from her teammates, the rest from spectators along the riverbank.

Hands tug her to the river's edge. As a teacher calls for a paramedic, the back of Pamela's head burns. Sunlight shimmers down the September sky. Chilly gusts makes her shiver. A Coyote River EMS truck arrives, and the two responders wrap her in a blanket. One dons vinyl gloves and gently probes Pamela's scalp. Silently she curses her fear and looks across the riverbank to a farm field. The smell of freshly turned soil calms her.

"Whoa," whispers the bear-like man who'd inspected her wound. He tilts one hand at the younger EMT. At the fingertips, blood coats the vinyl. "But there's no debris in there. So, gauze. Fifteen minutes."

An hour seems to pass before the junior medic releases the pressure on Pamela's scalp and removes the gauze. Wearing a fresh pair of gloves, the bear examines her again.

"Bleeding's pretty much stopped," he says. "We'll get the stretcher and take you to—"

"No, please," Pamela says. "I'm fine. So it's just a scrape. . . . I *have* to be here, it's important."

The medics protest, saying a doctor must examine her, but Pamela pleads again. They relent. She signs a waiver, and they urge her to go to an emergency room if she feels dizzy, confused, or drowsy; or if nausea or a headache develops.

She nods and thanks them but has no intention of leaving. She practiced hard in order to qualify for Coyote River's canoe team. The other two paddlers, both boys, showed their annoyance when she beat them for the *stern* position—the steering seat at a canoe's rear. Mohawk guys are so colonized, she thinks, that they conveniently forget the power of us Haudenosaunee women.

She glances at the members of Woodmore Academy's team. Two of the three are girls. Damn right, she thinks, it's about time.

Standing beside her, Melvin Brown clears his throat. With skin the colour of his surname, he's a wrinkled but fit elder along for the outing. He climbs the gentle slope leading to

CHAPTER 1

the farm field and turns to face the assembled high-schoolers. "Everybody, listen up!"

The canoes now lie on a bank of tussock sedge, and as the chatter fades, Melvin kicks one of the hulls. A sewn-on *Deadhead* logo adorns his camouflage jacket's breast pocket. Above it is a patch of the Mohawk Warrior Society's red flag, showing a fighter in profile against a yellow sun. And atop the badges, steel-grey hair juts from under Melvin's frayed baseball cap.

"This mishap," he says, "it ain't so good for Pamela Renard, the pride of Coyote River." The elder winks at her. "And you're all probably wondering why we put these"—he points to the canoes—"side by side in the river and told the teams to *stay* parallel, or try to, as they paddled."

A light prop plane, its engine roaring, passes over the assembly. Melvin pauses until the din subsides.

"Well, folks," he says, "here's my answer to that. The Mohawk are a tribe of the Haudenosaunee people, which means 'people of the longhouses.' The French called us *Iroquois*. We don't take kindly to that name. It means either 'black snakes' or 'killer people'—depending on who you ask. Anyway, a long time ago, in 1613, we made the Two Row Wampum Treaty between us and some Dutch traders. They were moving up the Hudson River into Mohawk territory. Those Dutch wanted a parent-child relationship with us, but we negotiated a treaty based on peace, friendship, and mutual respect between two *independent* nations."

From the satchel on his shoulder, he removes a wide belt three feet long. He holds it out horizontally, rawhide tassels at both ends fluttering in the wind. "And this ceremonial belt showed the idea—two sovereign peoples working as equals."

He runs his weathered fingers along the pebbly surface. "Tiny coloured beads called *wampum*. They're strung together. These two rows in purple here," Melvin taps each one, "represent the two nations, like two canoes sharing a river and never colliding, never interfering in each other's affairs—"

In a strong gust of wind, he loses his grip on one end of the belt, bends down, and recovers it. "I guess that's the Creator saying he don't like me being so long-winded."

To his deadpan look, everyone laughs.

"Anyway, that's the basics—*only* the basics—of the Two Row Wampum Treaty. Respect and friendship between two sovereign peoples. Now, to be respectful, it helps to be informed. So the reason we've set up the Two Row Exchange is to grow knowledge. Right, teachers?" Melvin tips his cap to the instructors standing near him.

"And you Woodmore Academy students," he says, "if you seen those flags flapping on the barricades when your buses rolled in here today, one of them looks like this." He raises the wampum belt above his head. "Two purple rows on white. But I'm getting off track, and trotting beside the canoes has tired me out."

Melvin returns the belt to his satchel. Looking up, he says, "Hey, Pamela, you're smart. Help me out with the history." He looks into the crowd and conspiratorially cups one hand beside his mouth. *"I read her essay for the scholarship competition. It rocked!"*

His hand goes down and he eyes Pamela. "So come on, Pam, get up here."

She starts up the slope and pauses, turns back to the assembled students. A hodgepodge of baseball caps, Tilley hats, tennis visors, and other headwear.

CHAPTER 1

"Wait a second," says a girl with shoulder-length auburn hair, her skin as light as her buff cowboy hat. She steps forward. Despite the wide brim above her eyes, she's squinting, her head tilted. "Why fly your two-row flag if you're going to throw rocks and beat people up? Because that's what's happening at the borderline with Ewing. We've tried being patient but—"

A Woodmore teacher, tall and blond, sprints to the redhead. His tense smile convinces no one. "Um, that's going on both ways, isn't it? On both sides—from both sides, I mean. " The man waves his hands at her in a vague appeal. "Look, Rose, why don't we all stick to the history topic, OK?"

"Whatever, Mr. Flynn," Rose says. "But I'm surprised they even let our buses through the blockades today." She turns and stares at Pamela. She curtsies deeply and extends her upturned right hand. A tight-lipped smile stiffens her face. "Over to you, *Ms. Scholar.*"

Nervous giggling flows through the group.

Who is this bitch? Pamela wonders, anger bubbling in her belly. But wanting the event to succeed, she resolves to stay calm, to simply ignore smirking Rose. She joins Melvin, scans the faces watching at her. The murmurs fade.

"Well," she says, "the year 1613—"

She halts, her throat dry and palms sweating. Pull yourself together, she thinks, you're a Mohawk woman! No one messes with us, nothing stops us.

She drags her tongue around the inside of her mouth, coaxes saliva to flow. "Sixteen thirteen. That's almost four centuries ago. But we Haudenosaunee have always regarded the Two Row Wampum Treaty to be still in effect. Like in 1677, it was the basis for our Covenant Chain Treaty with the British.

And again, over a century later, in 1794, it was the foundation for our Treaty of Canandaigua with the United States—"

"With the States?" someone asks. "But you're in Canada."

"Not all of us," Pamela replies. "Most Haudenosaunee are in New York State, but how this reserve came to be in Canada is another story. So, I guess that's all I had to say."

Melvin elbows her arm and turns to her. "No, don't quit now!" he whispers. "More about the Dutch."

"Oh, right," Pamela says, wishing Melvin would stop stage-managing. "Ever since 1613, we've considered the Netherlands as like an ally. In 1923, we called on Holland for support in a dispute with Canada at the League of Nations. That League was the precursor to the United Nations. Then later, I think it was in . . . 1977?"

The pause is long and the faces in the gathering show their confusion. *How*, she marvels, *can I have forgotten a simple year!* Panic circles over her like a bird of prey.

But Melvin is nodding at her. "That's right—nineteen seven'y-seven. At the UN."

"Right. Of course," Pamela says, mentally hugging Melvin for saving her. "That year we went to the UN and, again backed by the Dutch, asked for the Haudenosaunee passport to be honoured internationally. But only Holland actually does so—accepts our passport."

Confident now that she's covered the salient facts, Pamela signals to Melvin.

"Quite a history," he says. "Ain't the sunniest one."

Mr. Flynn, the lanky Woodmore teacher, raises his hand. "If I may add, I read a news article just days ago about some Iroquois—Haudenosaunee, I mean—high school students in Lafayette, New York. They used the Two Row Wampum

CHAPTER 1

to convince the school board of their right to wear their Onondaga regalia at their graduation."

"Now that story's a little sunnier," Melvin says. "Thanks, Mr. Flynn, for helping set up this whole thing. Great idea, putting some students in canoes. And, Pamela"—he turns to her, shakes her hand—"you give us some good history. Show your thanks, folks."

He starts clapping and applause builds, everyone facing Pamela. She glimpses Rose, whose arms hang at her sides, the cowboy hat hiding her eyes.

At the nape of Pamela's neck, a trickle. She reaches back, feels warm wetness. She looks at her hand. Flinches. From her fingers, blood drips.

Chapter 2

Oakville

Woodmore Academy betters any other private school in the city, whose average household's net worth ranks among Canada's highest. Pamela learned yesterday of the town's reputation, when her father mentioned it on the one-hour drive from Coyote River.

Her fingers touch the back of her head. The laceration is closed and healing, the bandage gone, and she fights the urge to pick at the scab.

She's sitting amid the cafeteria's hubbub with other upper-school girls, all of them wearing plaid kilts, white blouses, and navy blue neckties. Everyone is chatting, eating lunch. They occupy three long oak tables, one for each floor of Pilkington House. Windows fill one wall, soaking the cafeteria with daylight.

She looks outside. Across a manicured green sits a stone chapel, whose neo-Gothic arches hold stained-glass pictures filled not with Christian saints but with abstract designs. The patterns, where they allude to spirituality at all, suggest only

CHAPTER 2

flowers or birds or clouds or converging rays of light. Pamela has heard the school claims to be a multicultural, multifaith institution.

She turns from the windows and eyes Rose Molloy, the same Rose who interrupted—who challenged—elder Melvin at the canoeing exercise a few days ago. Yesterday, as everyone was moving into Pilkington House, Pamela recognized the auburn-red hair and her voice, as Rose gossiped with a couple of other Grade Twelves at one end of the third-floor hallway.

Pamela watches as a male student walks by with his plastic tray and ogles the cleavage peeking out of Rose's unbuttoned shirt. He trips on a chair leg and barely misses spilling his soup onto the tiled floor. While Pamela wouldn't mind if her own breasts were as big as Rose's, she herself would never dress like that. It's cheap. It reveals a lack of self-esteem, of self-respect.

Except for the dining-hall tables' flowery ornamentation, carved into their borders, the room is uniformly contemporary in whites and subtle greys, with a ceiling of square tiles and aluminum pot lights that would be oppressive if it wasn't so high, two storeys above the floor—an airy minimalist box, simple and severe. The space shares those qualities with half the campus's buildings; the rest were built in the early-1900s Collegiate Gothic style. Pamela researched the school's history. She pays attention to these details.

She *doesn't* know, however, anyone else at Woodmore Academy except her roommate, the elfin Amy Ling. After moving in yesterday, the two of them stayed in their room and talked until midnight.

Amy also notices Rose's bold cleavage choice when she sits next to her, and from across the table Amy gives Pamela a wide-eyed stare. "Hey, Rose," she says, wiping her mouth with a napkin. "Did you know Pam is here on a scholarship?"

"Like three days ago, on the rez," Rose says, tilting her head. "Everyone, including me, heard her speak at the canoeing shindig. So, yeah, I know."

"It's just a student exchange," Pamela says. But she thinks, *Pamela Renard, representing all Mohawk youth, everywhere*—well, all Mohawk youth from Coyote River, anyway. On the reserve last summer, Dad babbled on and on to her: *You're one of our best and brightest, and a model to your friends and your little cousins.* Every time he mentioned it, Pamela's chest tightened and her excitement about the exchange shrank. She feared that, though her friends might be jealous, her performance would be pitiful by Woodmore's academic standards.

"It's more than that," Amy says, putting down her fork. "OK, it's technically an exchange, but of how many students? Only two. You had to win a competition to qualify, didn't you? To me, that's a scholarship."

"Barely hear you two over this din," Rose says, but she nods her head, then turns to face Pamela squarely. "If I didn't know otherwise, your wavy bob would've fooled me." She leans forward, squishing her boobs against the table's edge, and motions to the other girls sitting nearby. "I mean, your skin's hardly dusky."

Pamela fiddles with her spoon. She wishes Amy hadn't mentioned the exchange. She wants to fit in with these girls, not have it separate her from them. But Rose's comment about dusky skin . . . Pamela chooses to ignore it and puts down her spoon. "This stew is lukewarm already."

Rose smiles but her eyes are hard. "Tell us more about the

CHAPTER 2

Two Row Exchange, Pammy."

"Yeah," says a shorthaired girl beside Rose. "Tell us." A silver ring adorns one nostril, and thumbtack-sized studs glint on her earlobes.

Pamela tries not to stare. "Wait a bit, and I will. In the chapel, I'm giving a speech about the Haldimand Tract."

"Whatever *that* is," Rose says, waving her hand dismissively. "You know, with that light brown hair, you could almost pass as white. Wow, from ten feet or less, I can usually spot trash from the rez."

"It's my natural colour." Pamela says the words evenly and strokes her hair, but her gut is plummeting. She just got here and the slurs have started, just as her father warned her. She scrunches her eyes to contain the rage and refuses to look at Rose. She's sick of being half Mohawk, half white—French Canadian. For four years, in the hallways of Coyote River High School, she heard the taunts of "apple" each time she walked by a competitor for boys, popularity, or grades. Now Rose is insulting her other half. Pamela turns her head and bores into the bigot's eyes. "Well, I guess you need a pair of glasses."

A sneer twists Rose's face. "And to force me to an optometrist, you're going to threaten me with a bow and arrow?"

On the far side of Rose, the girl with the nose ring sniggers and claps her hands.

Rose bows her head momentarily. "Applause appreciated, Joan."

Pamela's heart is bucking like an untamed horse. She takes a deep breath. "How did a Neanderthal like you get accepted to Woodmore Academy?"

Rose shrugs, and, for a second, hurt registers on her face.

The belligerent mask returns. "I pity the kid—Jordan Windsor, he's a nice guy—that Woodmore picked for your snooty student exchange. Poor Jordy, trapped, probably bored to death, on your reserve for a year." She shakes her head. "Let's be honest, race isn't the problem. It's Coyote River's land grab. My family lives right beside the rez, and your damn blockades—they've cut off access to my favourite riding trails, ones I helped my father to cut."

"So," Pamela says, "you're obviously from Ewing. How's things in the cultural capital of southwestern Ontario."

Rose gives her the finger. "And Coyote River's a metropolis."

"That's the *last* thing any rez wants to be."

"Things in Ewing are just dandy, thanks. Your damn barricades mean there's a ten-kilometre detour to my parents' ranch. My dad's losing money, like a lot of his neighbours. His clients are pissed off, boarding their horses elsewhere, getting their riding lessons elsewhere. If things don't change soon, we'll lose the ranch."

Pamela stares past Rose and through the wall of windows. The brittle corpses of leaves lie broken on a manicured lawn, and along tree-lined footpaths, gusts are stripping the maples, oaks, and chestnuts.

She turns back to Rose. "Think whatever you want, but the barricades aren't my fault." And they're not. Pamela recalls how, at Coyote River High, student council voted for no violence. For a peaceful protest. But the clan mothers must've called in the Mohawk Warrior Society, because stones were soon flying and fistfights erupting.

Rose gets up and pushes her palm toward Pamela's face. "Blah blah blah. Whatever, Pammy. Make up as many excuses as you want." She lays her hand on Amy's shoulder. "Got to

CHAPTER 2

go, homegirls. See you back at the dorm."

Pamela shakes her head as Rose and her entourage exit.

"Really sorry," Amy says. "If I'd known what shit was going to come out of Rose's mouth, I wouldn't have asked about the exchange."

"It's not your fault." But despite her soothing words, Pamela can't calm down. Being occasionally called an *apple* on the reserve always unnerved her. But not like this.

Beside the exit doors, a janitor is changing the recycling bins. He looks up at the two of them.

"That redhead," he says. "Last year I saw her bullying other girls. You did the right thing. Never back down from people like that." His nametag reads, *Sol*. He's young for a janitor—in his mid-twenties. With a recycling bag in each hand, he nods, then strides away toward the kitchen doors.

In surprised thanks, Pamela cocks her head and blinks three times. She turns and Amy follows as they exit Edwards Common, the dining hall. Leaves swirl across the open lawn. As the two walk the path back to Pilkington House, buttery sunlight heats the ground. They notice Rose's crew up ahead and stop a moment for the group to get further away. They've just set off again when Pamela's phone rings.

It's Luke.

"Oh, no." Pamela can't decide whether to take the call.

Last week, as she prepared to leave the reserve for Oakville, Pamela thought she might never see Luke again. His life in the gang was becoming more and more dangerous. A year before, the reserve police charged him with raping a Coyote River girl—Jane Taylor, a friend of Pamela's. When Luke came to her house and pleaded innocence, Pamela said she never wanted to see him again. But then the truth emerged:

another gang member was the perpetrator. After the actual rapist confessed, Luke and Pamela reconciled. Briefly. Jane was inconsolable, no matter how Pamela and other friends tried to help.

Linked to Jane in Pamela's memory is cousin Lillian, who a decade ago was raped and murdered, and the case never solved. Nicknamed Little Lily, the girl's physical beauty showed itself early; she only reached age thirteen. The whole extended family fell hard with the brutal loss. Dreams about it still trouble Pamela's sleep.

So, as much to celebrate Lily's spirit as to help Jane stand with dignity, Pamela organized a SlutWalk at Coyote River High School. Luke, brainless Luke, said the girl should have known better, "with *her body*, and always wearing like short shorts and crop tops." Pamela slapped his face and ended the relationship right there. She made him agree: *No phone calls, no texts.*

But Luke *is* on the phone, and he's angry. She can hear it in his voice, even over the shaky phone connection to Coyote River.

"You used me for fun," Luke is saying, "then fucking ditched me like you found something more exciting to do."

"You earned my ditching you, and you know it."

When Luke wasn't high, Pamela thinks, he could be so gentle and open. And none of her other boyfriends could keep up—literally—with her as he did, whether in canoeing, cross-country skiing, or off-road biking. The weed was OK, not something she'd do again. The sex was awkward, and she's mostly just glad she got losing her virginity over with, even if the bedroom action itself was tepid. But Luke, oblivious sexist and drug-dealer-in-training, was a lost cause with a

CHAPTER 2

dark future.

Into the shadowed entrance of Pilkington House, Rose and her troop disappear. Pamela hopes Luke is alright, that he's stopped selling or even using pot. Before she departed for her year at Woodmore, Pamela gave him no support or encouragement to avoid those pursuits. She could have tried, perhaps, but would the effort have helped? Not if the Hells Angels were pressuring him to push cocaine on the rez, which was what he'd told her. Poor Luke, a gentle soul beneath all the trouble.

Pamela wonders how much trouble *she'll* get into at Woodmore. With Rose to deal with, she's got enough already.

Chapter 3

June 2007

The bottom. Sol Fitzgerald knew his grade and hated it. At Woodmore, the other janitors held the same position, but Sol had lived his whole damn life at that level, and being a trash jockey came naturally, though not as instinctively as playing the piano, an activity which, in his teens, lifted Sol away from his rotten secret, which was also his family's private shame. Genetics, the good and the bad. In the Fitzgerald clan, especially the bad.

It was seven-forty on a Monday morning, and as Sol's work boots thudded into the quadrangle, the temperature was rising like a thunderhead. He approached Woodmore Library and scanned the building's entry. Where was Airstream Mechanical's technician? Jason something. The goddam guy had said, last thing on Friday, he'd be there by seven-thirty. At the entrance doors, Sol flipped through his key ring and was reaching toward the keyhole when he noticed them. To his right, where the wall turned and abutted a fenced garden, a man and woman lay on the flagstones. No sound,

CHAPTER 3

no movement from them.

Sol twitched. It must be a student prank, he hoped, mannequins stolen from a clothing store. Or else the pair *was* real; both of them had got drunk nearby, wandered onto the property, and blacked out. But who, other than folks like Sol, would have done that on a Sunday night?

He scanned the other buildings fronting the courtyard: the athletic centre, auditorium, and upper school. Nah, nobody hanging around any of them. Half in shadow from the low sun, the square itself was empty, the kids snoring in their dorms or gobbling breakfast in Edwards Common.

He inched nearer to the twosome. Plastic dummies didn't bleed, but these bodies were oozing. Ten feet from the wall, the woman lay on her back, left hand jutting awkwardly from under her right side. Sol stood for a moment by the body, then jerked back. He knew the person. But his brain refused to let him speak or even recall her name.

Then he swallowed. "Pam?"

A face of smooth caramel-coloured skin. Pamela Renard, her still-budding features looking more like a girl's than a woman's. Eyes staring vacantly at the sky. How could it be brainy, gifted Pamela?

Grey pulp bloated from her cracked skull, and blood had spilled through her wavy chocolate hair and over the paving stones.

Sol crumpled to his knees and vomited. Recalling the slurs and pranks Pamela had weathered, he pulled a rag from his uniform and wiped his mouth. The stunts began against her just after the school year started. And a few days into September, he had to repaint Pamela's door in Pilkington House to kill any trace there of the red-lettered racist graffiti.

He remembered yakking often, after that event, with her and Bobby in the upper school's hallways, and how the boy had put his arm around her shoulders and laughed at her jokes, even the lame ones. Pam, Sol thought, what the hell happened? Here he was sniffling, a fucking wimp, no matter how many fistfights he'd won.

Guessing that the effort was useless, Sol pressed his fingertip against her wrist. Chilly skin. He could hear the distant hiss of sprinklers on Taylor Green, the purr of traffic along Lakeshore Road. No pulse.

He turned to the man, who lay face down, three feet from the wall, an ammonia tang rising from the body. In dress shoes and a suit jacket, with a bald spot and greying hair at the temples, the body lay half over the flagstones and half beyond a low garden fence, one of the iron posts projecting from the guy's back, his tie hanging toward the ground, blood having run down the fine silk and dripped into the day lilies and yarrow. Sol felt bile rising in his throat but fought off another puking fit.

Someone whistled a tune. Footsteps sounded, and from around the corner, an entrance door rattled. "Wonder where Fitzgerald is?" said a squeaky voice.

Sol recognized it as Jason's. "Over here!"

In overalls with Airstream Mechanical stitched on the chest pocket, Jason strolled into view, his scrawny head down, his eyes fixed on a clipboard in one hand, his other gripping a metal toolbox. "Man, was the 403 ever backed up, or I would've got here sooner and—" As he saw Sol and the corpses, he dropped the toolbox, and it clattered against the pavement.

Chapter 4

To escape the Toronto rat race, Alison Downey accepted the downgrade from Detective Sergeant to Detective. Her career wasn't her raison d'être, as it was for most of the men, but even with the low profile, she feared bungling her debut case in Oakville.

She squinted through the aging GM Malibu's scratched windshield as she drove along Trafalgar Road. She couldn't stop the worry. Due to budget cuts, Regional Investigative Services had lost staff, and Norm Miller, the detective sergeant assigned as her partner, was off work with a rock-climbing injury, so Alison was working solo. If she messed up, what a wonderful first impression she'd make in the Halton Regional Police Service—as the sole detective who was both female and black.

She merged onto the 403 and headed west, then south on Dorval Drive, the air freshening as she neared the lake. You'd never smell that in Toronto, she thought. Smaller cities had their advantages. She turned onto Lakeshore Road in the vicinity of Old Oakville, which was well populated, though not entirely, by mansions on one-acre lots, with BMW and Mercedes models common in the driveways.

Last year, when planning her escape from Toronto, Alison

had driven through the streets of Old Oakville a half-dozen times, and on one afternoon she stopped at Lakeside Park and strolled down to the water's edge. To her left and forty kilometres away, the CN Tower gleamed silver. It poked above the smog like an Empire Loyalist's sword raised above cannon smoke, and she'd wondered how many of her ancestors—Black Loyalists, all of them Upper Canada slaves—had died for Britain during the American Revolutionary War.

Now, like guards keeping out the riff-raff, Woodmore Academy's stone gates loomed. The hoi polloi of Oakville, however, had succeeded in smashing some rails of the property fence, and someone had spray-painted two lines of graffiti on the stonework:

WOODMORE WANKERS
WOODMORE GIRLS SUCK MY WOOD

Beyond a two-aisle parking lot within the property, facades in brick and stone stood in shadow. Alison passed a chapel and the upper school before she noticed two patrol cars parked in front of the Administration & Admissions building, four storeys of faux-Gothic tower. As she parked in the drop-off circle, a stocky constable standing on the sidewalk waved. She walked over to him.

"Alison Downey?" he said, shaking her hand so hard her knuckles cracked. "Constable Dave Hicks."

The muscles of his bulldog neck rippling, Hicks cocked his head and gestured behind him into the campus. "I responded to a 9-1-1 from a janitor here. Two dead. Murder, murder-suicide, or a really bad accident. Scene's taped off, and I left a rookie guarding it"—he pointed along the walkway, toward a quadrangle—"outside the library." Hicks tipped his cap back and scratched his forehead. "Pandemonium before we got the kids under control. They were walking to their first class of the day, and, no surprise, a group of them saw the bodies and started a stampede." Hicks gestured toward a hulking boy leaning against the administration building's wall. "Him. Says he's the boyfriend of the female—"

The boy yowled, dropped to his knees and collapsed onto the ground.

"What's his name?" Alison said, taking out her notebook.

"The poor kid." Hicks grimaced and shook his head. "And he's the son—can you believe it?—of the male victim. Anyway, Woodmore's director has cancelled classes for the day. Kids are restricted to their dorms." Hicks focused again on his phone.

"His name?" Alison said.

"Oh, Bobby Havers. And his girlfriend was . . ." Hicks thumbed through his notebook. "Pamela Renard, from the Coyote River reserve."

She strode toward the Havers boy and was about to introduce herself when Hicks shouted, "Ident van's here."

Alison turned and straightened to her full height—six feet, in her work shoes. She took a deep breath, thinking, *Should I interview the Havers boy or walk the crime scene with the identification officers?* Both tasks were critical, but she knew that teamwork at the scene, with the accompanying flow of ideas, was better than seeing it later by herself. In her notebook, she scrawled a reminder to interview Bobby Havers soon.

As the two Ident officers took equipment out of the van, Alison nodded to them and introduced herself. Susan Roberts and Don Gatti. Roberts, tall and angular, stood only an inch below Alison. Gatti kept rubbing his paunch, and he had to look up at both women. His eyes swept appraisingly over Alison.

Her hands quivered, as they always did at a murder scene, but her apprehension didn't come from the violence or ugliness of the death. It came from the sight of a dead body. Any dead body. And every time, she felt as if she were back at the Parkdale apartment in Toronto, when she would find Kopal, her best friend in high school, lying on the pull-out bed.

Kopal had been pregnant when, disowned by her Pakistani-immigrant parents, she came to stay with Alison's family. But the Downeys' support wasn't enough. Kopal's final act of despair, or escape, was swallowing a truckload of painkillers. Alison had resolved then to do something with her own life to save girls like Kopal.

Walking now with the others toward Woodmore Library, she gritted her teeth.

Outside the building, Hicks led them past two blue-collared men sitting on a bench by the entrance, which was roped off with caution tape trembling in the breeze.

"These two workmen," he said. "Janitor and an air-conditioning technician. They found the bodies."

Another constable stood beside the pair.

Alison nodded to him. "Stay here. I'll talk to them later."

Hicks motioned for the others to follow him and walked around the corner of the building. Flies buzzed. Two bodies lay before the team, and Alison surveyed the figures. As the sharpness of ammonia wafted up, she scanned the wounds: extreme blunt-force trauma to the girl's head, a fence post

CHAPTER 4

spearing the man's chest. It came from the man. She donned gloves, bent down, and examined his pockets. According to the driver's license, his name was Ray Havers. A business card gave his job title, *Branch Manager, RBC Royal Bank*, and an address on Lakeshore Road.

Then, in a breast pocket of his suit, she found a treasure. A clear plastic bag, half full of white powder.

Alison passed it to Gatti.

She craned her neck, her glance sliding up the library's four-storey wall. "With the force needed to create those wounds," she said, looking at Roberts, "seems likely that one or both jumped. Or were pushed." She turned to Constable Hicks. "That's why you taped off the library entrance."

Hicks nodded.

At the young woman's body, Alison kneeled, swiped at the flies. She scrutinized bruises on the neck and skin under the fingernails. The girl wore a calf-length dress in a bright floral pattern, and an uneven chunk of the cotton was missing from the hemline, as though it had been torn away.

The image of a ripped shirt fluttered in Alison's mind. One evening, back in Grade Eleven, Kopal had buzzed from the apartment lobby, and Alison's mother let the girl in. One of Kopal's shirtsleeves was missing, and her bare arm bled from scratches. Her father—the girl explained as she sobbed—was literally pushing her out of the house when her mother kicked at him and held on so tight that Kopal's sleeve tore off at the shoulder seam. She'd never seen her parents again before she died.

Both Kopal and the dead girl now lying before Alison possessed the supple glowing skin that only youth provides.

"We move on?" Hicks said.

The team walked toward the entrance doors.

Hicks held up a key ring. "The keys to the ivory tower. Literally."

"To the limestone library, maybe," Alison said.

Hicks grinned and jingled the keys in his palm. "Got these from the maintenance manager." He gestured to a yellow-taped door off the foyer and led them up a concrete stairway, their footfalls echoing. He halted as they reached the second floor. "See, the administration building and the library are connected. The library takes up the first three floors, but administration has its own entrance facing Lakeshore Road, with executive offices running back along the fourth floor. They're situated above the library. And those offices share a fourth-floor corridor with direct access to a rooftop patio—café tables, umbrellas, trellises, the whole shebang." He waved at the others and resumed climbing. "We've got a rookie guarding the admin hallway up there."

At the top landing they faced a steel door. Hicks unlocked it, and the crew emerged onto a flagstone-paved patio, where sunlight reflected off the pavers in a blinding glare. Alison saluted to shield her eyes and scanned the scene: one long table for eight, a half-dozen café tables seating four, and, under an awning, a bar worktop. Above table umbrellas, a planted trellis spanning between wood posts freshened the air. A breeze cooled her skin and whispered through the hanging plants.

At the patio's opposite end, a wall of cedar studs and lattice screened the rest of the roof, which was a sea of gravel, A/C machines, and vent stacks. The admin corridor was clad entirely in windows and a glass double door, and Alison jumped when her reflection came into view. She took a breath, exhaled slowly, and noticed a string mop propped against a mullion in the window-wall. She kneeled beside it, smelled ammonia. Slid her knuckles along the strings. Still soggy, they were likely the source of the ammonia soaked into Havers's jacket.

"Don," she said and turned back to the patio. "We'll need to dust this mop handle."

Gatti gave a thumbs-up gesture.

In the distance to Alison's left, Toronto's skyscrapers jutted like jagged grey teeth above a yellow haze. She didn't miss the metropolis's frequent "smog days," but Oakville's air wasn't much better.

She shook her head and looked at the vista to the south—playing fields and tennis courts, parking, and a service road. Beyond, a ribbon of woods and the steel-blue lake.

To maintain the view, the south wall was merely a waist-high parapet. Easy enough to fall over it, she thought, if you aren't mindful.

And at that modest height, the parapet would allow a strong assailant to push someone off the roof. Road traffic hummed in the distance, and Alison's heels clunked on the flagstones as she approached the perimeter wall. She'd never liked heights, and as she gripped the metal flashing, her knuckles whitened. Alison looked over the edge. Two bodies, four storeys below. She stepped back and examined the parapet. A scrap of fabric hung caught by a seam in the sheet-metal flashing. About the size of a facecloth, the cotton displayed a printed floral design.

* * *

Alison interviewed the janitor and the A/C tech who'd discovered the bodies. But she'd have to postpone questioning Bobby Havers, the dead girl's grieving boyfriend: Constable Hicks had let the boy go home for the day. Hicks said Bobby was from Clayton Hill, a nearby neighbourhood, and could walk home in fifteen minutes.

Finally, in the Admissions & Administration building, Alison obtained Pamela Renard's parents' names and Coyote River address. But then she realized the death notification was outside her jurisdiction. An FNP Constable on the reserve would have to notify the girl's next of kin. She phoned the Coyote River Police and left the parents' details with an officer.

* * *

Heading back to Regional Investigative Services, she started the sunbaked Malibu and sighed. What, she wondered, were the key details? The AC tech Jason Beckwith seemed too much of a family man for his age, early- to mid-twenties, but he swore he'd been at home with his wife and kids on Sunday night. On the other hand, Solomon Fitzgerald, the janitor, was Beckwith's age but had shown attitude. Lots of it. Something was grim, very ugly, in his background.

Despite Fitzgerald's enigmatic past, he'd volunteered he was an ex-con for assault, and a "former" cocaine addict. And now, evidently, an alcoholic, because he spent Sunday night drinking alone at a downtown pub. Fitzgerald also offered that his live-in girlfriend didn't see him from Sunday around noon until this morning, so unless the pub's staff could vouch for him, he possessed no alibi. Still, the lack of one could only

CHAPTER 4

suggest Fitzgerald had opportunity for the crime; his assault conviction didn't equal motive. She had left her business card with him, "in case anything else comes to mind."

But other facts did implicate Fitzgerald. Even if his alibi stood, he *knew* Pamela Renard. He'd identified her body before Director Collier corroborated it, and he confessed to knowing both Pamela and her boyfriend Bobby Havers "casually." Which meant what? Alison needed to shadow Fitzgerald, but working with no partner meant proper surveillance wasn't feasible.

As she neared her townhouse, palms slipped on the steering wheel. Would the mugginess never end? She tried to relax, but her mind kept going over the day. Fitzgerald had stated he came to the library to let in Beckwith, so that the air-conditioning repairs made on the previous Thursday and Friday could be double-checked. Beckwith didn't have access to the library, as Fitzgerald did, and he was short and scrawny. Unless he'd turned into Superman, he couldn't have forced Ray Havers off the roof. The banker was six feet four and broad-shouldered. But Fitzgerald, though he was only of average height, had a young muscled body that could have been a match for the middle-aged man.

Another possibility was that Fitzgerald and Beckwith formed a team: the pair worked together on the library roof just two days before the murder. But that scenario seemed elaborate.

Instead, Alison wondered, *What's the simplest picture to begin with?* That image showed the banker pushing the girl to her death, then jumping to his. The reverse, Pamela shoving Havers off the roof, was the next plainest possibility. Many odds, little certainty. Unfortunately, Alison needed to solve the case pronto, to show the white boys at Homicide that she was more than middling, that she was there not because of some affirmative-action quota. But *pronto* and police work usually formed a contradiction.

Chapter 5

The day's events coalesced into a red ache behind Sol's eyelids. He peeled off his clammy uniform at his locker and got into street clothes. He buttoned his shirt and stared at a concrete block wall as blank as Pamela's eyes staring up from the quad's pavement. It was a fluke that he'd come to know her at all. A fluke. But Sol was grateful for the luck that introduced them to each other, and he marvelled at the humility he'd seen in someone so obviously gifted. Cracked images of her flitted through his mind: scrapping with Rose Molloy, laughing with Bobby Havers in a school corridor, lying on the pavement, lying broken. Gone.

He wished he'd somehow been able to prevent her death. If he ever found the culprit, he'd beat the shit out of them. Does that detective Downey, he wondered, care as much? Or is it just a job to her? Cops in general, they didn't give a damn how you felt. So she had launched right into finger-pointing and wanted his alibi.

Old Harold sat on the locker-room bench and whistled as he removed his work boots, then filed his fingernails, distracting Sol from his thoughts. "Hey, wasn't no easy day around here." He narrowed his eyes, inspecting his thumbnail, and filed it again. "No good for nobody. You OK?"

"It's like a nightmare, only it's fucking real."

Harold scratched his white beard, which he kept carefully trimmed, and stood up to tug a pair of running shoes from his locker, then slid them on. "Get some sleep. Shock like this morning don't leave you alone. And you got your la-di-da university test coming up," he said, chuckling. "Need your beauty sleep for that."

Sol slammed his locker door shut.

"Seriously, take care of yourself. I would've had a heart attack if I'd found them dead bodies."

"Thanks for your concern."

Harold nodded, not getting the sarcasm. He loved to razz Sol about U of T. So did Cheryl Malak, who dropped out of a nursing program two years ago when she got pregnant and the father abandoned her.

Sometimes Sol wondered why he'd ever started in the Academic Bridging Program. Tash had been the spur, and she'd been right. If he could just hang on and pass Canadian History. He did great on the quizzes—remembering dates, names, and places was easy—but his essays stunk and cancelled out the quiz marks.

The struggle reminded Sol of his limits in music. He'd shone at piano from an early age, and it helped that his lessons, given by his cousin Danny, were free. In Grade Five, Sol told Mr. Farrell that he played the instrument. The homeroom teacher, a grey-haired widower, took an interest in Sol and made sure he performed at every school assembly. The man also told Sol about the Royal Conservatory of Music on Bloor Street, and how it offered a course of exams you could take. But Sol's parent's couldn't afford to pay for those tests, so, against Sol's father's gripes about "not needing anyone's charity,"

CHAPTER 5

Mr. Farrell paid for each Conservatory exam as the gifted student progressed up the grade levels, and the teacher's help continued through Sol's high-school years. But during those years, when Sol burned to write his own pieces, he discovered he sucked at music theory: he barely passed that part of the Conservatory's Grade Ten exam.

Turning now from Harold, he vowed to study hard—certainly harder than he did in music theory—to improve his grasp of grammar and English composition. Because unless Sol did so, his essays weren't going to earn better marks.

Sol checked the wall clock. The next bus was due in fifteen minutes, so, looking forward to a stroll through Woodmore's grounds, he left the locker room. He needed to relax, to curb his fear that the cops were framing him, the suspect with a prison record, but instead, as he neared the front door, he saw Cheryl sitting with her ass on Peacock's desk. She giggled, tossed blow-dried waves of platinum blond. Peacock was married and twenty years older than her, so *surely* they weren't sleeping together. But honesty forced Sol to admit, he and Tash made a pretty unlikely couple. Walking out the door, he turned and saluted the lovebirds.

Chapter 6

September 2006

Sitting in their dorm room with Amy, Pamela feels rattled by her lunch-table fight with Rose Molloy, so she closes her eyes and tries to gather her energy. In thirty minutes, she'll have to give her speech. She wrote it during the summer, and she's rehearsed it three times, but her stomach is fluttering. She wishes the Two-Row Exchange's committee had instead created another activity like putting two canoes in a river—anything except having her give a lecture.

At two o'clock, while the whole upper-school student body finds pews in Woodmore's chapel, Pamela squirms in the itchy school-uniform kilt. The Director speaks about her lofty expectations for students in 2006 and 2007, and then Mr. Flynn, the Assistant Director, introduces Pamela to the assembly. He breaks the schoolmaster stereotype. He is fit, even brawny. When Mr. Flynn leaves Pamela standing alone at the oak lectern set up in the chancel, the pages flap in her shaking hands, and she worries her sweaty fingers will mar the two row wampum belt she's brought to illustrate her

CHAPTER 6

talk. She lays her papers on the lectern, but with the ceiling fans working vigorously, the top page flutters away and lands beyond Pamela's reach. As giggles flit through the audience, Mr. Flynn rushes to retrieve the misbehaving sheet. He hands it to her and touches her shoulder.

"Don't fret," he whispers. "You'll do fine, young lady."

Pamela clears her throat, a beehive buzzing in her chest.

"Director Collier, Assistant Director Flynn, teachers, and students, I'm thrilled to be here as part of the Two Row Exchange, and I hope *your* participant, Jordan Windsor, will enjoy his year at Coyote River High School and get to know the reserve. It'll be less of a jolt for him than you might think, because my reserve's the most populous one in this country, with about twelve thousand band members living there and a village, Tsorahsa, of thirteen hundred people. In addition to his required Ontario Grade Twelve courses, Jordan will take classes in Mohawk history, culture, and language.

"On the other hand, I don't need much education in settler culture: native people in this country have studied it, usually against their will, for more than a century. Have you heard of residential schools? One of them operated on my reserve from 1885 until 1970. But Canada's residential school system, an attempt to kill our identity and culture, is too big a topic to address today, so let me instead offer a crash course on the Coyote River First Nation and especially the Haldimand Proclamation."

Pamela feels it: the trembling in her voice has diminished. As she concentrates on relaxing her shoulders, she looks up at the chapel's vaulted ceiling, then glances out at the faces. Bobby Havers, a fellow Grade Twelve she met in the parking lot on move-in day, gives her a thumbs-up and smiles.

She continues. "Most of you know, I assume, that Coyote River First Nation is in a land dispute with the neighbouring town of Ewing—well, with *some* people in Ewing. Who's seen it on the news?" She gestures to the crowd. "Could I have a show of hands?"

Three-quarters of the students raise their hands.

"That's the elephant in the room, and my reserve's past answers the questions, 'What's behind the quarrel, and why is it happening?' So, here's a little history lesson. First of all, can anybody tell us when the American Revolutionary War took place? Don't be shy."

Except for the ceiling fans' whir and the swish of tree branches against the arched stained-glass window behind Pamela, the chapel is silent.

Mr. Flynn jumps up from his chair beside the lectern. "Anybody?"

A diminutive girl with ebony skin raises her hand. In a thick African accent, she says, "Yes, I believe that that war was waged from 1775 to 1783. And Great Britain lost. Obviously."

Chuckles and murmurs scatter through the space. Gesturing *stop* with his arms, Mr. Flynn calls for quiet.

"Correct," Pamela says. "During the war, several Iroquois nations, including the Mohawk nation, fought for and aided the British side. That group of Iroquois families originated in the Finger Lakes region of what's now central New York state. After the American Revolutionary war ended, Sir Frederick Haldimand, the British Crown-in-Council here at the time, granted them 950,000 acres along the Coyote River, and they moved north of the border. Nine hundred fifty thousand acres. Remember that number. Fast forward to 1793—"

"Who gives a shit?" someone says. A girl's voice, almost at

shouting volume.

As the sound bounces off the chapel's vaulted ceiling, Pamela looks around for the speaker. Must be Rose Molloy, she thinks, who else could it be? She wants to scream, *I give a shit, Rose. And so should you!*

Again, Assistant Director Flynn rises. "I won't dignify that rude remark by wasting time looking for the culprit. Really, students, you are all privileged to be here! This school expects more of you." He signals for Pamela to continue.

"In 1793, that's nine years later, the 950,000 acres granted by Sir Haldimand's proclamation is reduced by a British statute, the Simcoe Patent, to 675,000 acres. What? How did 275,000 of Mohawk land suddenly 'disappear'? But the worst was yet to come. Let's skip ahead by two centuries, to 1995. By that year, the area owned by Coyote River First Nation had shrunk by 95 percent to a mere 50,000 acres!"

She waits, expecting a collective cry of dismay, but the spectators remain silent. Thanks so much, Pamela thinks, for your understanding. She scratches her cheek, from anger not nervousness.

But a lanky boy stands up and says, "Why—why did that happen?"

"That's a tricky question," Pamela replies and looks down at her notes. "From 1980 to 1995, Coyote River tried to find out. Under Canada's Specific Claims Policy, my reserve submitted two dozen claims to the federal government, but as of today, only *one* of those petitions has been resolved. What the applications ask for, basically, is compensation and a full report on how the reserve's area shrank over the centuries since the Haldimand Proclamation."

She eyes the long-limbed questioner. "So, I can't answer

your question, except to say that with all but one of the claims still unresolved, we've got no consistent response yet as to *why* it happened. Only the government—hopefully—knows for sure."

And now, Pamela thinks, for the hardest part. Coyote River and the clash at Ewing's border have headlined the CBC news on television for months, and she's heard that the quarrel has been covered by media in Britain and other countries. She's unsure whether the tension, as strong as a bank-vault wall, is in her mind only.

"Which brings us to what's happening now between Coyote River First Nation and the town of Ewing, which adjoin each other. You've probably heard sound bites about it on TV, so I want to demystify the circumstances for you. This year a developer from Ewing started building houses on Coyote River's land—that is, within those remaining 50,000 acres. The builder thinks he bought it from the Ontario government. But Coyote River's band council disagrees. It has never recognized the government's title to the parcel. And that's why the roads are blocked with protestors and barricades. It's the only way my reserve can get the government—federal and provincial—to take notice and agree to fix the situation. We've lost enough land already, and Ontario is going to dishonour the Haldimand Proclamation even *more*? Not if we can help it.

"I feel bad for the developer. He's caught in the middle. In any case, tempers are flaring, and there's good reason. Coyote River's protests are causing inconvenience and hassle for drivers in the area, some businesses are suffering as a result, and so stones are being tossed and fistfights keep happening. The OPP have arrested people from both sides. Now that—"

CHAPTER 6

"What do you think it'll take to resolve the dispute?" says someone Pamela can't locate in the throng. "To stop the fights?"

"Beats me," Pamela says, grinning. *How about*, she thinks, *the government telling us honestly what the hell happened to 900,000 acres of the Haldimand Tract?*

Light laughter flutters through the room. This time some teachers, sitting on chairs behind Mr. Flynn and Ms. Collier, join in the levity.

"Now that you know the historical background," Pamela says, "I hope you can see that Coyote River's protest was launched for good reason."

From the heat of two hundred bodies crammed into the pews, the air has become stifling. Or perhaps only Pamela finds it oppressive, having presented a slew of uncomfortable facts—uncomfortable for non-aboriginals, anyway. She chides herself. It's them, not me, who should feel unsettled. I merely stated the truth. She turns her eyes to the Assistant Director.

In his chair by the reading stand, Mr. Flynn stares at the floor, rubs his forehead. He must be praying that Pamela's next topic is uncontroversial, and she obliges, finishing with a bit about how, in the Mohawk language, each of the first ten cardinal numbers hold double meanings, and in sequence they narrate the culture's creation story. Finally, she has everyone (except possibly Rose) reciting the numbers one through ten in Mohawk: *énska, tékeni, áhsen, aié:ri, wisk, ià:ia'k, tsá:ta, sha'té:kon, tióhton, oié:ri*.

A bland feel-good ending. Mr. Flynn is smiling now.

In the formal question period that follows, Rose is first to the microphone.

"So the British," she says, "had this guy Haldimand—colonial governor or whatever—grant Coyote River some land. Oodles of land. Here's some education for you: some years after the grant, your band council signed their names to a survey map of a smaller area. *Smaller*. Then, oops, that map got 'lost or destroyed,' and the rez has been trying to 'reclaim' its land ever since. Including right now at the border with Ewing."

Standing beside the platform, Mr. Flynn speaks in a raised voice. "Do you have a question, speaker?"

With a smirk, Rose turns and goes back to her seat.

Ten minutes later, Pamela has responded to a half-dozen actual questions, and Ms. Collier calls for thanks to the speaker and to the Assistant Director, who worked with Coyote River to create the Two Row Exchange. Amid the applause, and with three media people taking pictures, Mr. Flynn presents Pamela with flowers and a small replica of the two row wampum.

The clapping fades, and the students start filing out.

Director Collier, swathed in too-strong perfume, hugs Pamela. "We're so excited to have you at Woodmore. I do hope the situation with Ewing is resolved soon, but anyway, best of luck in your studies here."

Feeling that the speech went better than she imagined, Pamela strides back to her pew. Amy is congratulating her when Rose's braying laugh bursts from somewhere behind them and echoes around the chapel.

Chapter 7

June 2007

"Don't worry. You'll do fine," Tash said, touching Sol's shoulder as if he were a child. "My parents don't bite."

"You make this dinner sound like an audition." As he brought a piece of toast to his mouth, a glob of raspberry jam slid down his T-shirt.

Tash snorted. "Oh, my lovable slob."

"Fuck, it's not funny." He lurched from his chair and escaped to the bedroom to put on his running gear.

Once he was out of the apartment, he jogged into White Tail Park. The sun pounded like one of his opponents from back when he'd boxed as a teenager. Sweat dripped down his back, and though he wore a baseball cap, he knew his freckly Irish face would sunburn. Yet he ran, just as he did weights, whether he wanted to or not. His life demanded physical strength, because nobody was ever going to take advantage of him again.

Ten kilometres and a pail of sweat later, he got home and worked out on the multi-gym in the living room.

"See you tonight," Tash said, poking her head out of the bathroom doorway. "Umbria's a ritzy place, so dress for it." She glanced at Sol's battered upright piano beside the multi-gym. "I'm heading out for lunch with Sharon. Then we'll browse the stores, and after that I've got Ultimate. You're practicing this afternoon, right?"

"Three new pieces to learn." Sol groaned through a bench press. "I don't want to be sight-reading and flubbing every second note in front of the choir and getting dirty looks."

"Makes sense." Tash picked up her keys in the vestibule and waved. The front door clacked shut.

Grunting and hissing against the pain, he pumped iron. If Tash's parents ever saw the multi-gym, and how much space it took up, they would forever see him as a muscle head. She, at least, didn't mind his workouts as long as she could do her yoga in peace.

Months ago, she'd suggested he try it: "Come on. More than anyone else I know, you need a way to relax." She'd soon bought him a DVD, *Yoga for Beginners*.

His workout over, he towelled himself. On the TV stand, the DVD's case stared back at him. He hadn't even removed the cellophane from it yet. Whenever he saw Tash doing yoga, she looked so graceful, doing *warrior pose* or whatever it was called. Her face radiated calm.

Now he wished he felt that peace, but with his meet-the-parents dinner only hours away, calm dodged him. Why did Tash wait so long for him to meet her mom and dad? They lived in Oakville, not India. Was she scared of what their reaction would be?

* * *

CHAPTER 7

From hearsay or a news piece, Sol knew that Oakville enjoyed one of the top average incomes in Canada, but most of the place looked like any other suburb in the GTA: strip malls, asphalt, asphalt, asphalt, and apartment towers and single-family houses on streets curving like spaghetti. As a kid in St. James Town, he'd lived in a twenty-seven storey pillbox, but at least he could navigate his neighbourhood's gridiron.

If Sol was fair, though, Oakville wasn't totally covered by suburbs. The lakeshore sported an old-fashioned downtown and a belt of mansions, historical museums, and churches—Old Oakville. When he'd first ambled along the lakeside path and rubbernecked the grand houses, Sol remembered learning about the Family Compact, the ruling class that ran Ontario in the early 1800s, and he thought some of them had no doubt owned manors fronting the shoreline. He'd walked further west and seen where the lake met the mouth of Sixteen Mile Creek, a yacht club overlooking boats that dipped and rose with the water.

Besides his shoreline strolls, Sol's bus rides around Oakville gave him a sense of other neighbourhoods. The better ones tried to wall out the big-box stores, the 403's traffic, and the riff-raff crowded into Soviet-style apartments on Trafalgar Road, safely north of Old Oakville, old money, and the drowning-in-debt middle class. With his janitor's salary, Sol was absolutely a member of the fucking rabble.

* * *

Outside Umbria's glass and stucco wall, the honey locust trees threw shadows along Lakeshore Road and its shops and restaurants. Sol squinted against the low sun and glanced along the street. Where was Tash? He hoped her Ultimate game had ended early, so she'd arrive before her parents did. What the hell would he say to them if she wasn't there?

He pushed up the sleeve of his houndstooth blazer and checked the time. Dress slacks and a turtleneck completed the look. He tried to feel natural in the getup, but he should have worn a light cotton shirt. Heat clung to the fading afternoon.

Tash's shiny Jetta, a twenty-seventh-birthday gift from her father, slipped into one of the few open parking spaces near Umbria. She waved as she approached him. "My parents not here yet? Guess I inherit my lateness from my mother. She always gussies up like a teenager for prom."

"What about me? Dressed up enough?" Sol did a half-turn, like he was posing for a mug shot. "I want to impress your—"

Tash pointed to a late-model Mercedes that passed by them and parked farther down the street. "That's them." She scurried toward her parents and hugged her father, who wore a suit and tie, a full head of greying hair, and a black moustache. She squeezed her mother too and made introductions.

Showing teeth as blindingly white as Tash's, Mrs. Harishandra extended her hand to Sol. "The mysterious Mr. Fitzgerald. I was starting to think you were a figment of Tashi's imagination."

"*Moi aussi*," Dr. Harishandra said and combed his moustache with an index finger.

Inside the restaurant, they followed the maître d', walking under hanging amber lights and past a pianist playing a Rossini opera overture. Umbria was serious about being Italian.

The other diners' eyes tracked Mrs. Harishandra. She wore

CHAPTER 7

loose trousers, which looked like pajamas, and a silk scarf over a tunic. A *shalwar kameez*, she called the outfit. And it was attractive, but too tight. It probably fit fifteen or twenty pounds ago.

Amid the noise of voices and clinking cutlery, the maître d' seated them and distributed menus. The smells of Focaccia bread, pesto, and thyme spread through the restaurant, so even if the conversation was going to suck, the food promised to be good.

Tash's father looked up from his menu at Sol and cleared his throat. "My wife is wrong, you are not a complete mystery. Tashi tells us you want to apply for an undergraduate degree. I assume you do not want to remain a sanitary engineer, but you would be making a rather late start in academe."

"Don't knock janitors," Sol said, hoping his smile toned down the reply. "Woodmore Academy would be a pigpen without us. The kids are slobs, believe me, but this year Woodmore got an award for our health program. During the winter, our flu cases were 30 percent lower than any other school in Halton Region. Us janitors were the ones who pushed for hand-gel pumps and 'wash your hands' posters."

Tash touched him on the shoulder. "It was Sol's idea, and at the closing assembly last year, the director presented him with a health-and-safety award."

"Whoop-de-do," Sol said. He lifted his hand and twirled his index finger.

Dr. Harishandra frowned. "There is no need for modesty. You showed initiative and concern above your normal duties. Congratulations."

Tash nodded her head. "Yeah, Sol."

That winter, over half the students had caught the flu, and

he'd stood for five minutes one day in a boys' washroom and got woozy watching the kids' habits, like using the toilet stalls, then not washing their hands. He was no scientist, but hadn't these kids learned about germs in health class? Didn't they know that something you couldn't see could kill you? Years ago he'd learned, the hard way, to look past the obvious, the surface of things. You had to think carefully, step by step—like Tash did in her bioscience lab—to know the truth.

A waiter appeared wearing a goatee and a smug half smile. Not much to be self-satisfied about. Age forty at least, still slinging plates for minimum wage. From a bottle of Merlot, the guy filled everyone's glass except Dr. Harishandra's, who asked for orange juice. They gave their orders, and the goatee padded away.

"Me and Tash talked it over," Sol said, "and yeah, starting college at twenty-four is late. But Tash got to know her friend Sharon—you've met her?—when Sharon started university at *thirty*." He guzzled from his wineglass, and he could feel Tash's stare.

"Sharon," Dr. Harishandra said. "A hard worker, who helped Tashi through some difficult times. What did Sharon go into? Was it physiotherapy?"

"Yes, Dad."

"I want to major in kinesiology and phys. ed., with a minor in music," Sol said. "Then apply to teachers college."

Dr. Harishandra tilted his head, raised an index finger. "A noble profession, but these days, from what I heard, the competition for open positions is fierce. I wish you luck."

Sol noticed that Tash and her mother sipped sparingly from their first glass, but he tipped back his second one anyway and finished it. When he put the goblet down and reached

CHAPTER 7

for the bottle, Tash grasped his forearm.

"It's almost empty," she said.

In the resulting hush, Tash's folks fidgeted in their seats. She broke the tension with a story about her day at the lab. Everyone laughed, but another awkward lull threatened to never end. Sol wished he held something clever to say. He pinched Tash's thigh instead.

"So, how's your kitchen reno going, Mom?" she said.

The waiter came back with the dinners trailing steam.

"Virtually finished," Tash's mother said, cutting into her baked salmon. "If I could get your father to nail down the baseboards and paint the walls before the next millennium. Always trying to save a buck, my husband."

"I'd prefer to be a music teacher, straight up," Sol said. "But the province and the school boards keep cutting music because 'it's just a frill.' Bullshit."

Mrs. Harishandra turned to face Tash's father. "So, when are you going to finish the kitchen?"

The doctor wiped his mouth and frowned. "Music instruction, a 'frill.' That is indeed bullshit."

Maybe Tash's father wasn't a pompous ass after all.

"So," the doctor said, "where did you grow up? You are from Toronto, I understand."

"St. James Town."

"Oh, I hear periodically about that neighbourhood on the news." Dr. Harishandra stroked his moustache. "I understand that it is one of the country's oldest and largest social housing projects."

"And you know what *those* people are like," Sol said.

The doctor halted a forkful of *penne* before his mouth. "Which people?"

You know what I mean, Sol thought. Fuck, he needed another drink.

Chapter 8

It was Saturday afternoon, and Alison appreciated her townhouse's central air-conditioning. Would the heat wave ever end?

With the severe temperatures, Woodmore Academy's A/C repairs had obviously been a necessity, so that part of the janitor's story—his discovering the bodies while letting the air-conditioning tech into the library—was believable. But the anger emanating from Fitzgerald, and his record for assault, did nothing to lower him on the list of suspects.

Marcia had left by nine, and Alison, planting yarrow and delphiniums in the front garden, sweated through the morning. So Alison wanted a dry, comfortable afternoon. She grabbed her novel off the coffee table and plopped onto the couch. The characters were just coming back to her when the click of the front door's latch broke her concentration.

"Mom?" Marcia's voice.

"Living room, Muffin."

"It's *Marcia*."

"Don't start."

Appearing from around the foyer wall, Marcia cleared her throat. "This is Tyler. He lives down the street."

Beside Marcia stood a tall white boy, holding a laptop

computer and a book under one arm—a thin kid but with a developed upper body. Those sculpted arms marked danger. Testosterone. And where there's testosterone . . .

"Pleased to meet you," she said, crossing the living room to shake the boy's hand. His grip was as unyielding as a steel vise. If Sol Fitzgerald possessed similar strength, the janitor could easily have overpowered a bank manager, even a tall one, used to sitting at a desk all day.

She pointed to Tyler's book. "What you reading?"

"John Steinbeck. *The Grapes of Wrath*."

Interesting, Alison thought. At least his interests ranged beyond bodybuilding.

"We're parched," Marcia said, sweat shining on her forehead. "Going to chill out on the balcony."

"Lemonade in the fridge."

Marcia poured the drinks and led Tyler through the patio doors.

Alison tried to read, but she couldn't. The floral pattern of her daughter's shirt was identical to the one on Pamela Renard's torn dress. Well, it wasn't *identical*, but Alison closed her eyes and the design hovered before her, would not leave. The scrap of fabric, caught in Woodmore Library's parapet . . .

"Marcia," she said, loud enough for her daughter to hear through the glass, and motioned to come inside.

Marcia slid the patio door open.

"Just you," Alison said. "And close the door." She patted a couch cushion beside her.

"Tyler's mother teaches high school English."

Alison put the novel down and bit her lip. "I'm glad you're meeting kids in the neighbourhood."

CHAPTER 8

"She's really smart, I've talked to her."

Alison realized she was rubbing her palms together. "Can I ask you something?"

With the calm of a Yogi, Marcia sat down on the couch.

"You plan on going to movies or concerts—that sort of thing—with Tyler?"

Marcia shrugged.

"Be home by nine if you go out—"

"I'd barely get back from the *early* show by nine."

"Nine-thirty, then."

"Don't worry. I can take care of myself."

As long, Alison thought, as you don't mean like the Renard girl took care of herself.

* * *

On Sunday morning, Alison went with Shirley to St. Thaddeus's United. The activity held an extra benefit: Alison noticed two eligible-looking black men in the congregation. They looked roughly her age, but she didn't get close enough to check for wedding rings. She wasn't that desperate, was she?

Since the move from Toronto, Alison didn't mind going with her mother to St. Thaddeus's, a five-minute walk from the townhouse. She knew Shirley was lonely, having lost close neighbours and friends from church in Parkdale.

"We're home," Shirley said into their foyer as they returned from church around one o'clock. The oak stairway gleamed with polish, and the Pine-Sol she'd applied yesterday still wafted up from the floor tiles.

From Marcia's bedroom, the girl's voice emerged. "OK."

She appeared at the landing and looked up from the *Harry Potter* novel in her hands. "How was church?"

"I wish you'd come with us, dear," Shirley said. "When your momma was your age, she soaked up sermons and looked up Bible verses, and she loved choir. Singing is fun."

The pages of Marcia's book entranced the girl. "How can it be fun?"

"Take your nose out of your book when you're speaking to your gran," Alison said.

Marcia harrumphed. "You wanted me to read more often."

"You know what, dear?" Shirley said. "We're old Nova Scotia stock, Black Loyalist Anglican. Well, I was until I met your grandfather."

"Mom, if Marcia doesn't want to go to church, let her be."

The girl disappeared behind the landing, and her door clunked shut.

"You know," Shirley said, "St. Thaddeus has a youth group."

"Hmm. I doubt it'll make Marcia go to church again, but at least she'd meet the right kind of kids."

"Lucky kids, not better kids," Shirley said. She aimed a pointed glance at Alison. "Look at who grew up in Parkdale. But anyhow, the newsletter's on the fridge, and it's got the youth group's number on it."

A good enough idea. But Alison *first* needed to sway Marcia to join the youth group, period.

She was about to burst from church coffee followed by the lemonade, so she rushed to the bathroom. Washing her hands, she eyed her reflection in the mirror, the ceiling light illuminating crows feet at her eyes and creases near her mouth, and she wondered, *maybe I'm a good candidate for the plastic surgeons in those cheesy television ads*. She remembered another

CHAPTER 8

commercial, in which a woman's breathy voice delivered the slogan for an anti-aging cream: *Your skin isn't getting older. It's just exhausted.* Like the rest of her. But unlike Alison, getting older was a challenge Pamela Renard would never experience.

Chapter 9

September 2006

Early in the morning, Pamela hears the patter of Amy's slippers as the diminutive student leaves their room for a shower. But Amy doesn't reach the washroom: as soon as the door latch has clicked, a muffled shriek comes for the hallway.

Amy darts back inside and slams the door. "Pam! Something . . . something you've got to see."

Pamela is lying under her bedcovers, but Amy reaches under the sheets and pulls hard on her arm.

"Not so fast!" Pamela says, rubbing her eyes with her free hand. "I'm barely awake."

She stumbles after Amy into the hallway. Diagonally, in foot-high letters on the outside of their door, the word *squaw* drips down in red paint.

Amy holds her up by the armpits, which would be a comical pose—Amy being short and Pamela, tall—if the context wasn't so nasty. As Pamela's guts swirl, Amy helps her back into bed and leaves to find the housemistress.

CHAPTER 9

***

Though all of Pilkington House is scheduled this morning for Orientation Week's opening breakfast, Ms. Atkinson locks down the dorm. For half an hour, the ground-floor common room functions as an interrogation centre. The housemistress, in her vast floral-print dress, blocks the door.

"Breakfast or no breakfast," she says, with a posh British accent, "no one shall leave until the culprit announces herself."

Whining ensues, especially among the senior girls. "We're were starving," one of them says.

"Somebody better own up to it now."

After an eternity, a kid called Penny starts whimpering.

"It was me," she says, wiping her nose with her wrist. "I did it. I'm sorry."

Ms. Atkinson grimaces and shakes her head, the bangs of her steel-grey pageboy quivering. "By any chance, would you like a tissue?" She hands Penny one. "Are you protecting someone? Because, if you'll forgive me, dear girl, I can see you're not at the top of the social ladder here. Well?" The housemistress snaps her fingers.

Penny doesn't budge, stays silent.

Ms. Atkinson harrumphs and puts her hands on her roomy hips. Except for Penny, she excuses everyone to leave for Edwards Common.

***

Once the breakfast commences, Pamela sees that Rose now sits several tables away with her buddies. That's fine with me, she thinks. She doubts that Penny acted alone, or even of her own will. If the poor misfit *did* deface Pamela's door, someone bullied her into doing it.

Once the meal is over, Pamela and Amy walk with the rest of the floor to Pilkington House. At their door, they find Sol, the janitor they'd met in the cafeteria yesterday, working a paint roller over the offensive letters, plastic sheeting and sandpaper at his feet.

"Building matron couldn't get the paint off the door," he says and scratches his chin with his free hand. "I can imagine who the culprit is."

"Me too," Pamela says.

"Careful now, paint's still wet."

Amy pushes gingerly on the door handle and enters their room, but Pamela remains staring at the half-covered insult, feeling certain the perpetrator can only have been Rose Molloy. *That racist boor*, she thinks, *is due for some payback*. So much for friendship and mutual respect—things Pamela actually believed she'd experience at Woodmore. And she wants them badly, especially from people like Rose. Why? It's perverse. The question perplexes her, enrages her. Is she experiencing Stockholm Syndrome, in which hostages develop a bond, as a survival strategy, with their captors? Pamela wishes she were full-blooded Mohawk, not half. Her life would be—would always have been—simpler, if not less painful: membership in a downtrodden people would be her identity, but at least she'd unequivocally have *one*.

"Are you OK?" Sol asks as he picks up scraps of sandpaper.

Shaking her head, she walks past him and through the doorway.

***

CHAPTER 9

In the evening, Pamela phones home. Riding a current of anger, she recounts the graffiti incident.

After concluding the story, she says, "I'm going to sock whoever did it." Her fist tightens.

Mother's voice, its accent strong after twenty years in Ontario, is measured. "Me, I'd reproach them, of course, of course. But be quiet about it. Don't hit anyone."

Pamela's been sitting at her dorm-room desk, but she gets up and walks past her bed to the window, which is recessed above a radiant heater in one corner. Amy's half of the room mirrors this arrangement. Against the orange-pink afterglow stand the dark hulks of Woodmore's buildings and the black fingers of trees; the light is fading minute by minute. With the winter months approaching, these shadows will soon smother her.

"Pampam, you listen?"

"Oh," Pamela says, retreating from her thoughts, "yes, of course I'm listening." She turns from the window and sees Amy, who's wearing earbuds and swaying to the music as she writes in a three-ring binder, her other hand resting on an open textbook.

"You only been there a few days," Pamela's mother says. "Give it more time and make some more friends. You'll forget about the stupid person who play the prank. . . . But this exchange—you staying in Oakville—he won't always be easy. You have to be strong."

Her mother's words provide little comfort, and Pamela turns back to the window. The afterglow is gone, replaced by blackness.

Chapter 10

June 2007

Sol shielded his eyes from a sun-bright glare and groaned as blurry words fluttered above him. He forced his eyes open and strained against the windows' light as Tash ripped the curtains back, daylight ricocheting off the piano and the multi-gym.

"Get up. Son of a pig, the wine at Umbria wasn't enough?" Tash pulled an empty Seagram's VO bottle out of his hand.

"Was tossing and turning in bed. I couldn't sleep."

"So you came out here and *drank* yourself to sleep. Again, on the couch. You prefer being with the cat instead of me?"

Heat already pulsed from the windows, so the day would be a sauna, as some days in May had been already. He shut his eyes again.

"Get. Up," Tash said through clenched teeth. She stomped away, and the bathroom door slammed.

On the faded sofa, he lay on his side with Metchnikoff, rust red and purring, curled beside him. He remembered the day he'd first noticed her prowling around the dumpsters behind the building. She'd been filthy, scrawny, and sick, but when

CHAPTER 10

he brought her up to the apartment, Tash snubbed his idea of keeping the cat. His plan started with saucers of milk: each day at dusk, he'd leave one out by the dumpsters. A couple of weeks later, Metchnikoff seemed no better, so he took food out and waited, making sure a dog or another cat didn't push her away as she ate, and after she finished, he picked her up, and she purred in his arms. He tried again to sway Tash, without success. One summer evening, when she said again that he was being silly—they couldn't keep a cat in the apartment—he took a sleeping bag into the field beside the dumpsters and lay propped on one elbow to watch for the feline. Dusk fell. No cat. Under hazy stars he'd dozed off, and Metchnikoff had crawled in with him and curled up. At dawn the next morning he woke to see Tash standing over him. "You win," she said and bent down to pet Metchnikoff, whose head was poking out of the sleeping bag. "You're too cute and Sol is too crazy about you." The cat had crept out and rubbed its forehead against Tash's shins.

From the parking lot below, honks shook Sol into a sitting position. The annoying toots came, he figured, from returning night-shift workers locking their cars. "Oh, go to hell, you idiots! Why are people so stupid and thoughtless?"

"Calm down," Tash said from the bathroom.

He scratched Metchnikoff behind her ears, sat up, and rubbed his temples. "On a Sunday morning." He wanted to fall back onto the cushions and drift back to sleep. Being out cold—especially with help from booze—provided a favourite escape.

He tried to stifle it, but his belch sounded like a foghorn.

Brushing her hair at the mirror, Tash spun around and glowered. "Charming."

The air tasted stale on Sol's tongue, thick with strings of saliva. "Give me a break. Look, about last night. Your father—"

"He didn't dis your precious St. James Town. He was just curious about your life."

"He thinks I'm wrong-side-of-the-tracks material. White trash." Sol got up from the sofa. "Sometimes I wonder why you gave me a chance at all."

"He's just a family doctor, not a billionaire investment banker. And I can tell: he wants to like you, but you want him to hate you. That's how it seemed last night. Look, I know you had a hard time as a kid, but when are you going to grow up and stop prejudging people? Otherwise, what are we even doing together?"

Sol waited until Tash left for brunch with a friend, then got off the couch and phoned Miroslav.

* * *

An hour later, the two men sat on a bench at the edge of Lakeside Park, the breeze failing to give relief from the stickiness. Miroslav had brought two coffees. He passed one to Sol, who enjoyed the aroma before sipping.

"Thanks, man."

"Is not problem."

Beyond the promenade and a slope leading to the rocky shore, quiet ripples wrapped the lake, but Sol couldn't settle himself. He was fearful of losing Tash.

At the other end of the bench, Miroslav swigged from a coffee cup as big as pitcher of beer. He wore khaki pants and a white cotton shirt, and—sans his sauce-spattered Woodmore

Foodservices apron—the man would have cut a handsome figure if not for his paunch.

"Don't worry about parents," he said. "Your girlfriend is upset, but you yet haven't failed her testing."

Deep within the park, a merry-go-round was squeaking, and kids, giggling and shouting.

"Easy for you to say, Miroslav. Why was I in a testy mood and reaching for the bottle—or at least aching for it—in front of the one man I really need to like me? Now how am I going to fix this fucking mess?"

Miroslav's eyes fixed on Sol's. "Let father win. Apologize." He winked, and his smile revealed yellowed teeth, the bottom set caving in. "If you want to keep girlfriend, you must do. Be honest with father." Miroslav crumpled his coffee cup and raised it in a toast. "Good coffee, no? Not like crap at Edwards Common." He tossed the cup in a garbage can and saluted Sol. "See you tomorrow, comrade." He lumbered away, east along the pea gravel walkway: he enjoyed looking at yachts in the harbour.

Sol stared at the lake, a steel blue wall against the sky. Miroslav was right. Feeling wronged, by everyone and everything, wasn't going to work anymore, and it wasn't worth the damage, especially if Tash got harmed. Not worth it. With the sun sinking over Hamilton, shadowy smokestacks obscured by the afternoon haze, he took out his phone, found the number for *Harishandra, Dr. F.*, and made the call.

Chapter 11

The shockwave of Nathan's fart reached Bobby across their room where he was studying in Norton House.

"Gross." Bobby, at his desk, folded the textbook over his nose. "Go into the hall if you're going to incinerate half of Oakville."

"*Sorry*. It's not that bad."

Cursing, Bobby opened *Writing the English Essay* again. "Can't you read—and fart—somewhere else? This essay's due tomorrow." Nausea and panic. Like the evening before his chemistry exam. The night Pam died.

* * *

That night, he and Pam had sat at a library study-table. From the chemistry text in front of him, chemical formulas had scowled. He felt a growing knot in his stomach, like a prelude to vomiting. This is pointless, he thought, and he looked out the windows to see students walking through Trevena Way and around its little gardens. A girl leaned over a lilac bush and closed her eyes as she inhaled. It wasn't fair. He wasn't meant to sit on his ass with a book in his face. If his stupid father could only understand that.

CHAPTER 11

From the opposite end of the study tables, Rose Molloy, sitting with her clique, screeched her bimbo laugh. Pam turned her head in the redhead's direction. Rose winked back. The girl annoyed everyone, except a few lecherous guys at Norton House, who drooled at her curves, the way her bust filled out her blouse. Rose seemed to enjoy the attention—at least, she *had* done until one night at a party last fall, when the same Norton House pricks assaulted her.

"Ignore her. She's a stupid racist," he said. "I mean, *stupid* stupid. Rose sucks in chemistry as bad as I do. Pretend she isn't here."

Pam just shrugged, which was weird, because the hate between her and Rose was clear to all the Grade Twelves.

With the warm spring, the air-conditioning system had gone berserk and turned the library into a refrigerator. Some students now wore sweaters. Air-supply grilles hung exposed from the ceiling and whistled a tune.

Bobby glanced at Pam as she wrote down a formula. Books and papers strewn on the table, she'd helped him study for the past hour. How, he thought, did I end up in these circumstances? Bobby closed his eyes. The situation came into focus: he wanted to raise the child along with Pamela, but she refused the idea as a mad fantasy. Worse, she kept hedging about even completing the pregnancy.

So, trying to prepare for final exams as well, Bobby felt besieged. He'd struggled all term in chemistry, and he fought to understand it now. Beyond the windows, dusk faded into black. A welcoming void. The tightness in his chest wouldn't leave, because if he failed the course, his father would be furious.

"Earth to Einstein. Try working this out while I'm gone,"

Pam said and passed him a sheet of paper. "I'm starving. Taking a snack break, ten minutes, tops. Now get to work."

She walked toward the hallway leading to the foyer. Bobby knew her destination: the vending machine halfway along the corridor. She'd joked, when they first started dating, that the contraptions were an ancient Mohawk invention, and she was addicted to the salty peanuts they dispensed, which she would munch while perusing the hallway's notice boards.

Bobby read over the problem: *Given that the empirical formula of a compound is CH and the molar mass is 104 g/mol, calculate the molecular formula. . . .* I'm screwed, he thought. He was never going to get this stuff.

After trying and failing three times to get the right answer, Bobby looked at his watch. Twenty-five minutes were gone. He walked to the corridor, but Pam wasn't there.

"Hey, Pam."

Bobby strode to the far side of the vending machine. No Pam. At the hallway's other end, a glassed-in entryway and a stairwell door stood in silence.

He passed through the vestibule and walked outside. Lilac drifted in the air and, across the quad, the silhouettes of Coombes Athletic Centre and the upper school loomed.

"Pam?"

June bugs chirped in syncopation like a techno-pop drum track. Over the insects' song, something else. Heels snicking on pavement. Bobby turned in the direction of the footsteps and saw Pam, twenty metres away, running toward the entrance marked Administration & Admissions. A door was swinging inward ahead of her but she grabbed it before it shut. She went in.

"Pam," he yelled.

CHAPTER 11

Bobby jogged to the door and tried it. Locked. He rapped on the glass and peered inside. No one in the vestibule. In the dim security lighting, an open staircase spiralled up.

"Bizarre."

He waited for ten minutes, then shuffled back to the library. Moving toward the study tables, he shivered in the frosty air and wondered when they were going to fix the crazy air conditioning. He called Pam's cell number. Voicemail. A group of Bobby's friends were leaving, and he asked them if anyone had seen his girlfriend in the last half-hour. No one. He sat down and made a vain try at the same chemistry problem.

Rose Molloy appeared beside him and smiled.

He looked away from her. "What do you want?"

"I'm heading out of here. More studying doesn't help the stupid Irish like me." She stroked her hair and held a lock of it in her fingers. Held the gesture for a second too long. She'd tried the flirtation a dozen times before.

"Join the club." He scribbled another line on the scrap paper. "Seen 'Pammy' in the last few minutes?"

"The less I see of her, the better."

Behind Rose, some students gathered their laptops and books, and others were already shuffling out of the building.

Her clique walked by the table, one of the girls gawking at Bobby. "See you at the dorm. Don't do anything I wouldn't do."

As the giggling gang disappeared down the corridor, Rose looked at her phone. "Quittin' time, my fellow scholar."

She turned the screen toward him—9:58 p.m. Closing time was ten o'clock.

"I don't see *you* rushing to leave," he said.

"My, my, you're grouchy tonight. Romantic trouble with the Pamster?"

"I was about to pack up. Then *you* came along."

"Pardon me for living." Rose shifted the stack of binders and books she held in her arms, then turned and sauntered alone down the hallway.

He was by himself now in the building, except for the librarian, Ms. Moore, who was acting as study-hall monitor for the extended hours. Pam's books and papers lay deserted, her knapsack hanging on the back of her chair.

Ms. Moore rounded the circulation desk and approached him. "That's a wrap. Time to leave," she said, adjusting tortoise-shell glasses on her nose.

On his floor at Norton House, most guys called her "the foxy librarian." He agreed.

She came up to the table and pointed at Pam's things. "Take your friend's gear with you."

"I can't find her."

Ms. Moore turned and looked at the wall clock. "She probably forgot and went back to her dorm. Have you tried calling her?"

"Yes. She wouldn't just—"

"If she's not there in the morning, go to administration. They'll know what to do." Ms. Moore put her hands on her hips. "I'm going to be late picking my husband up at Pearson. He's arriving from Japan. Now, chop-chop."

As she strode back to her desk, Bobby tried not to gawk at her hips swivelling beneath her pencil skirt.

God, what a pig he was. And if not for his sex drive, he wouldn't need to convince Pam to go through with a pregnancy he was responsible for. Well, she was accountable for it too, but none of that mattered. If she didn't want to keep the baby—and she didn't—that was her choice.

As the thought of an abortion flashed through his mind, Bobby heard his mother's warning to him: *I got pregnant at eighteen, and I've never forgiven myself for having the "termination"—what a horrible word for it. If you and a girl ever get into trouble, keep the baby. Have it adopted if you must, but* don't *do what I did.*

Bobby had made his choice then, and he hadn't cared what Dad or anyone else thought of it: Pam *would* give birth, and he would raise the kid, no matter how scary that seemed.

* * *

Fear now engulfed him as he scoured the essay-writing text for a shortcut to fix his English essay, but with Nathan's reek finally dissipated, Bobby could focus. He scratched a paragraph onto the foolscap. He stared into space. If Pam were here, she would be his saviour on this assignment too, but she wasn't here and never again would be.

Chapter 12

September 2006

When she encounters Rose's Gang of Four in the hallway or the common room, they look away and either giggle or reJspond to her "Hi" with cold silence. Pamela bristles. She'll say, "Fine, and how are you?" as they walk away. But she also finds them pathetic, for the weakness they show as Rose's self-declared clique, their single rooms huddling next to Rose's at one end of the third-floor hallway. Thankfully, to Pamela and Amy, the other doors along the corridor are friendly.

Thursday afternoon, before everyone leaves for the weekend, a co-ed athletic event takes place. Each student gets their choice of team sport to play, and the players are then grouped by grade level.

Unsure of what to choose, Pamela walks around the sign-up boards. She sees Bobby Havers's name on the basketball list, and she wants to be on his team. Helping her with her things during the move-in, giving her a thumbs-up during her speech—she hasn't forgotten his actions. Later, during the game, she grows to like him even more: five minutes into play, Pamela sinks a basket, and he flashes a brilliant smile as—lowering his hand because he's so tall—he high-fives her.

* * *

With classes done for the day, she stumbles through the door and collapses on her bed. A yellow sticky-note lies on the arm of Amy's desk chair: the girl has gone yet again to the library, so Pamela is going to nap until dinner.

A month into her exchange program, Pamela has learned that the academic expectations at Woodmore are rigorous—not that they were a breeze at Coyote River High. There, her teachers pushed her to go beyond the assigned work when she sat yawning at her desk, having finished her reading or math problems or lab report twenty minutes before everyone else. One math teacher would, at such times, speak to Pamela only in Mohawk. Because of Mr. Knoll, she went from knowing four words of the language (*yes, no, mother, father*) to having short, rudimentary chats with him in Mohawk.

Now, as then, the pressure to use her talents exhausts Pamela. Her father's incessant calls to work harder, to do better, whisper to her while she's watching TV in the common room or throwing a Frisbee with some floormates on the expanse of Taylor Green. The plastic disc is floating on the wind and Pamela is running and jumping but can't catch it, when a distant mechanical *clunk clunk clunk* shakes the air. Drifting from the east, the sound recurs intermittently at Woodmore, apparently coming from a construction project at Oakville Harbour. *Clunk clunk clunk.*

Pamela opens her eyes. She slides off the bed and answers the door.

"Oh, you're alive, Ms. Renard. I've been knocking for the past five minutes," says Housemistress Atkinson. She's wearing another billowy print dress—white polka dots on navy blue. "Assistant Director Flynn needs to see you in his office." Ms. Atkinson snaps her fingers. "Straightaway."

She marches Pamela across Taylor Green to the administration building.

In Mr. Flynn's office, trophies and team photos weigh down display shelves, and a couple of Impressionist paintings hang on the wood-panelled walls. Yes, Pamela thinks, a perfect old-world headmaster's office, or at least a room that's trying to look like one.

"Don't fidget," Ms. Atkinson says from the chair beside Pamela's. "You could to damage the leather if you keep scratching at it. There's nothing to be nervous about."

Pamela looks down at her chair's arm and lightly closes her fist. She wills herself to relax.

On the Assistant Director's desk, a framed picture stands angled toward him. Always too nosy for her own good, Pamela leans forward in her seat: in the photo, Mr. Flynn and two other men stand smiling beside each other. Wearing hunting caps and Day-Glo orange vests, each holds a bow, and on the ground in front of them, an arrow juts from the carcass of a deer. Getting out into nature, she knows, is a good thing. Since Pamela was old enough to walk, Grandma Becky took her into nearby fields and woods, where the girl learned to identify, and to remember the uses of, wild herbs like valerian, blue cohosh, and echinacea. Often when she and Grandma got home from a collecting jaunt, Pamela's mother screamed about the mud they'd tracked into the house. If Pamela's father was in the living room, he'd chuckle (along with Grandma Becky) and say, "Joceline, Joceline . . . calm down. What, you don't want Pampam to learn about the land?" Despite the last name Renard, no one on his side of the family spoke French, and nobody knew how or when they'd come to have the surname. As Pamela got older, she learned that her father resented *having* the name. He joined of a committee advocating a return to the matrilineal, clan-based system of ancestry—not just informally but strictly, to be passed by the reserve council as a bylaw. The reserve's clan mothers supported him, but at the Renard's church (one of fifteen of various denominations in Coyote River), he got into loud arguments about the issue with other parishioners. Pamela wishes people could just get along with each other, like the three smiling men in Mr. Flynn's hunting photo.

"Pamela," he says, "can you inform me whether, besides the disturbing graffiti incident, you experienced any trouble with Rose Molloy during orientation week?"

Her heart thumping, Pamela blurts out the words: "You're pursuing the bigoted little bitch. Thank you!"

Ms. Atkinson snaps her fingers. "Ms. Renard, watch your language! Consider yourself warned."

The only other thing on the Assistant Director's desk is a miniature American flag, its staff anchored in the pen holder's oak base. Where is the Canadian flag? Pamela wonders.

"OK," she says. "Rose Molloy and I got into an argument at lunch the day before my door was defaced. But she started it. Threw every Indian stereotype and slur at me. Rose blames *me* for the blockades at the building site in Ewing."

Ms. Atkinson combs her fingers through her ash-coloured pageboy. "Right. That then provides her motivation, although no excuse exists for such a hateful act."

"I'm cognizant of the land dispute," Mr. Flynn says, "but I still do not understand."

"The Molloy girl is from Ewing," Ms. Atkinson says. "Her parents operate an equestrian ranch on the town's outskirts."

"I see." Mr. Flynn gets up from his chair and gestures for them to do the same. "Well, with that information, I believe the case is wrapped up, as it were. Rose Molloy not only vandalized a dormitory door with hate speech, but she coerced another student—Penny Long, is it?—into taking the blame."

Turning to look out the window, he scratches his chin.

"Ms. Atkinson," he says, "Rose is hereby suspended for tomorrow. She's not to be in any classes or extracurricular activities. See to it that she stays all day and evening in her room. And should she again attempt a similar deed—or derogate Pamela's heritage in any way—she'll be sent home for a week. Apprise her of that possibility."

As Mr. Flynn holds open the door, Ms. Atkinson says, "I understand the care you're taking. It would be a shame to see this incident undo all your work on the Two Row Exchange."

Mr. Flynn *had* worked hard on setting up the exchange. Pamela remembers him being at Coyote River High School last year when they interviewed the keeners (including her) for the scholarship.

She's almost out the door when a question occurs to her, and she turns to face the Assistant Director. "So, Rose actually confessed?"

"No. After several interrogations," Ms. Atkinson says, "*Penny* conceded that Rose had blackmailed her with photographs, taken when Rose and her friends cornered the poor girl and pulled her underwear down. If Penny refused to

CHAPTER 12

vandalize your door and assume all guilt, Rose would post the photos on Facebook. But in the end, the scheme failed because Rose had carelessly texted the blackmail note from her own phone to Penny's."

Mr. Flynn nods as he returns to his desk. "And Pamela, to be absolutely sure, we had the police verify that the blackmail text did indeed originate from Rose's device."

Standing in the doorway, Pamela laughs. "What a lightweight."

With Ms. Atkinson glaring at her, she turns and catches the Assistant Director smiling.

* * *

At dinner, she glances over a few tables to see Rose, slouching with her head down, her friends consoling her. When Rose looks up and notices Pamela, her stare could bore through a concrete wall.

Pamela shoots a smirk back at her.

Chapter 13

June 2007

In the night, each hour seemed like twenty-four. Sol lay on his back, his hands clasped behind his head. Beside him, Tash snored. His eyes explored the ceiling's cracks and flaking paint; he mapped its water stains—some so faint they were barely visible, others shadowy and growing darker, bigger, blacker.

Two corpses are rising from Trevena Way, it's dark, and you smell lilac and cut grass and lavender from the gardens. Under a streetlamp's weak green glow, black juice flows from the girl's skull. The man's tie, hardened with dried blood, stands out like a hard-on. Zombies in a B-movie, the pair trudges toward you, their arms outstretched.

Someone shaking his shoulder.

"It was just a dream," Tash said. "Sol, you were dreaming."

He got up to pee, and outside the bathroom window, through smog along the horizon, a fiery eye glared. His T-shirt soaked with sweat, Sol shivered.

CHAPTER 13

***

The upper-school boys were pigs. Early afternoon and Sol was working in a first floor boys' washroom. He cleaned the toilet stalls and the urinals. When he was finished, he put on UV safety glasses, turned off the room lights, and switched on his Versalume lamp. The ultraviolet gadget cost a couple of hundred bucks, and Peacock had refused to pay for one out of Maintenance's budget, so Sol bought it himself. In the darkened room, splotches glowed in blue and violet on the wall, beside and below—even above—the piss catchers.

Pigs, spoiled little brutes. Either that, or they were the clumsiest kids in the GTA. He purged the wall of their dried piss and turned the room lights back on.

He didn't care that Howard and Cheryl laughed at him when he'd first showed them the UV lamp. They'd nicknamed him Captain Ultraviolet. The workload already demanded enough, they'd said, without them hunting for phantom pee like science nerds.

Nerdy or not, Sol did an in-depth job. Always. His porter father, a luckless saint, had done odd jobs and lugged suitcases around Union Station for thirty years, and he'd said that painstaking work was its own reward, even if no one praised you for it. Sol knew that no one ever would, anyway.

He moved to the sinks and noticed the paper-towel dispensers were empty, so he went down the hall to the janitor's closet, which faced, across the corridor, a glassed-in stairwell bursting with daylight. As he picked stacks of paper toweling from the shelves, voices and laughter echoed behind him. He turned. A group of teenage boys stood within a right-angled triangle of space under the lowest flight of stairs, and that opening formed a 3-4-5 triangle, the stringers making the hypotenuse. The Pythagorean Theorem was one of the few things Sol remembered from elementary school. From high school math, he recalled nothing.

He was about to turn back to the closet when, between the boys' navy blue suit jackets, a flash of white and orange shone. Rose Molloy. The white of her blouse, the glint of her red hair. And a sound, her sobbing. Sol turned on his phone's audio recorder and opened one of the stairwell doors, which swung silently, and he saw Rose backed against a brick wall under the stairs, the boys forming a half circle around her.

"You guys are animals," Rose said, her arms crossed in front of her.

In a bass voice, the tallest boy said, "Come on, Miss Tits. Don't just tease us—show us what you got."

Sol cleared his throat. "Sorry, guys. This floor's overdue for a mopping."

The hulk turned around and looked Sol over. "This won't take long."

"Look at the grime in the corners, it's gross," Sol said, stepping to within an arm's reach of the boy. "Can't have students getting sick from mould."

"Looks pretty clean to me." The teenager waved his hand in front of him. "Hey, no harm intended. We're just having some fun." Without warning, the boy drove his palm into Sol's chest.

The push drove Sol backward and would have toppled him, but he'd tensed his muscles before the shove came. The kid, who'd obviously never fought before, left himself open to attack, so Sol launched a half-hearted punch to the face but followed by kneeing the kid hard in the nuts.

CHAPTER 13

With their leader curled up and moaning on the terrazzo, the other boys cowered. Rose marched past them and rushed up the stairway.

"Hey, loser," the kingpin said, struggling to his elbows. "Do you know who my father is? We'll charge you with assault, asshole, so you're going to lose your job."

"I don't think so," Sol said, pulling out his cellphone. He played back the recording. "Now get to class or wherever the fuck you're supposed to be."

Chapter 14

At 21 Division, Alison's desk in Homicide sat cluttered with file folders. Her concentration wavered because the image of Pamela, the broken girl lying on paving stones, sliced through her thoughts. Dead at age eighteen, only five years older than Marcia.

Rather than years, Alison's experience at Halton Region amounted to weeks. Not yet living in Oakville during the first two of them, she commuted an hour each way, and the cars and trucks had literally moved at two kilometres per hour for minutes at a time.

But now, she drove for only fifteen minutes to get to work. Bliss.

Getting up from her desk chair, she inhaled the carpet's chemical smell as fluorescent lights buzzed overhead. Morning sunlight blazed through the windows.

In the kitchenette, Detective Constable John Ruvinsky poured coffee into his cup, decorated with an image of deer antlers over the words, *Hunting: Nothing Else Matters*.

"Morning," Alison said.

He faced the window. "Yeah."

As Alison filled her cup, Ruvinsky dumped cream and three teaspoons of sugar into his own. His thinning hair, seen

CHAPTER 14

against the bright window, formed an upside-down halo.

"So, how long have you been with Halton Region?" Alison said.

He walked away from her toward his desk. "Too friggin' long."

Nice chatting with you too, Alison thought. In her three weeks at Halton, Ruvinsky's behaviour was only the worst of the pack at Homicide. All guys. Even Randal McWilliams, with skin darker than hers, reinforced the Wall of Silence. And Ed Loams, Detective Sergeant, who'd been cordial to her so far, just sat in his office with the door closed.

The men of Homicide guarded their secrets well, but Fitzgerald possessed no such ability. His background was easy to unearth, and from phone calls and database queries, Alison confirmed that he'd spent six months in jail for aggravated assault. The conviction had come three years ago, when Fitzgerald was twenty-one. Earlier, at the end of his teens, he went through detox and came off cocaine. Yikes, she thought, and the guy must have an addictive personality, because last year he spent a night in jail for drunk and disorderly.

According to the trial transcript, Fitzgerald once beat a man unconscious. Fractures to the cheekbone and two ribs.

But the transcript also showed mitigating details. A woman filed an attempted rape charge against Fitzgerald's victim, Roger Franklin, on the same day police charged Fitzgerald with assault. Supposedly, Franklin and an accomplice had roughed up the woman, Tashi Harishandra, and they'd started to go further. Which was when Fitzgerald jumped Franklin. Harishandra testified that Fitzgerald was acting in her defence. And I thought chivalry was dead, Alison thought. If she'd been the judge, she would have given Fitzgerald a medal, not a jail term.

She looked up from her papers and stretched her arms. Ruvinsky noticed. He scowled and exhaled, and the sound was like air being let out of a tire, likely because a honey cruller filled his mouth, some crumbs stuck around his lips.

Double-desk work pods filled the office, which was crowded with computers, file cabinets, and people.

Results from Ident lay beside the trial transcript. She'd perused them already: pathology put the time of death for both victims at around ten o'clock, Sunday night, and both deaths were from physical trauma—to Renard's head, Havers's heart. No trace of cocaine showed up in the banker's system, nor any illicit drug or alcohol, in the girl's.

But the pathologist found a surprise in Renard. A fetus. Gestation was, at most, two or three weeks, and the father was . . . the killer? If so, Bobby Havers rose to the top of the suspect list.

The fingerprints on the bag of cocaine belonged to neither Havers nor Renard, and they yielded no matches in the CPIC database. Havers's dealer could have slipped the baggie into the suit jacket as they completed their transaction. That was the most plausible explanation, but maybe the killer planted it as a diversion.

Whether he was framed or not, Havers had no defensive wounds, but the bruising on Renard's neck was consistent with attempted strangulation. Which would explain the skin under her fingernails; the DNA samples, however, were in a queue at the province's Centre of Forensic Sciences, and any municipal force expecting next-week turnaround was fantasizing. Much more likely, the findings would come back after a month or longer.

CHAPTER 14

Why, in the first place, was Havers up there—apparently with Renard, a schoolgirl—drinking on a Sunday night? Maybe Bobby had accompanied them.

The fingerprint examination, though, pointed away from Bobby toward an unknown someone. From the roof patio, the wineglass shards yielded a thumbprint—with a zigzag scar in the ridge formations—that wasn't Havers's and matched no records in CPIC. But it did pair with impressions left on the coke baggie in Havers's suit jacket.

As shadowy as the print owner's identity, Alison realized, was the conflict on the roof before the victims were pushed. It could have been a drug deal gone bad, or a twisted love triangle exploding, but both possibilities were guesses. In what direction did the evidence point? Both victims' clothes contained lime-green filaments of a cotton-linen blend, which could have come from the killer when he or she struggled to push them off the roof, but the threads could have been transferred from somebody at a party or other group activity, or by some other means entirely. Another bit of data seemed clearer: the back of Havers's jacket was wet with ammonia from the mop on the roof, but that fact seemed too neat, shouting *setup* (unless Fitzgerald was dumber than he seemed). And if Fitzgerald was being framed, then his and Beckwith's recent trips to the library were simply a coincidence. To start excluding the possibilities, Alison resolved to check Beckwith's alibi herself and have Ident examine Pamela's dorm room and Ray Havers's house, with a focus on gathering fibre samples.

She called Jason's home number and agreed to a time with his wife. As she got up to drive to the address, an electronic grasshopper cheeped, and Ruvinsky scrabbled around his desk for his phone.

"Yeah," he said into the Blackberry. "Sweetheart, relax. Speak slow." Packed with staff, the open-concept office gave no privacy, and yet Ruvinsky whimpered like a puppy. "What does that *mean*, 'The tumour is stage four'? How many stages are there?" he said, wiping his nose on the back of his hand. Then he crumpled forward on his desktop.

"Is everything OK?" Alison said.

"Like you care."

* * *

At a townhouse complex in Oakville's suburban north, Becky Beckwith let Alison in. Wearing a Toronto Blue Jays T-shirt and sweatpants, the young woman cooed to a baby wailing in her arms, while a little boy hugged her knee. "Taylor, say hello to the nice lady."

Taylor buried his face in Becky's thigh and whimpered. She brushed back a strand of straw-coloured hair and smirked. "Oh, the joys of raising kids."

Alison smiled. "I have a daughter myself. What happened at Woodmore Academy is so disturbing."

"Jason's still freaked out from what he saw. He's barely slept."

"I understand," Alison said. "Forgive my abruptness, but I have to ask some personal questions. Have you and Jason been having any marital problems?"

Becky shooed Taylor over to his toys. With the baby now nodding toward sleep, they sat down on a toy- and blanket-covered sofa.

"What sort of . . . problems?" Becky said.

CHAPTER 14

Alison let her silence speak.

Becky sniffled. "Jason was great after Taylor was born. He really was. . . . But he's been—I don't know—not 'there' since this one came along." She smiled at the baby, then shook her head. "Distracted, sort of."

"Distracted by what?"

Becky shrugged.

"And that's all?"

"OK, OK. He's not here much in the evenings." Becky wiped her eyes with a baby blanket. "And sometimes he comes home plastered. Or shirks the chores he'd done gladly when Taylor was a newborn."

Alison decided to be blunt. "So is he drinking with his buddies or having an affair?"

"Every payday, he contributes to a savings account, going toward my tuition for dental hygiene at college. You know, for after the kids are in school. How could he be having—"

"Would you say you're a light sleeper?"

"A floorboard creaks, and I'll wake up. And now, with these two munchkins—and whatever's up with Jason—getting a decent night's sleep is a vague memory for me."

"I see. Has Jason ever mentioned a man named Solomon Fitzgerald?"

"Nope. Never heard of him."

"Alright. Can you remember where Jason was last Sunday night?"

Becky sprang toward Taylor, who was sucking on a USB memory stick. She snatched it and returned to the couch. "For a change, Jason was home with me and the kids that night. We went to bed a little after ten o'clock."

"Any memory of Jason getting up during the night?"

Becky laughed. "Only I get up for the kids now, and Jason sleeps like a log."

"Does Jason own a lime-green shirt?"

"Lime green?" Becky hooted again. "We don't have the money for hip clothes, and Jason wears his shirts until they're as thin as sheer curtains."

Chapter 15

Woodmore's campus was Alison's oasis from the afternoon sun. From the landscaped islands of Trevena Way, only the cries of blue jays broke the stillness. Her footsteps echoed along the deserted walkway, classes being underway after lunch. Whether classes were in session or not, she was going to interview Bobby Havers—boyfriend of one victim, son of the other. Love was the most dangerous emotion, and Alison primed herself to watch his body language.

She strode into administration's board room to find Bobby sitting in his Woodmore uniform beside a man who wore brogues, dress pants, and a crisply ironed button-down shirt.

"I'm Herman Flock," the man said as he rose and shook her hand. "Housemaster of Norton House. And this is Bobby Havers."

The boy shook her hand with a bear paw. His wild hair clashed with the preppy jacket and tie, and he stood at least six feet four. Ray Havers's height matched his son's, but the man was thin, not brawny like this kid. He would've lost a pushing match with Bobby.

The boy plunked down in a padded chair.

Alison took a seat across the table, which gleamed, reflecting two rows of ceiling pot lights. Spreading her hands over the tabletop, she wondered if it was real mahogany.

"Bobby," she said, "I'm very sorry about your father's passing."

"And my girlfriend. My girlfriend's 'passing.' " Reddened skin encircled Bobby's eyes; steel edges surrounded his words.

"I'm here to ask you some questions about the death of your father and Pamela Renard."

"Please be reasonable," Herman Flock said, smoothing the cotton of his shirt. "The suffering he's going through."

"OK, Bobby, you're friends with Mr. Fitzgerald, a janitor here?"

"More like colleagues."

Herman Flock raised an eyebrow.

"Sol's into classical piano," the boy said, "and I'm in a rock band. We just talk sometimes about music."

"Where?" Alison said. "At Woodmore?"

"Yes."

"How do you know him?"

"Through Pam."

"And how did *she* know him?"

The ceiling grilles hissed, and Alison shuddered in the cold downdraft.

"From the day Pam moved into Pilkington House," Bobby said, "this girl on her floor, Rose Molloy, started throwing slurs at her. For being Indian—Mohawk." He grasped a lock of his hair and chewed on it. Flock glared at him, and the teen brushed the strand back. "Sol witnessed it. He was the first person at Woodmore to help Pam. Like tell her what a screw-up Rose was, tell her to stick up for herself. One day, after Pam and I started hanging together, she introduced me to Sol. I remember, he was mopping a corridor, and she just

CHAPTER 15

started talking to him like they were old friends. Which I guess they were, in a way."

"They had a romantic relationship?" Alison said.

"What?" Bobby chuckled. "No, no. Just that Pam never forgot his helping her deal with Rose, back when she had no network at Woodmore."

"Pamela never hinted they'd been more than friends?"

"The guy's a *janitor*."

How open-minded of you, Alison thought. Pampered little ass. "Why were your father and Pamela up on the roof garden on Sunday night? The evidence suggests they were drinking together."

"That's ridiculous."

"Why? They'd never met?"

"She had dinner a couple of times with my mother and father and I."

"So your relationship with her was a serious one."

"Stupid me, I *thought* it was serious."

"Were you intimate with each other?"

Bobby pushed himself against the chair back. "I thought you were here to find out who did this."

"In autopsying Pamela's body, the pathologist found a fetus—"

Bobby's hand whacked the table. "I'm the father. Happy now? I wanted us to keep the baby, raise it together, but Pam never decided. She was clear about not wanting *me*, though."

"When was the breakup?"

"I'm missing a chemistry class to be here, and I'm already behind in the course."

"Have you heard of a charge called 'obstruction of justice'? You can go to jail for it."

Flock joined Alison in glowering at Bobby.

"Last week," the boy said. "Thursday or Friday."

Alison wrote that down. "OK. Other than Rose Molloy, did Pamela have any enemies? Other kids here who might want to harm her?"

Bobby shook his head.

"Was Amy Ling jealous?"

"The roommate? She's obsessed with getting high marks," Bobby said. "Not boys."

"Your father. Was he in any trouble?"

"I really have to get to chemistry class or I'm going to flunk."

"We're talking about your *father* here."

Bobby stared at his hands on the table. "He and Mom have fought for years, but they seemed happier, calmer with each other."

"Happier for how long?"

"Like the last year or so."

"What changed?"

"No idea."

"How did your father and you get along?"

"You think I killed my father."

"I'm not saying you did anything."

"I guess I can kiss a passing grade in chemistry goodbye. My father was on my case about school. It's my last year, and he had the illusion I'm going to be a doctor or lawyer. He wouldn't hear of me majoring in music. Things weren't rosy, but I wouldn't kill him over it."

"What were your whereabouts on Sunday night?"

Bobby sighed, then squinted. "Around 7:30, Pam and I met at the library to study for final exams. I suck at math and science, so she was helping me cram for the chemistry final.

CHAPTER 15

It was like 9:15 when she took a break and headed down the corridor for junk food from the vending machines. But she like . . . disappeared. After half an hour, I went looking for her. Look, I'm not even sure whether I saw what I *think* I saw, but I walked out of the library and glimpsed her, to my right, going into Administration & Admissions. The door closed behind her, and I called out and ran to the admin building, but when I got there, the doors were locked, and I could see that the foyer was empty. I rapped on the glass and shouted. Five minutes went by. I banged again on the doors, but nothing happened. It was so strange. I went back to the library."

"You didn't wait any longer? Presumably you'd have wanted to find—"

"Look, the library was about to close. Ask the librarian, Ms. Moore. When I left at ten o'clock, me and her were the only people in the building."

"She and I," Flock said.

"And where did you go after that?"

"Straight to the dorm," Bobby said.

Flock leaned forward. "Every night, a student monitor on each floor of Norton House does an inspection just before lights out at eleven. I would have immediately received a report if Bobby was absent. But I obtained no such information."

Alison stood up. "Thank you. That's it for now."

As Bobby and Flock walked out the door, she glanced at her notes. According to what Bobby said, no motive drove him, and he had an alibi for after ten p.m., unless he'd snuck out of the dorm later. And what about his seeing Pamela walk into administration's entrance, which would've been locked at the time? The statement made no sense or else hinted at something very odd. Perhaps speaking with the girl's archenemy, Rose Molloy, would unlock the weirdness and provide a simple explanation. Regardless, Rose's hostility to Pamela made the bigoted girl a suspect, and Alison circled her name and wrote *Interview ASAP* beside it.

* * *

After querying an office worker in administration, Alison phoned the housemistress of Pilkington House, the dorm Rose Molloy was staying in. She told the woman, a Ms. Atkinson, of her need to interview Rose and asked if the girl would be available by the end of the afternoon. But Atkinson said Rose hadn't been seen since the previous night—not at breakfast, not at lunch, not in any of her classes. So, the housemistress was checking with Rose's teachers and Director Collier to see whether the girl had been sent home due to a family emergency or illness.

Strange, Alison thought. As odd as Pamela Renard disappearing into the locked administration building on the night she died.

Ms. Atkinson promised to call as soon as she learned Rose's whereabouts.

With no other interviews slated for the afternoon, Alison still wanted to make good use of her time at Woodmore, so she asked the way to the roof garden, knowing she needed to get another look at it after Monday's rush with the Ident crew. She followed directions from another worker she'd asked and walked down a corridor marked *School Officers*. Along one side of the hallway, light from floor-to-ceiling windows blinded her, and wood-panelled doors with brass nameplates

CHAPTER 15

dotted the opposite wall. At a glass door halfway along, caution tape and a young constable guarded access to the roof garden, which lay beyond the window-wall. She guessed its main purpose was to impress parents and investors. Give them the VIP treatment, tea on a roof garden overlooking the lake.

The constable unlocked the door and pulled back the tape, and Alison stepped onto the roof space. At one end of the roof garden, a steel door marked *Fire Exit* nestled in the stone wall. It was the door to the library stairwell she'd been in yesterday with Hicks and the Ident duo.

Alison went into the stairwell and descended, her heels echoing on the concrete. OK, she thought, the administration building was locked over the weekend—the admin manager confirmed it—which rules out access from that side. But at the library stairwell's top landing, if the roof-garden door is always locked, how did Pamela Renard or Ray Havers gain access? And what was Havers even doing at Woodmore late on a Sunday night? Assuming a murder-suicide scenario, another key question involved motive.

To pursue its answer, Alison drove to the exclusive Clayton Hill neighbourhood, not far from Woodmore. Interviewing Debra Havers might crack the conundrums. But if the woman knew why Ray's spare-time activities included drinking with a schoolgirl who happened to be his son's sweetheart, getting Debra to admit such an awkward truth could be gruelling.

Alison's concern was warranted. The interview yielded little. She wondered whether Debra was simply in shock from Ray's death, trying to hide compromising realities, or a combination of both.

* * *

On Sunday evening, Alison had knocked on Marcia's door and convinced the child to join St. Thaddeus's youth group. Half an hour passed before the girl agreed.

Now, after just two days in Spirit Seekers, Marcia stood in the foyer with yet another boy, Carson. After introductions, she summarized the Seekers' activities that day. Then—speaking quickly, as though fast words would dodge Alison's radar—she asked if Carson could stay for dinner.

Alison knew what her daughter's reaction would be, but she made an excuse anyway about an aunt and uncle arriving soon, and that ploy let Carson leave without awkwardness or hurt feelings.

Marcia's jaw plunged. "I don't get it. Carson's from Spirit Seekers. He's really nice."

"It's hot out, I know," Alison said, looking up and down her daughter's cut-off jeans and crop top. "But if you showed any more skin, you'd be naked."

Marcia sucked air through her teeth.

"Let the girl be," Shirley said, standing by the kitchen stove. "She's only being practical, because it's as hot as Hades."

Marcia ambled up the staircase before either adult could say more. Her bedroom door clicked shut.

Shirley leaned on the counter and shook her head. "Youth group or no youth group, child's just exploring."

"Of all people, you should know what can happen when young women go 'exploring,'" Alison said. Shirley had bailed her out one night, when Kopal and Alison were arrested for underage drinking and causing a disturbance. As they neared the end of their teens, the girls dared each other with

CHAPTER 15

shoplifting, drinking, and boys. They hadn't finished their escapades until it was too late for both of them.

Was Pamela Renard—living at Woodmore, away from the constraints of home, and unsupervised by her parents—reckless as well? Despite what Bobby Havers said, maybe Pamela had flings with all three men: Bobby, his father, and Fitzgerald. Like throwing sparks on tinder.

Chapter 16

Sometimes, on a weekend evening, Sol and Tash would drive thirty minutes west from the city and up Mount Nemo, and after they made out on the ridge, they would watch the sky darken over the lake, the grids and curves of Burlington's streetlights glimmering below, beyond a patchwork of farms and woodlands. The lights spread along the lakeshore. Toward the east, they merged into Oakville. If Sol watched those sparkles for long enough, his breath softened. He was alone. No thoughts. No anything.

The mood never lasted long enough, and he'd turn back to Tash, Oakville lying beyond her, high-rises blurred in fuzzy silhouettes. The buildings were pipsqueaks compared to Mount Nemo, but that rock wasn't a mountain: it was a stretch thirty metres high of the Niagara Escarpment. Sol held no inkling what "escarpment" meant, but he didn't want to sound stupid—he'd taken so much dope in high school, he barely passed Grade Twelve—so he stifled the question.

As if she were psychic, Tash provided an answer the first time they went up Mount Nemo. It seemed then that she was apprehensive about the two of them being found by a police cruiser on patrol, because after their first kiss in the car, Sol wanting more, Tash pushed him away.

"Niagara Escarpment," she said.

Sol rubbed her back and leaned toward her face. "What about it?"

"It's a dolomite spine, four hundred and fifty million years old. Harder than the limestone around it." She gestured to the landscape, a quilt of farm fields and woodlots and two-lane roads, that spread out below them. "The rock we're parked on weathers way slower."

"You're making it up."

"We're talking millions of years. Weathering through geologic epochs and then across multiple ice ages."

Sol mimed smoking a cigarette and put on aristocratic accent. "Absolutely fascinating, my dear."

Tash chuckled and this time didn't resist Sol's advances.

Anyway, real backbone ran through that rock. It was tougher than Sol, who—when the stakes really mattered—buckled like a second-rate boxer punched in the gut. He took an interest in the ridge, read up on it. Like the curve of a horseshoe, the Niagara Escarpment ran north from Upstate New York, through southern Ontario, and into the Great Lakes through the Bruce Peninsula and Manitoulin Island. Then it crossed the border into the States again and reached across northern Michigan into Wisconsin, where it hugged Lake Michigan's shore for five hundred kilometres, ending near Milwaukee.

A big piece of rock. Sol dreamed of someday hiking the whole thing with Tash.

* * *

Sol got home late from work, microwaved a tray of frozen

lasagna, and he and Tash ate in silence, except for dull chatter about how each other's day had gone. Anything to avoid talking about her parents. About her father. There was a silence, which seemed to last an hour until Tash broke it.

"You're as quiet as a ghost," she said.

"And you aren't?"

"Any news about the . . . the scene at Woodmore?"

Sol pushed down the flutter in his stomach and the image of Pamela's broken skull in his mind. "The library's open again, and the bodies are gone. But yesterday, that detective, hinting that *I* was the psycho-murderer. I felt numb. Sleepwalked through work."

He cleared the dishes from the table, but as he leaned down to kiss Tash's cheek, she turned away. Dickens United and accompanying the choir would be a welcome escape.

* * *

Willing himself to make the request, Sol bounded up the steps of Dickens United, nestled in the suburbs north of downtown. Along the church's nave, he padded toward the waiting choir. Dickens was small, but to Sol, its arches were as sky-high as the music he got to play and hear there.

As he approached the piano, Minister Frey waved. Strands of her shoulder-length hair, closely streaked in black and silver, fluttered in the breeze from an upright floor fan. "Thank God you made it."

Assembled behind her on a stepped platform, the choir members laughed.

Sol bowed to them.

Minister Frey opened the sheet music on her lectern. "OK,

CHAPTER 16

let's wrestle this beautiful monster to the ground. Or up to heaven. That would be better." More chuckles from the choir. "Summer's coming fast, and a lot of you will be who-knows-where for the next two months. But we want to knock them dead with this in September. Get those bums in the seats, because this church needs money. Badly."

The next hour provided a bolthole from the daily bullshit. As Sol struck the keys and the choir sang, the *Cantate Domino* rang out like rays of sunlight filtered through clouds. And he thought, If only everyday life were music.

After the practice finished, the singers filed down the nave, and Sol folded up his sheet music.

Minister Frey leaned against the piano. "The usual?"

He was going to ask. He was. But falling into their routine came so easy. "Uh-huh. One more hour. Practicing here is great, with how the sound echoes off the ceiling." Sol took out the Bach keyboard Partita he was working on. "You know, I'm obliged for—"

"Forget it. You're the best accompanist we've ever had. So practice away. I'll be in my office."

She left, and Sol went through the six movements, breaking them down, searching for an interpretation. The process was like using smaller and smaller chisels to find a statue within a chunk of rock. He chose which notes to articulate in a phrase, tried it out and picked different notes, or changed a pause to an accelerando. He experimented with dynamics: where to play loud, where soft, and how to transition between the two. Cousin Danny had taught him well.

The Partita's first and last movements were challenging and showy, but Sol preferred a middle one, the dark Sarabande, which sounded divine on the Steinway grand, the notes clear and strong, filling the space and reverberating for seconds. The keyboard's responsiveness was superb. He appreciated his luck, because before he'd answered the *Accompanist Wanted* ad posted at his local grocery store, he'd only played so-so upright pianos, usually out of tune and with a few sticky keys.

When Minister Frey had auditioned him a year ago for the position, she'd asked for references. He blurted it out, that he'd only been out of the Milton Hilton (a.k.a. Maplehurst Correctional Complex) for a year. He said he might be able to get two references: an assistant director of Woodmore, and the owner of the Green Dot Restaurant (where Sol worked for three years before his assault conviction). Minister Frey didn't mind. She'd said she "saw something" in him, and they would try it out and end the arrangement if any problems surfaced. None had.

The minister appeared from around the doorway to her office. "Time's up, maestro. As usual, a divine sound. It's nice to have it when I'm working on a sermon."

Sol closed the Bach book and spun on the piano bench to face her. "Uh-huh. Glad you like it." The thumping of his fist against his abdomen gave him pluck. Finally. "You went to university, right?"

"Yes," she said, glancing at his belly. "Why do you ask?"

Sol eased his abdominals and stopped tapping on his stomach. "Well, I'm thinking of . . . thinking about going myself."

"Music major?"

"Phys. ed. Figure that'll give me a better chance in the job market."

"But you'll keep up the piano."

"I want to minor in music." The grain of the oak floor

suddenly fascinated Sol. "Since I'll be a mature student, there's a test—"

"What test?"

"Well, it's more than just one exam, really. At U of T, there's this thing called the Academic Bridging Program. You do coursework, go to lectures, and you have to get at least 73 percent—that's a B grade—to then start a full-time degree. Academic Bridging's a year long, part time, and I'm almost finished. I just don't know if I'll make 73 percent."

"You seem like a bright enough guy to me."

"Come on. I already told you, I barely squeaked through Grade Twelve English with a D-minus, the lowest to pass? My other marks were no better."

A shrug from Minister Frey. "So what? You don't have to be an English scholar if you're in phys. ed. and music."

"Yeah, but first, I got to get that frigging B."

"Hey, no swearing in here." The minster brushed back a tress and pointed upward. "You'll upset the big guy, or gal, upstairs."

"I really need help with the damn thing—oops. Me and Tashi tried, but she has no patience. And you're good with words."

"You think I'm patient?" the woman said, grinning. "We 'people of the cloth' don't sit around all day communing with angels."

"The final exam is coming up in—"

"Don't worry. I'll go get my schedule. But there are two rules. One, call me Imogen. I hate formalities, which I guess is a bad quality in my profession. Two, be patient with yourself. With writing, if you put your mind to it, there ain't nothin' can stop you." Her wink was devilish, and Sol would follow her down to Hell if it got him the 73 percent.

Chapter 17

Coyote River First Nation

Ms. Atkinson hadn't called yet about Rose Molloy's whereabouts, so Alison started the workweek by driving out to the reserve to interview Pamela's parents. She was optimistic. Perhaps they'd have a different perspective to share, one that might open a new avenue of inquiry.

She was pessimistic, however, that DC John Ruvinsky would contribute anything, but Detective Sergeant Loams had insisted on an officer accompanying Alison for this interview. "The case Ruvinsky's been assisting on is in a lull. Take him along. But you only get him for today. Two officers—it'll show respect," Loams said, "and that we're taking this case as seriously as any other." The reality was that only Alison was working it. *When*, she thought, is Detective Norm Miller going to be fixed up from his climbing accident? If not for Miller's hospitalization, he and Alison would be partnered, and she would be under much less pressure.

Passing first through the suburban sprawl of Burlington, then by the smokestacks and apartment towers of Hamilton, her Malibu entered the countryside. Expansive fields rolled by, dotted with farmhouses, silos, industrial-scale chicken houses, and the occasional feed-processing plant—corrugated metal silos linked by crisscrossing shafts and conveyor belts—to rival any work of high-tech engineering.

"Holy shit," Ruvinsky said, gawking out the passenger-side window. "No quaint family farms 'round *here*."

Alison nodded. "You grow up on a farm?"

"What? *No*." Ruvinsky seemed offended she'd even asked.

"God, you're touchy. What's up?"

"You wouldn't understand."

Fine, mister grumpy, Alison thought, *I'll shut up then*.

Under a heavy sky, they drove the next fifteen minutes in silence. A concrete bridge appeared and beside it, a road sign.

WELCOME TO COYOTE RIVER FIRST NATION TERRITORY

The Malibu's tires thudded as they went across expansion joints, and the car passed over three hefty pilings anchored beneath the river.

Past the far bank, Alison turned right at the first crossroad. Ruvinsky checked the rural-route number of each driveway against directions provided by Coyote River Police. When they reached Pamela's, the roadside bushes partially revealed a yellow-brick house set a hundred metres back from the road. Two-and-a-half storeys high, the building looked custom-designed, and it occupied at least three thousand square feet. The structure dwarfed the humbler dwellings they'd seen along the way.

The interior was no less impressive, with its double-storey

CHAPTER 17

great room, the hardwood floor reflecting tall round-arched windows. Sitting with Ely Renard and his mother Rebecca around a coffee table, Alison thanked him for the coffee. She repeated the condolences she'd expressed in the vestibule. Ruvinsky cleared his throat and adjusted his suit jacket.

"Joceline had an emergency call," Ely said, crossing his beefy arms on his chest. "She's a volunteer firefighter."

"That's OK. We can interview her later if it's necessary." Alison sipped her drink to help hide her disappointment: Joceline Paquette could well have key information to give.

"Well, don't be too late," Ely said, wearing a supercilious smile. "Grafton Flynn, from Woodmore Academy, has already been here to give us his sympathy—"

"The school's Assistant Director?" Alison said.

Ely nodded. "A good man. He's holding up Woodmore's end of the Two Row Exchange—and at this rate he's going to find my daughter's killer before you do."

"Well, we'd better get started then," Alison said, hoping her irritation didn't show.

The discussion lasted fifteen minutes, Ruvinsky contributing little to the effort. As the gloom deepened beyond the windows, white-haired Rebecca dabbed a handkerchief to her eyes. "I'm not surprised by what's happened, not one bit." She took off her glasses and waggled them toward her son. "I warned her, Ely."

"So did I, Mom."

"To think," Rebecca said, "some high-and-mighty white man . . ."

Ruvinsky shifted in his chair. He stroked his tie and sighed.

"There's no evidence of sexual assault," Alison said. "Nor have we confirmed foul play at this point."

Ely laughed bitterly. "Right, of course."

Alison shook her head. "I know that doesn't give Pamela back to you."

She asked if they knew of any enemies Pamela had, and Rebecca mentioned a couple of high-school girls with whom there'd been altercations. "But last year that pair calmed down, and Pam hasn't talked about them again. I think, after she started going out with Luke Daveneau, the two placed her some notches lower on their social ladder. Luke is *persona non grata* at Coyote River High. So, these girls 'won.' In their minds, they're hanging out with the cool but *respectable* boys now, and Pam isn't. Or wasn't."

Rebecca's statement, while not proven, reinforced Alison's view that the resentful-rival slant was unlikely. She'd pursue the angle only if every other lead failed. So, time to move on, Alison thought.

She revealed that cocaine was found at the scene, and Ely bristled, raking beefy fingers through his short black hair. "That boy . . . I thought Pampam's getting off the reserve—and away from Luke—would make her safer. What a fool I was. But, yeah, it wouldn't surprise me if he's involved, even if only indirectly. I mean, who knows what the gangs he associates with are capable of? Luke Daveneau runs with some local fools selling drugs to our children, but the same bozos think they can play with the Hells Angels."

Alison made a note to interrogate Daveneau. Nothing more of substance came from Ely or his mother, so Alison concluded the chat, and she and Ruvinsky left.

In the car, she phoned the Coyote River Police about the young gangster. She got through to the Chief, Zach Wilson, who corroborated Ely's assessment of Daveneau. But the

CHAPTER 17

officer dashed any plans Alison conceived to question Luke: Pamela Renard's former boyfriend was absent from Coyote River and had been so for a week.

"His buddies are tight-lipped," Wilson said. "But I'll call you if Daveneau turns up."

Chapter 18

October 2006

Oakville

In phys. ed. class today, Ms. Steele has the girls set up archery targets on a soccer field. She tells them the basics and takes five demonstration shots. What a markswoman, Pamela thinks. Leave Ms. Steele in the woods with a longbow and she could easily survive.

"Let's have a volunteer, eh?" the teacher says, her voice gruff. "Amy, show us how it's done."

Amy shuffles forward. "Wearing glasses and having good aim are mutually exclusive, Ms. Steele."

"Nonsense."

Amy's shot goes wide of the whole target. She giggles, along with the rest of the class, and gets a stare from Ms. Steele. The teacher's severe personality informs her hairstyle, which is closely cropped, with a spiky plume at the front.

The boys, who are shooting on an adjacent part of the field, cheer Amy. More like jeer. They holler and jump, pumping

CHAPTER 18

their fists in the air, and Mr. Flynn shouts at them to settle down. Among the boys is Bobby Havers, who raises his arms to call for silence, and his buddies settle down.

Ms. Steele's whistle chirps. "Girls, listen up, eh? Stand behind Amy and me, and observe carefully."

Her bow loaded and drawn, Amy practices her stance. Ms. Steele points out the flaws: string-side elbow too low, instead of in line with the arrow, and shoulders too high and tense. Amy's tongue protrudes from a corner of her mouth as she aims. She releases the bowstring, and the arrow whacks against the target, the shaft protruding from within the concentric red rings. The girls applaud.

Score ring eight, Pamela thinks, that's pretty damn good. Right now, it feels great to be a Woodmore girl, same as the rest. She's almost forgotten about Rose when, as the clapping fades, the whinnying laugh pierces the air.

"Calm down, everybody," Ms. Steele says, beaming. She cracks chewing gum between her teeth. "Can anyone tell me Amy's score for that shot?"

Rose Molloy raises a freckly arm. "Eight. The eight ring."

"Correct. Very good, Rose," Ms. Steele says and hands Amy another arrow.

What a joke, Pamela thinks. How hard is it to count target rings, one to ten? Well, at least the redheaded pest is competent at *something*.

Amy raises her bow but Rose interrupts. "Hey, Pam's from Coyote River, she must be a pro at this. Come on, Pam, show us the 'Mohawk method.'"

Pamela's fingers press like a steel vice against her bow's grip.

Ms. Steel digs her fingers into her spiky mop. "Not another

105

word, Rose. Unless you *want* another suspension."

Rose, standing three steps away from Pamela, continues, "But Ms. Steele, it's like in Pam's blood. You know? Cowboys and Indians, bows and arrows."

Pamela lets go of her bow's grip and seizes the tapered lower limb with both hands. She bounds at Rose and swings the bow like a baseball bat. When the hardwood whacks against Rose's upper arm, the girl squeals. Rose rubs the skin, which is already forming a welt, and grimaces. "Ms. Steele, did you see what she—"

"There, do you like that?" Pamela says. "It's the 'Mohawk method' for shutting up your vile mouth!"

Towering over the rest of the class, big Joan steps between the two combatants, plants her feet firmly, and crosses her thick arms. She's facing Pamela and she scowls. "Leave my—leave her alone!"

"Not another word," Ms. Steele says, "from any of you." Turning from them, she shouts, "Mr. Flynn, could you come over here? I've got gals here who are *way* out of line. I'm taking them to Ms. Collier's office, so if you could look after—"

"What seems to be the problem?" the Assistant Director says as he jogs toward them. He takes out a tissue and blows his nose but still has to wipe his nostrils on the back of his hand.

Pamela raises an eyebrow and thinks, What a *model* of good manners.

Mr. Flynn eyeballs the mark on Rose's arm, and as if on cue, she blubbers and gingerly touches it. "What happened to Rose?" he says.

Ms. Steele turns to face Pamela. "Why don't you tell him?"

CHAPTER 18

"Pamela?" Mr. Flynn says, his brow low and creased.

"Um, well, Rose was going on about my genetic ability with a bow and arrow, about the 'Mohawk method' of shooting," Pamela says. "Sorry, but I lost my cool and hit her—she deserved it."

"She used her bow like a club!" Rose says, whimpering.

"Are these accusations—on both sides—true?" the Assistant Director says, looking at Ms. Steele.

"Yes," she says. "On both sides. I'm very disappointed."

"Indeed," Mr. Flynn says, frowning at Pamela. "If you do not mind, Ms. Steele, let us forgo informing Director Collier." He approaches Rose. "The only reason you are not being suspended again, young lady, is that if you *were*, I would have to do the same to Pamela, and thus possibly exacerbate the enmity between you two. So, please, celebrate with each other your escaping punishment—this time. If something like this happens again, however, you *will* be disciplined. One or both of you." He looks at his watch. "Alright, the period is virtually over, so let us all head inside."

As the students walk toward Coombes Athletic Centre, Ms. Steele gestures for Mr. Flynn to stay. Pamela looks back at them and strains to hear their conversation.

"No disrespect, Grafton," Ms. Steele says, "but there's a protocol for physical violence. Shouldn't you have taken the pair to Ms. Collier and let her decide on—"

Abruptly, Flynn turns and paces ahead, speaking over his shoulder to Ms. Steele, "With regard to discipline, I have the same authority as the Director. And I don't want this incident to sabotage—even slightly—the Two Row Exchange."

The period bell sounds as the students reach Coombes.

Inside, in the gym's storage room, as Pamela is putting away her equipment, she sees Bobby Havers standing in a corner by the exterior door. All the other students have left the room and entered the gym, and she and Bobby are alone.

"I agree with what you did out on the field," he says. "She had it coming."

Pamela shrugs and looks at her running shoes. "Thanks. I just wish she weren't at this school."

"Forget about her." Bobby pauses, and when Pamela looks at him, he's blushing. "In fact, to help get her out of your mind, why don't you go to a movie with me this Friday night?"

"I don't know if it will help. Anyway, I'm going home early Saturday morning. There's a Two Row Exchange activity I'm needed at."

"Oh, I've heard nothing about more doings for that."

"There was only so much money raised, so this one's just for me and my Pilkington floor-mates, plus Jordan Windsor and the homeroom class he's placed in at Coyote River."

"I don't see a conflict. We'll just go to the early show on Friday."

Unsure whether she can trust Bobby, Pamela downplays her interest in him. "OK then, I guess. But I have to be back by nine. I've got stuff to pack."

Bobby rakes his fingers through his spiky hair and asks for her phone number.

* * *

On Saturday morning, Pamela's parents pick her up at eight, and an hour later their van arrives back in the Coyote River reserve. She spends the morning at home and has lunch there. Sitting at the table with her parents and Grandma Becky, amid

CHAPTER 18

the comforting aromas of coffee and homemade soup, she wonders why she was so intent last spring on winning her way into the Two Row Exchange. Why? She wants to be back with her family and the community she's always known. She wants to pretend this is just another weekend, just another noon-hour at home, that she never left for Oakville. She wishes Woodmore Academy, with Mr. Flynn's idea for the exchange, had never approached Coyote River's band council.

This afternoon she has to attend a lesson Melvin Brown is giving at Coyote River High. When the elder's talk is over, she'll have this evening and Sunday morning here. But then it's back to Oakville. Not enough time.

Wind buffeting the van as they drive west, Pamela's father drives her to the high school, where Jordan Windsor is standing by the entrance with about twenty-five Coyote River Grade Twelves—his classmates for the exchange's duration. Pamela first met Jordan the day of the Two Row canoeing activity, just before the school year commenced. She exchanges greetings with him and says hello to a couple of her friends in Jordan's group. Seeing them makes her realize how much she misses them. Everything would be so much easier if she'd stayed here. What illusions had clouded her vision, made her think she'd flourish off the reserve?

In a separate group, Amy and the rest of the girls on Pamela's floor stand beside their bus. Jordan turns toward them.

"Hey," he says, waving his arms overhead, "come on over!"

When the two clusters have formed a common crowd, Rose Molloy approaches, and, exchanging a glance with Pamela, says, "Hi, Jordan. How are you surviving here?" Rose pulls him aside and the two converse. Pamela is relieved to be out of her way.

109

Melvin Brown, having arrived on his motorcycle, dismounts and joins the gathering. The teacher waves to him and tells everyone to follow Melvin around the building to the playing fields. The wiry elder bounds ahead of the group, and he's wearing the same outfit he had on at the canoeing exercise. Melvin is known around the reserve for his "uniform": work boots, jeans, camouflage jacket, and frayed baseball cap.

They reach the rear fields, but Melvin keeps walking toward an adjoining woodlot. When everyone has joined him at the edge of the woods, he sits down, his legs crossed in front of him on the grass. "Everyone, let's form a big circle," he says, gesturing with outstretched arms. "And mix together, folks, I don't want to see no half circle of Coyote River kids and the other of Woodmore."

An awkward minute passes with people sitting down, only to move, then move again. When they're all intermingled and sitting in a rough circle, with the Coyote River teacher seated opposite from Melvin, the elder waits until silence prevails. "Circles make sense to Indians," Melvin says. "They're how we understand life. But we don't know nothing about straight lines or lists. They don't make no sense to us. Now, you know how to count to ten in Mohawk, right?"

Though the wind is coming from the west, the woodlot acting as a buffer, Pamela wishes she'd worn a sweater. She shivers, crosses her arms in front of her and hunches forward.

Like a partial replay of her speech in the Woodmore chapel, Melvin leads the group in reciting the numbers one through ten.

"Énska, tékeni, áhsen, . . ."

When the group has finished mumbling through to *oié:ri*, Melvin says: "Some of you Coyote River people will know this. Others won't. Anyways, those words we just said are not arbitrary. They mean something important to the Haudenosaunee. And since I started by talking about circles, I'm going to explain how they form a circle."

He details how the word for each digit signifies a part of the Haudenosaunee creation story. The number ten refers to "making a full circle."

"So, even our math relates to the circle," Melvin says, "but I've skipped pretty fast through that story, so let me give it to you proper. You see, when Sky-woman come to Earth, this planet was all water. It didn't have no land. So, the birds helped her to—"

"Sorry to interrupt," someone says. It's Rose, sitting one person away from Melvin. "But something smells really awful." She looks at the students on either side of her. "Don't you smell it?" Rose turns and points behind her into the woods. "Seems to be coming from in there."

"It don't bother me," Melvin says. "Some animal that's died in there, most likely. Actually, this might be a chance to show you more about them circles." He stands up and saunters toward the woods. "Follow me."

Everyone does, and beyond the scrub at the border with the playing field, the woodlot lot opens up. A partially decomposed deer carcass lies in the undergrowth.

"See, it's an old one. Look at that grizzled face, the long nose," Melvin says. "Poor thing. But this is part of the circle of life."

"Gross," Rose says, pinching her nostrils.

Some other students echo the reaction, but Pamela has hunted with her father. She understands and accepts death. And suddenly Pamela realizes, she's worthy of her mother's words—that she must to be strong at Woodmore.

Chapter 19

June 2007

To help reduce Alison's workload and expedite the double-murder case, Detective Sergeant Loams assigned Ruvinsky another task—to interview the staff at Havers's RBC Royal Bank branch, from tellers to mortgage-and-loan people to the assistant manager. Ruvinsky's notes led nowhere. Apparently, everyone at the branch saw Havers as a stand-up guy and a mentor. None of the business salespeople could think of any customers—like those turned down for a loan—who'd be angry enough to harm Havers physically.

There was only one lead, if it could be called such. Beth Lang, Assistant Manager, had worked with Ray Havers for twenty years, and she'd noticed a recent change in her boss's behaviour. For the last couple of months, Havers seemed preoccupied, unfocussed, and at times worried. About what, Lang didn't know. When she tried to coax him to be honest with her, Havers had laughed and said, "Everything's fine. *You*, Beth, are the worrier."

The ambiguity around Havers's mental state frustrated

Alison. Either the banker recently faced emotional strain or he didn't, but even if Havers suffered mentally, he hadn't told Lang *why*. All of which, despite Ruvinsky's efforts, left the case no further ahead.

* * *

As Alison stood watching on a basketball court in Coombes Athletic Centre, a girl caught a long pass and scored a goal, teammates cheering, slapping the player on the back. Beside Alison, and cradling a basketball under one arm, was Grafton Flynn.

"OK, ladies," he said. "Put it back into play."

The smell of sweat pervaded the gym, and running shoes squeaked on oak floorboards as the girls ran and circled and jumped.

"Will this take long?" Flynn said. "My lunch break begins now."

"How much do you know about the victims?"

Flynn blew his whistle and commanded that the balls be returned to the storage room. "And ladies, do not just bounce them through the doorway and scuttle off. You know, all of you can read English, so deposit them in the bin labelled 'Basketballs.' I am tired of seeing the equipment cast around as if a tornado had passed through."

In a lower voice, he said to Alison, "Would you mind if we went outside? I need to escape this malodorous sauna."

From the Coombes building, they strolled into the sunlight and sticky air of Trevena Way and the quadrangle. Students marched in a hundred different directions, and Alison spoke over their chattering and giggles and footfalls. "First, can

CHAPTER 19

you tell me, has a student named Rose Molloy been located? She must be interviewed, but I've heard nothing from her housemistress, Ms. Atkinson, who was to call me as soon as Rose turned up."

"You will have to enquire with Director Collier, as she insisted on dealing with the family personally," Flynn said, waving to a student who'd called to him. "But to my knowledge, Ms. Molloy's whereabouts are still unknown."

Alison and Flynn sat down on a bench in one of a dozen scattered gardens, whose edges cut neatly into the flagstones. Serviceberry trees rustled, casting shadows over Flynn's tanned face. Outdoorsy, as though he sailed, hunted, or rock-climbed.

"I'll follow up with the Director then. Anyway, still on the topic of Rose Molloy, I understand that you talked with her and Pamela Renard about the racial taunts."

"Yes, and I had to suspend Rose. Woodmore prides itself, you know, on global thinking and inclusiveness."

"So, apparently Rose was determined to stand out as racist, but why?" Alison said. "Surely she would've guessed the likely consequences?"

"That was my stomach growling," Flynn said and palmed his abdomen. "Woodmore's board perhaps did not consider the complications of establishing the Two Row Exchange."

"What complications?"

"Well, mutual respect and friendship is what the Two Row Wampum agreement was all about, so the intent behind the Exchange is that the Woodmore community learns about Coyote River First Nation, the reserve learns about us at Woodmore, about Oakville, and we're all better for the exercise."

"But?" Alison said.

"I already told you." Flynn sniffed and wiped his nose with a tissue. "Rose Molloy is from Ewing. You know, the land claim by Coyote River has simmered for years—for a few centuries, actually—with legal merit, apparently, on the reserve's side. And now the quarrel has reached a flashpoint again." He cleared his throat. "I hope that explains things, because I really must go. I have a tuna sandwich spoiling in my office."

"You could be spoiling in an interrogation room."

"What more do you need, detective? Well, let me provide you with a clarification of Rose Molloy's behaviour. She told me this when I was deciding the length of her suspension from school.

"Her family lives on a rural route of Ewing that borders Coyote River territory. Not surprisingly, I guess, her father, Dylan Molloy, is a vocal critic of how the Ontario government has handled the clash over Peaceful Meadows Estates. He alleges that the OPP treats the Mohawk protestors with kid gloves, which action leaves the whites bordering the housing development open to harassment. Which is to say that Rose hates anyone from Coyote River."

Hates enough to kill? Alison wondered.

Flynn yawned and bent to tighten his shoelaces—his feet were boats—then rose from the bench. "You know, I really have to—"

"What can you tell me about Ray Havers? Did he have any enemies?"

Flynn rolled his eyes and sat down. "I didn't know him. He sat on Woodmore's board of directors. Come to think of it, in a couple of meetings, Havers and Gwen Collier, the school's Director, got into shouting matches—vicious ones.

CHAPTER 19

You see, Havers was the major donor for some renovations to the library, but he had to pull most of his money. So, I can see how Gwen would feel, her professional credibility tarnished because of him."

"From what she told me," Alison said, "they'd patched things up."

"Not that I ever witnessed. Several board meetings took place after Mr. Havers's funds disappeared, and, during those gatherings, one could have shivered at the chill between him and Director Collier."

From the interview in the Director's office, Alison remembered Collier's words: *A regrettable tiff. We were both a bit embarrassed*. So, either Flynn's impressions were wrong, perhaps just premature, or Collier had lied.

"One more question. Would you know if Ray had a drug problem? Cocaine was found on his body. Were there rumours? Or what about Pamela Renard? Since you've already visited her family at Coyote River, you may—"

"How did you—"

"Another detective and I interviewed Ely Renard and his mother the other day. They mentioned you'd been to see them since Pamela's death. So, as I was saying, you may know her former boyfriend on the reserve is involved in pushing drugs there."

Flynn shook his head. "Ray, Pamela. No, I have neither seen nor heard anything involving either of them and illicit substances. Detective Downey, um, I have got to get out of this sun, so if you'll excuse—"

"What about Woodmore's teachers? Or students?"

"What do you mean?"

"Drugs."

"Well, no Woodmore teacher of whom I'm aware has taken forced leave—or been fired—for a drug problem," Flynn said, smiling. "But, or course, upper-school students have occasionally been found with small quantities of marijuana. The usual experimentation that goes on. Nothing more serious, I can assure you. But we discipline the offenders strictly, and that precedent makes our potential potheads think twice."

And, Alison thought, you're certain of this *how*? Granted, the student drug-pusher angle was unlikely, but it was still a possibility to be cognizant of. She closed her notebook, got up, and handed her business card to Flynn. "Enjoy the tuna sandwich."

Chapter 20

High school is a dress rehearsal for the rest of your life. Sol searched vainly for where he'd heard that saying, but it was true. On every shift in Edwards Common, he saw the cliques: the good-looking girls, the jocks, the artsies, and the science geeks and assorted nerds. This lunch hour was no different.

As Sol was reloading a garbage bin, the end-of-period bell rang. Among the herd of exiting students, half a dozen teenage girls approached from their table; some whispered with cupped hands to ears. He recognized Pam's roommate, Amy something, among them. A book under her arm slipped and she tried to catch it and her food tray crashed to the floor. Cream-of-tomato orange splattered over the white tiles. The other girls shrieked, but a second later, they returned to their hushed talk.

Amy tipped her soup-soaked tray over the bin. "Come again, Mahima, I can barely hear you."

"Shush," said an umber-skinned girl. Hair like black onyx swayed across her shoulders, and she spun around and stepped toe to toe with Amy. "Rose isn't here. The girl is missing." She pronounced "here" as *h'yah*, and "girl" as *gull*.

"Everyone on the floor knows that," Amy said. "Her room's been empty since Monday morning. What'd she do, take a horsey break at her parents' country estate?"

"No, no. I was saying"—Mahima's voice dropped to a whisper—"that yesterday evening, I was alone reading in the common room, and Director Collier knocked on Ms. Atkinson's door. They didn't see me. Collier told Ms. Atkinson that Rose's family doesn't know where she is, that she never turned up at their horse ranch, and her car is missing from student parking."

Amy's jaw dropped open. "What? That's crazy weird." She stumbled behind the rest of her floor-mates. "At least she's not here to bother Pam."

Missing since Monday morning, Sol mused. Wherever Rose went, she'd vanished right after the murder. That was unlikely to be a fluke. Rose must be hiding: why would she go underground if she wasn't involved in the killings? If Rose had a credit card—surely Mommy and Daddy had given her one—she could be holed up at any hotel or motel in Oakville, or maybe she'd gone to Toronto or farther east to Kingston or Montreal.

"If I'm right, then Rose Molloy . . ." Sol said to an empty dining hall. "What a sad excuse for a human being."

He wondered if Mahima knew more than she'd said, but he couldn't simply ask her. She didn't know him at all, certainly not like Pamela had and Bobby did. But if he was ever going to get that Halton detective off his back, he needed all the info he could dig up, and the quickest way to start was to talk with Amy.

* * *

The girls tittered and eyed him. A group of them had just

burst from a Pilkington House exit door. He recognized two of them from Pam and Amy's lunch table. As the clutch walked away, Sol continued his approach to the dorm. He hoped it was almost empty. He didn't want to be seen, but if anyone asked, he'd say he'd come to pick up a broken vacuum cleaner from the janitor's closet.

He climbed the stairs to the third floor hallway. Sol located Amy and Pam's door, which he remembered from the "squaw" graffiti episode, and knocked.

Amy opened the door, tripped backwards and dropped her physics textbook. "Yes?" A Woodmore jacket swayed on her skinny frame, and her shirt and tie seemed too grown-up for the gawky kid. She eyed Sol's name tag and looked past him, into the hallway. "What're you doing here again? And where's your cart? If the housemistress sees me with—"

"Sol Fitzgerald. Start of the school year, they had me paint over some graffiti on your door, and I got to know—"

"Pam. I remember. She like introduced us."

"OK, for Pam's boyfriend and my hide, I'm trying to crack what happened, because according to the cops, him and me are suspects. I need to ask you some questions about it, so could you meet me tomorrow? In the library or Edwards Common. It'll only takes a few minutes."

"Um, I don't know." Amy looked down at the door handle, turned it back and forth. "I shouldn't be—it wouldn't look good for me to—oh, just step in now. But make it quick, or I'll kick you out of here."

As Sol entered the room, he checked a smile. Amy was trying so hard. But she'd never be a "cool" kid, never be a tough one. Maybe she'd felt bitter about Pam's good looks and basketball chops. But not, he hoped, bitter enough to *kill*.

"Were you and Pam close?" Sol said.

"She was one of the few friends I have here."

He looked around the dorm room. Pam's side was as stark as a nun's quarters. On the wall above her bed was a poster print, which showed a turtle depicted as though it were a continent seen from outer space, its head and legs portrayed like land masses jutting into a blue-green sea. A map of North America was inscribed on the turtle's shell.

Amy's half of the room displayed no maps, but visitors needed one to steer around the jumbled stacks of books. An electric fan, perfume bottles, a smartphone, contact lens solutions, and a laptop computer crowded her desktop, opposite a rumpled bed. Perfume must have spilt onto the desk, because a cloying scent hit Sol's nostrils. He spied the pages of an unfinished essay—three of them were crumpled into balls, partly hiding a family photo. In the picture, Amy smiled, her expression so different from the frown she now pointed at him.

"You really weren't bothered," he asked, "that Bobby was, as you say, 'one of the cutest guys at Woodmore'?"

She tipped her thick glasses toward him and smirked, showing metal braces on her top and bottom teeth. "Well, just look at me. I'm Supernerd. It wasn't like Bobby ever considered me to be girlfriend material. If there'd been a race for him, I'd never have qualified for it."

Her bony legs stuck out from a mid-thigh plaid skirt but with the glasses gone, Amy's dark eyes blazed above high cheekbones. Sol could imagine boys mooning over her when she wore her contact lenses. She replaced her glasses, and the lenses extinguished much of the fire.

"But Pam wasn't superficial like most people are," Amy said.

CHAPTER 20

"We hung out together from the day we moved in last August. Sometimes she helped me with schoolwork. And she didn't drop me when her basketball chicks showed up, or after she and Bobby hooked up."

Hip-hop artists stared from posters above Amy's bed. Sol pitied the girl, who was clearly straining to kick down the dweeb fence around her. "Can you think of anybody at Woodmore—besides Rose Molloy—who had a grudge against Pam? Did Bobby have to reject another girl to date Pam?"

Amy shook her head.

"If anything else comes to mind . . ." He took a scrap of paper from the desk and scrawled his phone number and email address.

Amy periscoped the hallway and whispered, "OK, go *now*. Before Ms. Atkinson sees us together and busts my ass."

He stepped past the doorway, but Amy tugged at his sleeve. "I almost forgot," she said.

"Yeah?"

She waved him back into the room. "It didn't seem like much at the time, just the challenges of relationships. But in the last few weeks, Pam and Bobby argued a lot. One day, they were sitting on a bench in Taylor Green, and I could hear them from like thirty metres. And in our room, Pam kept having crazy angry calls with him."

"About what?"

"She spoke in code, like she didn't want me to hear. Or she gave only yes-or-no answers, to questions I couldn't hear. Whatever the trouble was, they'd hit a serious snag, you feel me?"

Amy scanned the hall and whispered, "Go go go."

Sol jogged to the exit door and pounded down the staircase.

No, he thought, I don't "feel" you, and I hate that phrase. He knew that a trusting kid like Amy could fall into trouble fast. He hoped she stayed safe through her youth. Not like him.

Chapter 21

Alison felt the teens eyeing her. Edwards Common buzzed with student talk and adolescent hormones cresting on late-June fever, an itch for school to end and true summer to arrive. Spiffy for a cafeteria, she thought, as she ordered the maple salmon.

Having found an empty table, Alison munched on the fish, which came with rice and peas. Steam rose from the plate, and as she stared at the vapour trails, a daydream emerged. She's sitting alone in an empty coffee shop, a soulless franchise joint, on a Sunday, or a maybe it's a holiday. She's sitting alone because she *is* alone. Shirley died five years ago, and Marcia's married with her own children now. So Alison's come here to talk to someone, *anyone*, even if it's just the boy behind the cash register. She's fifteen years older, pudgy, and getting pudgier: the cheesecake she's eating is three-quarters done. She wishes for more cake, but there'll never be enough of it to fill the void. It's late, and beyond the windows, black sky reigns.

A peal of teenage laughter brought her back to Edwards Common and the kids eating around her. It was time for business. She considered the coming interview with Director Gwen Collier. Just how serious was the Director's tiff with

Ray Havers? Serious enough to give the woman motive to kill him? Alison doubted it, but another motive could be lying below the surface.

But before Collier's interview, Fitzgerald needed questioning, and she decided to try the your-fingerprints-are-on-it ploy. In reality, she'd learned his prints matched nothing from either crime scene: Trevena Way or the roof garden. If the lie worked, she'd save time and avoid a lot of spadework.

She phoned Peacock, the maintenance manager, Barry Peacock, and waited while he checked his schedule.

"Ain't you lucky. Fitzgerald's doing the gym floor in Coombes Centre. He'd better be there by 1:30, or you call me. I run a tight ship."

Alison chuckled.

"Ain't funny."

"Have you ever noticed—when Fitzgerald's in his street clothes—if he owns a lime-green shirt?"

"I seen him in lots of brown and beige ones, like he wants to blend into the woodwork."

* * *

Ammonia fumes burned. At the far end of the gym, a man in blue coveralls stood beside a cleaning cart. As Alison approached, her footsteps echoed in the cavernous space, and Solomon Fitzgerald glanced at her. From a yellow plastic bucket, he picked up a string mop and turned away to slosh grey juice across the floor.

She herself had pushed a mop for pay. In the summer after third-year university, she'd cleaned tony houses in Rosedale and Forest Hill. The maid service rotated her around, and she saw that the whole neighbourhood was white, while her fellow maids were black, Asian, or Filipino. Anything but WASP. She accepted that her sample wasn't statistically significant, but the realization had made her shove the vacuum cleaner so hard against a dining room wall that the china rattled.

Fitzgerald projected a defiance of his own.

She gave up trying to make eye contact. "A few more questions."

He turned, his eyes shadowed under a baseball cap. "I'm running behind. Last month they fired a janitor, who won't be replaced." Fitzgerald turned away again and swished the mop over the floor.

"You've said your girlfriend didn't see you that night, including when got back to your apartment, so other than the Blue Lion's staff—who may or may not have noticed you there—no one can say you *weren't* on the library roof on Sunday night. And even you, with your blackout, remember virtually nothing about the evening. Were you really that drunk?"

"I won't deny it," Fitzgerald said. "It's a problem I'm working on."

"OK, but that doesn't help you here. Quite the opposite. The crime scene team found wine glasses at a table on the roof garden." About to launch a ruse, Alison cleared her throat. "They've done the fingerprint analysis, so what if I told you that your prints match the ones on a wine glass and on a baggie of cocaine we found in Ray Havers's jacket?"

Fitzgerald clinched his jaw, his lips pressed together.

"Well?" Alison said. "We also found a wet mop up there, and guess what else? The mop and Havers's jacket were soaked in ammonia."

"I don't know anything about the coke or the fucking ammonia. Stop lying to me, because with *my* record, if the those fingerprints were really mine, you'd be here with some burly backup. To arrest me."

Alison hoped her face revealed nothing of her bluff's failure. "That's all for now."

Fitzgerald turned and went back to work.

***

Woodmore's Director wept. Gwen Collier admitted the truth, but her eyes swerved from Alison, to the office windows, to an abstract expressionist painting on the wall. "Yes, I admit that Ray Havers and I had been angry awhile with each other. I came to Woodmore only a year ago, and I was—still am—anxious to increase private and corporate donations. When Ray joined Woodmore's board, the unspoken agreement was that he would, personally and through his connections, generate endowments."

Collier cupped her hands over her face and continued to sob. From a Kleenex box on the desk, Alison passed the director a tissue.

"I can't believe Ray's gone," Collier said, folding and unfolding the tissue absently. "He was a banker, as you know, but he'd got into real estate development. Everything was fine at first, but starting in March or April, I think, he started yammering about financial fraud—something about financial derivatives and subprime mortgages—going on in the States. He obsessed over it. In Woodmore board meetings, he spent half his time grimacing as he read financial websites. And then he almost pulled his funding of upgrades—badly needed

CHAPTER 21

ones—to the library."

Before driving to Woodmore that morning, Alison asked around Homicide about the school: were there any recent headlines that might relate to the Renard-Havers case? No. But DS Ed Loams possessed a wealthy friend with a kid at the school, and the acquaintance had witnessed a nasty board meeting spat between Havers and the Director.

"So I've heard," Alison said. "Did you patch things up with Ray?"

"We did," Collier said, stroking a lock of walnut-coloured hair. Strands of grey flashed through her mane, which cascaded over the lapels of her tweed jacket. "A regrettable tiff. We were both a bit embarrassed."

The woman was over age forty, Alison figured, but that *skin*: she must have had a chemical peel. "What turned things around?"

"Woodmore prides itself on community, and that includes everyone: faculty, staff, students, and parents. And alumni, of course. A former student, who made millions in the 1990s, in the dot-com boom, came forward and volunteered to give us half of the library upgrade costs. Ray was happy with that and contributed the other fifty percent."

The Director rose and leaned on a windowsill, which framed a view including Trevena Way, the athletic centre, a wing of the upper school, and a wall of steamy clouds beyond. The window was open an inch, and chatter and shouts wafted up from the walkway four storeys below. "We'd both been under pressure, but it was over. I apologized to Ray, he apologized to me. And he's still on the parent committee—was still on it."

Sitting in one of three visitor chairs by the desk, Alison

took notes and surveyed the room: a modest wood desk, a round meeting table for four, a photo of Collier gliding bent-kneed on a snowboard, and two walls of built-in bookshelves. Simple modern lines defined the woodwork.

By contrast, the aroma of a used bookstore pervaded the office. The shelves held volumes with tattered, faded spines, not trim leather-bound tomes. This babe of a headmistress, Alison thought, doesn't put on airs. But why was Collier looking, half of the darn time, at the windows and the walls? What was she hiding? "So you and Havers were buddies again."

"We were never 'buddies.'" The director returned to her desk chair. "It was a professional relationship only." At the word *professional*, Collier clutched her wedding ring as her eyes flicked down.

Alison kept her expression neutral. "You and the other administrators on this floor have direct access to the roof garden, from that corridor," she said, gesturing beyond the office's doorway. "So could you tell me where you were last Sunday evening?"

Collier's look registered an affront, but her response was calm. "I was at Sound Body, a fitness club, from seven-thirty to nine, as I am on most Sunday nights." She smiled. "I like to be relaxed when the you-know-what hits the fan on Monday mornings. Sound Body is a big, busy club, so I'm not sure anyone would remember me being there or not."

"OK. I'll follow up on that." She gestured with her phone. "Do you have a recent picture of yourself?"

"Only group shots taken at school functions." Collier primped herself. "Go ahead."

Alison snapped the photo and put down her phone. "What

CHAPTER 21

can you tell me about Pamela Renard?"

"It's terrible. The girl held so much promise, and we were delighted to have her for—"

"The Two Row Exchange program. Mr. Flynn mentioned it."

"It's a trial run of sorts. Not yet a year. Assistant Director Flynn is our liaison with Coyote River. And, I have to say, none of us dreamed we'd experience the ugly racism that Rose Molloy displayed."

"What, exactly?"

"Racial slurs aimed, in public, at Pamela. Then the word 'squaw,' painted on Pamela's dormitory door. In red. Disturbing, because Rose is basically a good kid, I think, but—from what Mr. Flynn and the housemistress, Ms. Atkinson, have told me—the girl has a mean streak, of which Pamela was the unlucky target."

"Rose is, of course, a suspect. Can you arrange for me to interview her?"

"That would be a problem."

"Why?"

Collier looked down at her hands and sighed. "For the school's sake, we're trying to be discrete, so what I'm about to say can't go beyond this office." She gestured to the four walls around them.

"This is a murder investigation," Alison said, "not a high-school gossip session."

Collier narrowed her lips. "Rose was supposed to drive home Friday evening to stay with her family. They live in the country west of here—near, as it happens, Coyote River. But she never showed up at her parents' ranch, and on Sunday, they reported her missing to the OPP. Then they called me."

The Director ran her sweaty palms against each other. "She keeps a car on campus, and it's missing."

***

Alison parked a couple of blocks west of Trafalgar on Lakeshore Road. She walked into the Blue Lion and waited for her eyes to adjust from the sunlight on Lakeshore. When she could see again, amber light from faux gas-lamps revealed a bar and tables, and, on the opposite wall, leather booths. A solitary drinker read a newspaper at a table, and two older men sitting in a booth played chess over their beers. A door at the far end of the bar swung open, and a bald man walked toward Alison. She showed her badge and asked whether he or any other staff members had worked during the previous Sunday night.

He gave her a weary grin. "No sleep for the wicked. Or pub managers." He extended his hand. "Jamie Boswell, manager."

From her bag, Alison produced Fitzgerald's mugshot from his arrest for assault.

Jamie shook his head. "It was crazy busy that night. A big crowd was watching a soccer match, and folks who'd normally have been out on the patio came inside because outside was so muggy."

"You sure? Take another look."

The manager scratched his chin as he scanned the photograph. "Sorry, I've got nothing. But Mack is here—hey, Mack," he called to a rear corner, "you worked Sunday evening, right?"

A cleaning rag and spray bottle in his hands, Mack approached, his pendant earing swinging. He laid his materials on the bar and stroked his closely cropped beard. "Jeez, too many people were in here. Lots of people his age. Oh, wait a second. Yeah, he's a regular."

"What about on Sunday night?" Alison said.

Still rubbing his whiskers, Mack grimaced. "Sorry, the place was hopping."

"The other waitstaff—can you give me some names?"

"Tara phoned in sick at the last minute," Jamie said, "but Martina was here.

After getting Martina's phone number, Alison thanked both men and left. She called Martina, who lived only a block away in an apartment building and was in, but when Alison showed her Fitzgerald's picture, the fiftyish woman yawned and rubbed her eyelids.

"Sorry, I been doped up on pain meds. Often am, for my back," Martina said and took the photo in her hand. "Yeah, he's a regular. You know, we split the floor into zones, and I worked in the rear all that night." She passed the snapshot back to Alison. "Didn't see him, but also the space is sort of L-shaped, and the lighting's dim."

* * *

Alison was sitting at her desk in Homicide. When she noticed herself biting her fingernails, she lowered her hand. The nervous habit had begun in university, and it returned whenever her workload, professional or domestic, became unmanageable.

Among Alison's domestic worries, Marcia refused to open her bedroom door the previous evening and said nothing at breakfast today. If only Alison could find the time or energy away from work, they could do things together again: hiking, mini-golf, or horseback riding. None of that was going to happen. Not yet. Woodmore demanded first priority, or the first impression she'd leave at Halton Homicide would be "slacker," "dimwit," or both. Not a good thing for her job security. So, what could she do quickly for Marcia, quickly about the no-dating-till-you're-fifteen rule?

At her laptop, she googled the words *summer camps southern Ontario*. Over the murmurs of coworkers and ringing of phones, she managed to find a promising website—Camp Bayhead, two hours north on Lake Simcoe. Squinting at her screen through a shaft of afternoon sunlight, she learned that the camp was for girls only and was oriented to fine arts activities.

Perfect.

The cost of Bayhead's two-week programs, however, dulled Alison's enthusiasm. Then she noticed a three-day workshop program, in which participants chose to focus on one art among dance, music, drama, sculpture, or painting. Alison could "afford" the $650 price: what were credit cards for, other than racking up more debt than you could—in one month—comfortably pay back? But Marcia loved to paint, and she wanted to try outdoor landscape painting. Best of all, Bayhead was all girls, all the time.

One day remained to register for a workshop, so Alison's mission was clear: convince Marcia and register her online. Tonight.

Getting Marcia to and from Camp Bayhead posed another hurdle. With the Woodmore case hounding her, Alison couldn't spare the hours for two return car trips to Lake Simcoe, but a solution emerged. The good Professor Tim, she thought, my ex-partner for life, wants to see Marcia beyond his current one weekend per month, so he can be—as he says *ad nauseam*—"a real father to our daughter."

If only, a decade ago, he'd been a real husband instead of an adolescent in a man's body.

* * *

Belying the stuffy-bibliophile stereotype, Director Gwen Collier was apparently a bodybuilding fanatic. Either that, or she liked to gawk at musclemen, because they formed the majority of members at Sound Body, where Alison was walking from the vestibule to the registration desk.

Alison showed Collier's photograph to the manager, Tammy, who confirmed being on duty during Sunday evening. Although the woman recognized Collier as a regular, she held no recollection of seeing, or not seeing, the Director that night, and Sound Body owned no surveillance cameras.

"We opened only a couple of months ago," Tammy said. "Budget's tight, so we've only put in a basic alarm system so far. There's no video, no swipe cards yet. Sorry."

Tammy, Alison thought, should also be apologizing to Gwen Collier, because Woodmore's Director just lost her best chance at an alibi.

Chapter 22

At the end of his shift, Sol pictured himself writhing in quicksand. A trite image, he realized, but it summed up his grasp on who might be the killer and why they did it. He returned to the Janitor Can and approached Peacock's desk. The frames of the photos on the desktop showed a film of dust.

Peacock's broad behind, splitting the seam of his polyester pants, faced out from a filing cabinet, where he stood filing forms. Sol leaned an elbow on a cabinet underneath the whiteboard.

Peacock turned. "Smudge that schedule, and I'll cut your fingers off."

Sol supressed a smile. His boss also guarded the rickety chess table in the corner. Peacock occasionally asked Sol to play. The combat usually happened on a Friday after five, but even with the guy's keen interest in the game, Peacock got checkmated every time.

"I mean it, Fitzgerald."

"Seriously, Barry, can I pass something by you? See what you think?"

"Please, not more lady problems."

"No. It's about the killings. I heard—"

CHAPTER 22

"I don't mean no dig, but ain't you a suspect?" Squinting, Peacock scratched his neck. "Don't know if we should be talking about it."

Sol sighed and closed his eyes. "You know that I knew Pam Renard a bit, so excuse me for giving a crap about what's happened."

Peacock chuckled, but his eyes were steady on Sol.

"Look," Sol said, "I just heard some gossip. There's a student, Rose Molloy, who's been missing from school—and home—since Monday morning. This Molloy kid, she's the one who vandalized Renard's dorm room door."

A steel drawer squeaked as Peacock pushed it into the cabinet. He shuffled toward Sol, his BO hitting a high note over the background ammonia. "Yeah, so what?"

"The kid was like a sworn enemy of Renard. Isn't it dodgy then? Rose goes AWOL on the day the bodies are found?"

"No idea. Everyone I've chitchatted with thinks it's murder-suicide. I can see the headline: *School parent diddles student, kills her, then jumps.* Old story. Foxy jailbait meets dirty old man."

Sol shook his head. "That's offensive."

"You want *my* opinion," Peacock said, "well, supposing you can find her, I think it's too early to make a citizen's arrest—and a fool of yourself. What aim could this Molloy girl have to kill a schoolmate?"

"They weren't 'mates,' believe me. I saw up close what Rose Molloy did. I hope the cops aren't going tunnel vision with the first 'obvious' answer, Ray Havers. Rose is wicked, and she hightailed it out of here. That says something."

"Suit yourself." Peacock went back to his desk.

Sol walked into the locker room. *Who am I fooling?* he

thought. The most likely people aren't just Bobby's father and Rose. Coyote River Luke sounds like a rough customer, and is the guy really over Pam? He admitted that Bobby was too involved not to be a suspect. What, though, would spur the kid to commit such a sickening crime—a love triangle between him, Pam, and his father? Sol shook his head. No, that was too grotesque.

He sat down on the bench and stared out a puny window. Something else about Bobby tugged at his brain—Amy Ling's tale about the telephone spats between the boy and Pamela. And besides, on Sunday night at the library, Bobby was with Pamela. Just before she disappeared.

***

Sol lied. He told Tash that the choir practice at Dickens United was an hour-and-a-half early tonight. In fact, he'd found the schedule for an Oakville AA group, and he was going for his virgin visit. If he survived the meeting, he'd tell her—and ratchet down the tension between them. But if he couldn't hack the program, well . . . He avoided the thought, said goodbye, and took the Tashmobile.

At the meeting, in a church basement lit by fluorescent tubes—some flickering, others burnt out—he sat with a bunch of people he didn't want to know. Worse, he was going to face a roomful of tired eyes and admit, *I'm an alcoholic*. When he walked to the front and actually said the words, he felt like a fortress whose mortar was crumbling, or had crumbled, its walls falling down. About Danny, he said only, "I was abused by my older cousin when I was a kid." But everything else flowed: the tailspin of his marks in high school as he took up

CHAPTER 22

boxing and coke; kids cheering, and teachers not reporting him, as he beat up bullies; and his mother's crying, when she checked her seventeen-year-old son into a rehab centre.

The rehab got him off cocaine, but booze filled the void. He made sure his parents never discovered the new habit. He had stayed free of obvious trouble for a decade, but two-and-a-half years ago, he spent six months in prison for assault, for the crime of defending a woman, Tash, against two men in a nightclub parking lot. The conviction *would* have been for aggravated assault—Sol broke one man's jaw, knocked out some of the other's teeth—but the judge reduced it because Tash pressed charges against the bastards for attempted rape.

From high school onward, he never kept a girlfriend for more than a month or two. Each of them told him he "had problems." And now, when he finally enjoyed a long-term relationship, he'd just alienated his girlfriend's parents and shown them he was a drunk.

"So the only reason I'm here tonight," he said, "is that I can't lose her. Not this girl."

Chapter 23

After the AA meeting, Sol drove to Dickens United and was working with Minister Frey and the choir on John Rutter's *Cantate Domino*. He'd tamed the piano part at home, so his playing was relaxed, Rutter's music at times making the hair on Sol's back and shoulders and neck stand up.

The practice ended and as the singers filed out, she pointed at him. "OK, first tutoring session, right? Follow me."

When they'd both sat down in her office, Imogen—she insisted he use her first name—spun in her chair and scanned the bookcase. She pulled out *Practical Grammar*, a thin paperback, and showed him the cover.

In spite of his worry, he smiled.

Flipping through the pages, Imogen said, "OK, let's gauge what we can cover before your final exam. How much time's left?"

"I write it next Tuesday night."

"In six days?" Imogen said. She raised her arms high like an Old Testament prophet.

* * *

In the Janitor Can's storeroom, Sol grunted like a prisoner on

CHAPTER 23

a chain gang as he grabbed a beat-up toolbox, then shouldered a rolled-up tennis net. During the night, vandals had painted a fat green dollar sign on one of the tennis courts and shredded its net. And the doers—probably the same kids who'd sprayed graffiti on the front gates—even cut the net's support cable in two. It couldn't have been easy to cut steel braided wire. They were determined little fuckers.

As Sol trudged by Peacock's desk, the man looked up. "Don't dawdle out there. Looks like a storm's coming."

Sweat already trickling between his shoulder blades, Sol elbowed the door open. "I don't care if I get wet, as long as the rain clears this humidity."

He strode east along Service Lane. To one side, the student parking lot lay filled with cars too expensive for high-school students, but he knew that one spot was open—Rose Molloy's. On the other side of the road, tennis courts fading into the haze, he found the wrecked one and dropped the toolbox and net there.

Doubting Bobby's word made Sol wince. But checking into the boy's whereabouts after Pam disappeared on Sunday night was a necessity. So, before leaving the Janitor Can, Sol had checked Peacock's whiteboard: garbage pickup at Edwards Common was slated for two p.m. He could go there now, unnoticed, and confront Bobby's roommate, so he checked along Service Lane. No cars, no pedestrians. Time to make his move. He trotted across Taylor Green and took the rear Service door into Edwards Common, where the breakfast racket echoed and the waft of a dozen menu choices sickened him. Steeling himself, he wheeled a cart out of the janitor's closet.

From the bin closest to where Bobby and his housemates

were sitting, Sol took out the garbage bag. He'd timed his action as close to the bell as he could, and, before the clanging stopped, kids began leaving. Bobby approached.

"Can't talk," Sol said. "I'm way behind schedule."

"We'll catch up at noon. The lake woods." The hulk turned and jogged back to his friends.

Months ago, Bobby had introduced his roommate Nathan to Sol. And now Nathan, morbidly fat, waddled behind the rest of the Norton House boys. Checking that Bobby was beyond the doors, Sol motioned Nathan to the garbage bin and grilled him.

Breathing heavily, Nathan said he remembered Sunday night: in their dorm room, he'd started playing *World of Warcraft* around nine o'clock and was still playing when Bobby staggered through the door and asked if he'd seen Pamela in the last half hour. He remembered the time, 10:06, because he'd glanced at his alarm clock and asked if it could wait five minutes, since he was close to reaching Level Nine. But Bobby pressed the power button on Nathan's laptop. Nathan swore and tossed the computer on his bed. He said he hadn't seen Pam because he'd been playing since nine o'clock. Bobby explained that Pam was missing and flopped onto his own bed. After five minutes, Nathan heard him snoring, and when the pudgy gamer got up to brush his teeth just before eleven o'clock, Bobby had still been snoring.

"Was he sweaty?" Sol said. "Did he look ruffled, clothes wonky, like he'd been in a fight? Cuts or bruises?"

Nathan laughed, the rolls around his waist jiggling. "Only an idiot would pick a fight with a guy—a football player—as big as Bobby."

If the athlete had killed his father and Pam, he somehow

got up to the library roof, forced two people off of it, got back down, and ran back to Norton House—all without getting punched or scratched by his victims, and all between ten o'clock and 10:06. Not likely.

Sol thanked Nathan, who shuffled toward the doors. Whatever the trouble between Pam and Bobby was, it hadn't driven the boy to murder, according to the alibi. On the other hand, Bobby could have threatened his roommate with a beating or worse if Nathan didn't lie for him.

* * *

Noon came, and the sky darkened to muddy green. Hoping the storm would wait while he and Bobby ate lunch, Sol went into the lake woods. That morning, he'd installed the tennis net and tried removing the dollar-sign graffiti from the court, and, though a ghost of the mark remained, it would have to do. He spent the remaining time cleaning windows on the middle school's long south wall facing the football field.

Now, at nature's safe house, he and Bobby sat on the boulders. His guilt over checking Bobby's alibi plagued him, and as thunder boomed, he despaired. They ate for awhile in silence. Pam Renard, he thought, didn't deserve to die so young. And Bobby has lost his *father*.

"If we want the truth," he said, "we've got to think how your father was involved, as a victim or as the—the killer."

Bobby was staring at the dense clouds moving above the forest canopy.

"I know it's awful," Sol said, "but fuck, we have to at least think through the possibility."

Bobby fidgeted with a button on his school jacket. "Pam

had no reason to be interested in a middle-aged man, and my father—he was a jerk about some things—but he'd never force himself on anybody. Can we stop talking about this absurd 'possibility'? I can't stand it. As far as I know, the only person Pam had dated before me was some guy named Luke, on her reserve. Luke Daveneau. She got into smoking marijuana with him; he had an ample supply of weed because he was in a gang."

"Doesn't sound like Pam's kind of boyfriend," Sol said.

Bobby shrugged.

Sol leaned forward and put his hand on Bobby's shoulder. "OK. Your father—did anybody want to even a score with him?"

"A neighbour got cheesed off when Dad put an addition on our house. You know, a lot of dust and noise for a couple of months. But *really*? That's not a motive for murder."

"What about someone at work. A customer, a worker, his boss?"

"Dad *was* the boss. If he had been having trouble at work, he sure kept it on the down-low, from me and Mom."

"Would your mother know anything?"

Bobby's head sank forward, and he closed his eyes. "On tranquilizers. Leave her out of this."

"OK. How could we learn something from your father's bank branch?"

Bobby stopped slouching, looked up again at the churning sky. "I could just go there after classes and talk to a few people. I've hung around there since I was young, waiting for rides and so on from my dad. They know me there." Bobby fished his phone from his pants pocket. "I'll call the assistant manager, my Aunt Beth. Not a relative, but she's known me

CHAPTER 23

since I was—"

Above their heads, thunder cracked, and a flash blinded them. Fat drops smacked Sol's head, slowly at first, then faster and faster, so the two darted out of the woods.

Chapter 24

In a break between classes that afternoon, Bobby phoned Aunt Beth at the RBC Bank, and she agreed to meet with him in her office at four thirty. With the thunderstorm gone and dry air replacing mugginess, Bobby parked his bike outside the RBC building; the structure's red bricks reradiated the sun's heat. On both sides of the façade, exclusive stores lined Lakeshore Road.

He went inside and stood under the twenty-foot ceiling. Tellers and their clients murmured, the sounds reverberating in the airy room like prayers in a cathedral. Bobby thought of speaking to the tellers but—when two of them pointed at him and whispered—decided against that avenue. If one of them harboured a vendetta against his father, they would keep it hidden. His watch reading 4:27, he told the man at Information of his appointment.

Bobby sat down in the waiting area and reached for a magazine. Something moved in his peripheral vision. A petite, uniformed woman pushing a janitor's cart gestured for him to approach. He had chatted with her a few times in the previous year and learned she was a South Korean immigrant, but he'd never asked her name. Bobby rose to greet the tiny cleaner, but just behind her, Aunt Beth appeared from the admin corridor and shook his hand, so he followed the Assistant Manager down the corridor.

In Aunt Beth's office, all the papers and binders on her desktop were at right angles to its edges and to each other. The banker leaned her elbows on the writing area, which was operating-room clean, like Ray's desk at home.

"Oh, Beany," she said, "we're still numb around here. I can't imagine what it's like for you and your mother."

"I've got school to keep me going, and Mom's got her job. We're OK." Bobby cleared his throat. "Can you tell me a little about Dad? I mean, how things were lately for him at the bank?"

Aunt Beth frowned, her eyes owlish behind her reading glasses. "Ray's work here has no bearing on what happened at—"

"Did he have like trouble with anyone? Customers? Staff?"

"Isn't that a question the police, not you, should pursue?"

"Everyone knows, the cops can screw up cases, like when they focus on the wrong person. And who knows what else? I've got to keep that from happening, which is why I'm asking. You think my father had enemies? Other problems? I have to know, because I owe that much—a grasp of what happened between them—to my dad and Pam."

"You mean the scholarship student? The police told me you knew her."

"She was my girlfriend."

"Oh my God. I didn't know."

"You've known my father for a long time. Did you notice anything different with him recently?"

"He wasn't the kind of person who made enemies." Aunt Beth smoothed the sleeves of her business jacket. "In the last few months, Ray did seem a bit distracted, maybe a bit anxious. I asked him about it, but he answered with flippant jokes. And that wasn't like him."

"Thanks. That helps."

"Forget about it. You've got so much to deal with already."

He got up and closed the door after him. Down the corridor, the tiny custodian vacuumed the carpet. Bobby waved to her.

She flipped a switch, and the machine's whine faded. "Eun," she said, tapping a forefinger to her chest. "My name, Eun Kim."

"I think I've seen you once or twice around—"

"I am sorry about your father. I see on TV."

Eun signalled for him to approach. She pointed to the far end of the hallway, to the frosted glass door of his father's office. "On my night shift. The door was open. Shout with a man."

"Who was where?"

"Father. Shouting. Two, three times, on my night shifts. Shout with a man."

"What man? What were they saying?

Eun shrugged. "I not know."

Chapter 25

A car engine's rumble grew beyond the kitchen windowpanes. Spectacles on her nose, Shirley left her Sudoku puzzle on the table and strode to the counter to look. "Your ex-husband is here. Finally. I wasn't letting on how worried I was."

"Eight o'clock," Alison said, rolling her eyes. "Only two hours later than he promised."

She went out the door and down the townhouse steps. In the driveway, Tim Boswell helped Marcia get her bags from the trunk of his 1992 Lincoln Continental—he'd owned the car since before he and Alison divorced.

Tim's whiskers glinted in the slanted light. He approached, his eyes as piercing as a husky's, just as they'd been when he first seduced her. She was a twenty-three-year-old student, and he, her thirty-five-year-old professor. Too late, she learned that Tim's real personality wasn't as smooth as his public veneer.

"Marcia had a good time," he said. "Kids need to get out into nature." Tim looked at his daughter. "On the drive back, Muffin, you chattered incessantly about your new friend and plein air painting."

"Plein air *what*?" Alison said. She noticed that Marcia allowed Tim's using *Muffin* go unpunished.

"It means 'painting outdoors,' Mom. It was awesome."

Alison wished Tim would get in the car. "Well, miss social butterfly, we'd better get you inside and—"

"Al, could I have a word?" Tim clasped his hands.

Alison wanted to go inside, not have another meandering talk with this man. She glanced at Marcia. "Hey, those bags must be getting heavy. Go in and give your Gran a hug."

Marcia said goodbye to her father and trotted up the steps.

Tim leaned against the Lincoln. "I don't want to bother you. I know we agreed on paper, but I miss her so much. One weekend a month, it's . . ."

"I'm going to lose my mind." Heat spread into her neck and face. "You wanted it that way, said you didn't have the time. Career took precedence."

"Yes, *took*. Past tense. Things have changed."

Alison crossed her arms over her chest. "Uh-huh."

"In two years, I'll be fifty," Tim said, picking a speck of lint from his khakis. "That and my hypertension—they have changed my perspective. Please, Al. One weekend a month isn't enough anymore."

"You pleaded with me that you didn't have the time. You signed the agreement." She turned and went up the steps.

"Al, don't do this."

"Marcia must be dying to tell me about camp. See you, Tim. Same time next month."

Inside, Marcia and her grandmother sat at the kitchen table.

"So who's the new friend your father talked about?" Alison said.

"Elly Lawton. She's an awesome painter, and she lives in Oakville."

Thank you, God, Alison thought. This Elly girl could be

CHAPTER 25

the solution to the Marcia problem. But Tim, and his sudden yearning for more time with their daughter, posed a threat, leaving Alison to shake her head. In his requests and actions, her ex-husband usually hid an ulterior motive.

Father and daughter. Father and son. And motive. Was Ray Havers *also* shielding a hidden aim, Alison wondered, when he'd been on that roof with Bobby's eighteen-year-old girlfriend? Possibly to get rid of his son's "problem"—the fetus and the young woman carrying it—to make sure no bastard babies would be born under the Havers name? Ray's impulse to avoid disgrace would have been even stronger under a different scenario, in which he himself fathered the baby. If that were true, though, it made no sense that Bobby would lie for him, except through shame, grief, or misguided love. Those possible motives were both just supposition, Alison realized.

So, could any of the circumstantial evidence help clear Ray? She considered the lime-green fibres found both on his and Pamela's clothing. They *might* point to someone else as the perpetrator, but, just as easily, whoever or whatever left the strands could be a red herring. Two clear facts existed about the green filaments: the Ident team's searches of Pamela's dorm room and of Ray's house yielded nothing; but, on a visitor's chair in the banker's office, the crew had found several matching threads.

A mechanical growl made the kitchen windows buzz. Alison looked out to see Tim's rusting Continental turning out of the driveway. She could feel her pulse slowing.

Chapter 26

Sol knew that the impression he'd made on Tash's parents, especially her father, was less than sparkling. One weeknight, while Tash was vegging out by the TV, he braced himself and made the call, and Dr. Harishandra agreed, amazingly, to meet him the same evening at a downtown coffee shop on Lakeshore Road.

When Sol got there, the doctor was standing outside the café, angled sunlight flecking its wall. Sol wore old jeans and a T-shirt, and Tash's father was wearing another fancy suit. The guy probably went backpacking in a suit. Along Lakeshore, traffic hummed, and people chattered on the sidewalk and at café tables in a cobblestone square off the street. A Haydn string quartet wafted from Tempo, a CD store that stocked only jazz and classical music.

He pulled himself away from the sounds and followed Dr. Harishandra into the café. The doctor insisted on paying.

From their window seat, the clock behind the service counter read 7:35 p.m., but outside, the street bustled, and Sol liked the vibe. Dr. Harishandra took off his suit jacket, loosened his tie. From behind the counter, a grinder whirred, and the smell of coffee laced the air.

When the grinding stopped, Sol forced his gaze to meet

the man's eyes. "Thanks for seeing me. Sorry about dinner last Saturday. Maybe I was out of line, but I go for the booze when I'm nervous." He looked down and stirred his coffee.

"Not a problem." Dr. Harishandra said and ran his hand through his salt and pepper hair. "I understood you would perhaps be uneasy meeting us for the first time."

"That's not why I wanted to see you. I have a drinking problem, just started with AA, and I want you to know I'm trying." Sol turned to the window. Couples ambled along, one mother tugging at the harness on her toddler, who wore camouflage overalls, while a father pushed a baby stroller as big as an SUV. Sol wished he could mosey arm-in-arm with Tash along the sidewalk, like these people. But he would never be so carefree. Laughing and smiling. No worries. No nightmares.

"Wasted years. I had them too," Dr. Harishandra said.

"Wasted years?"

"Drinking. I stole all that time from my wife and children, and from myself, for that matter." He undid the top buttons of his shirt and reached down between the collar and his chest, and a round medallion on a chain emerged. On the metal surface, a triangle with words around it glinted.

Sol raised his eyebrows. "But Tash never said that—"

"She hasn't told me about *your* drink trouble either, so I guess Tashi learned from me and her mother to avoid speaking of it. This number *20*"—the doctor pointed to the centre of the pendant—"it's the number of years I have been sober. Like climbing Mount Everest—that is what the first five years of AA were like for me. I still regret the damage to my family, and I won't have you thieving more precious time from my daughter." He jabbed his finger into Sol's chest.

"You have a choice to make, work to do. Yes, you bordered on insolence at dinner, but I won't accept your apology, not yet. Not until you can show me your 30-day token."

On the sidewalk, a couple sitting on a bench squabbled. Even through the café window, the spite in their voices crackled, then the woman stood up and stormed off. The man covered his face with his hands.

A brown hand waving in Sol's face. "What are you staring at?"

"Nothing."

* * *

When he got back to the apartment, Sol watched TV with Tash, the apartment's air conditioner brawling with the heat. Lame gags and canned laughter issued from the television. "Isn't this the third time we've seen this episode?"

"Come on, *Friends* stays funny, every line of it."

Spread out below the living room windows, pinpricks of light twinkled: a million streetlamps, the headlights of cars, and the lit windows of buildings. Sol scratched his chin. "I've got stubble, and I don't want to rush in the morning." He got up from the couch and headed to the bathroom.

"That gives me control of the remote," Tash said, waving the gadget.

"Go nuts with it."

After shaving—and checking that the bathroom door was closed tight—he called Bobby.

To Sol's question, Bobby said, "Aunt Beth wasn't much help. She said Dad was easygoing, the sort of person who doesn't make enemies."

CHAPTER 26

"That's it?"

"No, there's something else. I saw it too in my dad, for the last few months, but I wanted to ignore it at the time."

"Ignore *what*?"

"He seemed stressed out, distracted. I never confronted him on it, but Aunt Beth did, and she said he was evasive to her. Never told her what was bothering him."

Sol sighed and combed his fingers though his hair. "That's fucking great. Your father *seemed* worried."

"He *was* worried," Bobby said. "I'm sure of it. I just don't know what was making him anxious."

From the living room, Tash giggled, and the TV laugh track swelled. Then silence, followed by three raps on the bathroom door.

"I've got to pee," she said. "What have you been doing in—are you on the phone?"

"Just a second." Sol cut his voice to a whisper. "*Later. Can't talk now.*"

Learning more about Ray Havers's predicament would have to wait. Sol pressed End, shoved the phone in his pocket and opened the door.

* * *

The next morning after breakfast, Sol, as he sometimes did, paused to look at the Ramayana album painting that hung on the living room wall. The image—which showed good guys fighting an evil, ten-headed giant—stirred him. The poster showed five figures, including two with olive-and-pink monkey faces and one with ten blue faces, on an open field under a blank cerulean sky. They fought each other with fists, axes, daggers, spears, and bows and arrows. Tash had explained the picture to him shortly after they'd first met, and as he stood now in front of it, he counted the wicked king Ravana's arms, *all nineteen of them*, each limb wielding a different weapon, so the heroes Rama and Hanuman were seriously outgunned.

Outgunned—Sol felt like that with Tash, who was lounging, reading the *Globe & Mail* on the sofa. Her weekend morning routine. She rustled the newsprint, sipped her coffee. In the bending of her elbow to turn a page, or in how she put up with a train wreck like him, Tash showed grace.

A year earlier, on the day they first met, he'd heard her whistling before he saw her. He'd started a dishwashing job at a bland Kelsey's restaurant, and Tash was already there waitressing, to save money for a trip abroad, which she was planning to take after her Master of Science degree. Tash had just started her shift and was waiting outside the kitchen for an order. Leaning her elbows on the pass-through counter, she whistled with solid pitch, ending each phrase with vibrato. With genuine feeling. The melody was from an old Roberta Flack song, and Sol remembered the words: *The first time ever I saw your face / I thought the sun rose in your eyes*. It was true. It was how Tash's delivery of the tune, and how she herself, affected him, haunted him, till he'd found the nerve to ask her out for a coffee.

He ignored the tightness in his belly and reached to the top shelf of a solid oak bookcase, which separated the apartment's living and dining areas. They'd bought the piece at a flea market after Sol moved in: his collection—music history books, crime novels, and sheet music—needed storage space. Tash owned as many novels and science textbooks.

CHAPTER 26

Wanting Tash to look at him, he groaned as he grabbed four thick hardbacks with one hand and fished out a bottle of Black Velvet whisky with the other. The bookcase wobbled, and he sucked in his breath as it almost fell over. But it didn't, and his ploy worked.

"What the hell, Sol?"

He didn't answer but moved, with Tash following, onto three other stashes. The finale was his yanking a dozen 50 mL mini bottles from under the night table. He placed the flasks with the others in a recycling bin.

Tash's frown was as focused as the laser he'd seen at her lab. "How long have you had all this stuff?"

"Something's waiting for you to see on the dining table." Sol strode to the tabletop and pulled out a chair. "Take a look."

Tash sat down. She faced Sol as he poured the liquor into the kitchen sink. Then she scanned the papers before her. "You joined AA?"

"Haven't had a fucking drink since Wednesday," he said, whisky *glug glugging* out of a bottle.

Tash tilted her head and her teeth flashed. "That's great. But why not just tell me."

Sol shrugged. "I want you to see I'm serious about this."

"I'm glad." Tash got up and hugged him. "You'll overcome it. But please, please, no more hiding anything. And I mean more than bottles. If it gets difficult, *talk* to me."

Sol still hadn't cleaned out his beer stash in the lake woods, but he would. He would.

Chapter 27

October 2006

The white-and-gold angel costume itches Pamela's arms, and the weight of its plastic wings pulls the polyester tight against her shoulders. She only cares that it was inexpensive and ready-to-wear.

A week ago, when she and Bobby had their movie date downtown, she spotted a party-supplies store and bought the outfit. She knew a Halloween bash was coming: Ms. Atkinson and Norton House's Mr. Flock announced a Grade Twelve "Woodmore Witchery" for Saturday night. The parents of one boy, Charlie Eaves, volunteered their big country house to hold the event. Big party or not, Pamela had too much studying to do to waste time making her own getup.

Amy, on the other hand, is leaning over her desk in their dorm room, taping, painting, and gluing her Halloween ensemble—a bulky 1950s-style TV, made of cardboard and topped with drinking-straw antennae.

"Hurry up," Pamela says, "the buses are going to be here in fifteen minutes."

CHAPTER 27

She walks out of the room and along the corridor—except Rose's end of it—to see what others are wearing to the party. Three girls sport identical Harry Potter costumes. Pamela grins, thinking, *A wizard must have had triplets*.

Halloween is celebrated in Coyote River, but traditionalists like her dad disapprove of the festival's European connection. On the other hand, Christians—a dozen churches dot the reserve—object to their kids playing ghouls and wizards. "Satan beckons!" those parents say.

Baffled by such feverish emotion, Pamela thinks religion is more alike between cultures than many believe. From what she's learned from the Internet and Grandma Becky and church, strange overlaps exist, like the parallels between Skywoman in the Mohawk creation story and UFOs in Scientology. Both stories are about extraterrestrials coming to Earth. Or like when Skywoman's daughter has twins, Skywoman *dislikes* one of those siblings. That situation, to Pamela, is like Genesis in the Old Testament, where God favours Abel over Cain—in Cain's opinion, anyway.

Though the details are unrelated, she believes it's all the same in a crazy way. So, what's wrong with honouring a pagan festival like Halloween? Pamela adjusts her wings and turns to see if Amy's made any progress with the glue gun.

* * *

On one of two packed school buses rumbling along dark country roads, Pamela is sitting beside Amy. The trip began an hour ago, and they finally pass a road sign for Annandale. A couple of minutes later, beyond the other side of the town, they turn onto a gravel driveway and arrive at the Eaves's house. The students disembark. As she walks with the crowd toward the sprawling residence, Pamela notices how appropriate the scene is: the dwelling and outbuildings form black silhouettes, chimneys penetrating the red afterglow.

Inside, the space is humongous, perfect for a dance. Ms. Atkinson and the Norton Housemaster stand as lookouts at each end of the room, and they're wearing costumes, Ms. Atkinson dressed as Superwoman, Mr. Flock as Einstein. They take turns bopping to the music, which everyone takes as a signal to go wild.

Of course, Rose Molloy needs no signal. She's dressed in a black leotard that shows half her butt cheeks, and with orange hazard cones over her boobs. Rose is the first to step onto the dance floor. Her cones waggling, she raises her hands to her head, as if she's crowning herself.

In contrast to the spry dancer, Pamela has felt queasy since dinner, and after she and Bobby dance a few times, weakness makes her sway. She walks up to Ms. Atkinson and circles a hand over her own stomach.

"I think I might be sick," Pamela says, shrugging one shoulder where the wing strap is chafing her skin. "Could I go out on the porch to get some fresh air?"

Her pageboy tangled from dancing, the stout Superwoman rearranges her cape. "We don't want you vomiting all over the dance floor." She snaps her fingers. "Go ahead, but come to me if you feel any worse."

Outside, leaning on the porch railing, Pamela moans from cramps. The smell of manure doesn't help, but at least it's a warm night for Halloween. Luckily, the porch is deserted but for her. After half a dozen loud farts, whatever it was passes. She sits back in a Muskoka chair and closes her eyes.

CHAPTER 27

She must have dozed, because screaming jolts her awake. From a barn across the yard another shriek erupts, followed by shouts. Pamela runs down the porch stairs and toward the yard, but, as she does, two girls stumble out of the barn and walk toward the back of the house. The taller of the two is limping. Fully alert now, Pamela follows them. As one girl fumbles to open the rear door, the long-limbed one leans against the wall and touches the skin around her eye. She winces.

"You OK?" Pamela says, recognising it's Rose's friend Joan, from whose nostrils dark blood has trickled to her lips and chin. "What happened to you?"

"I tried but—go help Rose," Joan says. "In the barn, there's . . ." Joan faints, sliding down the wall to the concrete patio pavers.

The other schoolmate bends down and gently shakes Joan's shoulder. "Joan, Joan, wake up."

"What—what's . . ." Joan says, slurring the words.

Voices, male ones, drift from the barn, and Pamela spins around. As she jogs toward the hulking structure, she says over her shoulder, "Stay with Joan. Let her rest a bit. I'll get help."

Inside, the smell of horse droppings. Pamela creeps through the darkness with her arms out ahead for protection, but the gloom dissipates, and she's approaching a lighted corner stacked with bundles of hay, in front of which are two orange highway cones. One is upright, and the other, laying on its side. Pamela's pulse clangs through her like an end-of-period bell at Woodmore.

She doubts what her eyes show her. It seems surreal, but the smell of hay grounds her. The scene is eerily similar to a nightmare that has assaulted Pamela periodically since she was eight, the dream prompted by her cousin Lillian's disappearance and death. The girl had been found, days after she vanished, sprawled on straw bales in an abandoned Coyote River barn. She'd been raped and strangled, and the perpetrator was never found. Now Rose, naked and whimpering, is also lying on bundled feed. Alabaster skin and plenty of curves. Past the hazard cones, the rest of her costume is scattered across the concrete floor. Four boys, their backs to Pamela, stand in front of their prey.

One of them kneels inches away from Rose, his dick poking out from his fly. "Come on, Rosie. You've been giving us wood for years. You're such a tease, but it's time to even the score."

"Don't," Rose says. "Please, no."

"Don't worry, we'll keep it on the down-low." Moving over her, he laughs.

His friends hold their phones up for the best angle.

Pamela, feeling like she's been punched in the gut, staggers and her footsteps echo off the rafters. A couple of the boys swivel toward the noise, but Pamela is far enough from the single lightbulb that dimness hides her.

"What the hell was that?" one of them says, his arm still raised, holding his phone.

His phone.

Pamela sees her chance. No one, not even Rose, deserves this.

Hands shaking, she readies her Blackberry's camera and steps out of the shadows. "Hey, guys. Say *cheese!*"

The rapists spin around and she snaps a photo, the flash blinding them, but only for a second. The many sprints

CHAPTER 27

Pamela has taken on basketball courts save her, because she outruns the cowards back to the house. She steps onto the front porch, calls 9-1-1, but one of the bastards hops the railing on the porch's opposite end and charges at her.

"You're next, bitch," he says.

Before the rat reaches her, Pamela is through the front door. Compared to the silence outside, the music—Michael Jackson's "Thriller"—is thunderous. Heading for Ms. Atkinson, she races around sweaty dancers while saying to the dispatcher on the phone: "Could you hold on for a second?" She reaches the housemistress and grabs her arm. "Ms. Atkinson, Ms. Atkinson, what's the address for this property?"

The woman steps back and frowns.

"Rose Molloy and Joan—it's an emergency," Pamela says.

"What? What kind of emergency?"

"The *address*. Now!"

Ms. Atkinson has the evening's schedule rolled up in her hand. Wide-eyed, she unfurls it and points to the address. Pamela relays it to the dispatcher.

His voice is tinny over the connection. "The nature of the problem?"

"One person injured, lost consciousness, and another assaulted—sexually."

Ms. Atkinson's jaw drops. "What?"

"Yes," Pamela says. "Just what I said."

The culprits have slipped back into the house, she knows, because she recognizes several of the boys, who emerge from the dancing crowd and try to look casual. When Pamela points them out to Ms. Atkinson, they narrow their eyes and puff up their shoulders.

"Where are Joan and Rose?" the housemistress says.

"Rose is in the barn, Joan is on the back patio. Those boys there"—Pamela says, pointing—"they stripped Rose naked and would have followed through if I hadn't scared them off at the last second. We have to do something, and I have proof."

She takes out her phone and shows the photo the Ms. Atkinson. The housemistress turns to face the culprits squarely, and, receiving her glower, their bravado wilts. With a stare and a half raised arm, Ms. Atkinson signals to Mr. Flock.

Through the room's sudden electric stillness, he approaches, his Einstein wig squashed on one side and his fake mustache lopsided. "Yes, Ms.—"

Sirens echo from the direction of Annandale. After apprising Mr. Flock, the housemistress leaves for the barn. The housemaster corrals the culpable foursome in a corner, the mechanical wailing growing louder and louder, and the police and medics arrive a minute later. At the front door, Flock directs the responders—two officers and two medics—and what was a boisterous party becomes only nervous chatter among the students.

Fifteen minutes later, Pamela, standing in the vestibule, sees the medics lift a stretcher containing Rose into an ambulance in the driveway. Then Joan limps to the vehicle, and they help her get in. The two cops enter the house with Ms. Atkinson, and she draws Mr. Flock into her conversation with them. Then she signals for Pamela to come over, asks for her phone, and shows the crime-in-progress photo to the police.

When the officers turn and face the guilty boys, a couple of the would-be rapists try to dash out the rear, but they're tackled. One of the pair says his mother, a crown attorney, will be suing for police brutality. Ms. Atkinson rolls her eyes.

CHAPTER 27

* * *

The next day, Rose isn't around at Pilkington House, and neither is Ms. Atkinson.

But not long after, during Tuesday's lunch period, Rose reappears. She's sitting, looking like a statue amid her buddies in the cafeteria. Pamela almost feels sorry for her, and against the stares of Rose's friends—and her own instincts—she approaches their table. "I told the cops everything I saw, Rose. It'll help nail those boys for what they—"

"Yeah, yeah," Rose says. "I heard about what you *supposedly* did at the Halloween party. How do I know you didn't put those little fuckers up to it?"

Pamela shakes her head. She wanted to be civil, to help Rose cope with the assault. But she won't, not after what Rose just said. "Really? That's how you thank me?"

"Get out of my face."

Oh, Rose, Pamela thinks, it's *you* now who's showing bravado. But your face is flushed. It's aimed away from your pals, and your eyes are wet.

Chapter 28

June 2007

Coyote River First Nation

Seen from a single-engine Cessna that droned as it flew over the reserve, the western half of Coyote River First Nation was a patchwork of woods and farms with a sprinkling of houses, churches, and the occasional factory or warehouse. The river itself curved through the territory's southeast corner, ripples on the water flashing in the morning sun.

Eight kilometres in from that corner, which abutted the town of Ewing, lay the reserve's village, Tsorahsa. The settlement's older roads formed a grid; its newer ones curved and looped like any post-World-War-II suburb in North America. And in a house on Dreamcatcher Drive, three tween boys had just turned off their video games and decided to play outside.

"What you guys feel like doing?" Wayne said, closing his bedroom door and gesturing to the rear of the house.

As he and his friends Timothy and Joey ran out the patio

door to the backyard, Wayne hoped they'd play "Crime Scene: Coyote River" or another game that kept them outdoors and away for hours from his snooping mother, who was always scared he'd get hurt in their hijinks or hit by a car. She was a worrywart. "We might as well be in a Toronto suburb," she'd said to his dad when they'd moved from her family's Coyote River farm into Tsorahsa last year. Well, Wayne wasn't going to let her spoil his fun today. The boys jumped off the deck and sprawled laughing on the grass, chilly dew wetting their jeans and T-shirts. Feeling the sun on his skin, he squinted up at the horsetail clouds swishing in the blue.

"How about Crime Scene?" Timothy said, a beanpole looming over pudgy Joey.

But Joey—who'd just turned thirteen, one measly year older than Wayne—rolled his eyes and picked up a lacrosse stick from the grass. He grunted with the effort, because he was as wide as he was tall. "You still on about that kiddies' game?" He shook the stick at Wayne. "You got any more of these? We could pass a ball around."

"Only child, remember?"

Joey threw the stick to the grass. "Never anything fun to do at your house."

Timothy wandered to the rear fence. "Hey, you've got huge rot here." With his fingers, he wiggled one of the pickets and pulled away a chunk: powder fell from the squishy wood. More rotted boards surrounded it. "And these branches resting on the fence? The rain slides down them onto it. Your parents should cut them down and replace the rotted stuff."

Timothy was the smartest kid in class, and this was one more example of his brains.

"Look at this thing," Joey said, kicking the fence. "Sure ain't no concrete wall." He screwed up his face and punched a hole through the wood like it was paper. "Sweet. You could jump and crash right through. Yeah, this could be like a reality show—call it *Balls of Steel*. So, you got the balls, Waynie? Dare you to jump through it."

"My mother just rented some DVDs. Got the latest *Harry Potter*."

"Don't be a wuss, man. Fence got to come down anyway. Why not have fun doin' it?"

"I'm dying to see that *Harry Potter*," Timothy said.

"Blah blah blah," Joey said and narrowed his eyes. "Always the tight-assed Police Chief's kid." He turned to Wayne. "So, you goin' to do it, *witto Waynie*?"

Wayne fought the urge to slug Joey, always strutting around like he was gangster just because he'd turned thirteen. Instead, Wayne launched himself like one of the rocks he'd seen thrown at the barricades. He exploded through the boards and landed on the other side of the fence, wood chunks and splinters settling over the ground.

Timothy, standing closest to the fence, coughed as grey powder whirled in the air.

As the cloud dissipated, Wayne got to his feet, took off his glasses and wiped them on his shirttail.

Joey laughed and eyed Wayne. "Know where you're standin'? Whose land?"

"Um, not sure exactly."

Timothy stepped through the hole in the fence and stood beside Wayne on the other side. "Out here on Dreamcatcher, the rez borders Ewing, doesn't it?"

"Holy shit, Timothy Wilson, you're actually *wrong*." Joey said, his eyes wide with pretend shock. "This is Coyote River land, just like 'Peaceful Meadows Estates' is, where the stupid Ewing builder thinks he can put houses on our ground. My uncle showed me on a map, and that's why he helped put up the blockades—to take back land England 'gave' us in the 1700s."

"Thanks for the speech, professor," Wayne said.

A grin spread across Joey's face. "Goin' to take a shit on this Ewing 'property.' Get back at them for Uncle Len."

Timothy combed his fingers through his hair. "How many times do I have to tell you, Joey? At the building site, your uncle almost killed that Ewing guy—permanent brain damage, the hospital said. It doesn't matter that the man jumped over the fence and threw the first punch. He was a jerk, yeah, but he didn't deserve *that*."

"Easy for you to say. You ain't in jail. And your stupid father helped the OPP bastards arrest my uncle." Joey spit on the ground and walked further into the woodlot. Paper birches and big silver maples murmured, patches of sunlight flickering on the ground. "So long, wimps."

Joey's bulk faded into the green shadows.

Wayne and Timothy looked at each other.

"Never listen to him," Timothy said. Five seconds later he stamped his foot and shouted, "Joey, get back here."

No answer.

Timothy made a fist. "Let's go find him and get out of here."

They strode forward, jewelweed and cardinal flower swaying past their thighs.

A couple of yelps pierced the air.

"Yikes," Wayne said. "What was that?"

Timothy ran ahead and forked left behind a red elderberry. Wayne sprinted to catch up and found Timothy with

Joey, who was kneeling before a lady—no, a girl, or part of one—lying facedown in the jewelweed. Her plaid skirt and white blouse were mostly torn away, shreds lying nearby.

Joey was pale, his eyes wobbly, and his forehead shiny with sweat.

Wayne saw why. Two arrows lay angled from the ground to the body's back, in which two wide holes revealed ribs and jumbled, fleshy strings. A putrid stench. His legs shaking, Wayne moved closer. Fanned out from the girl's head, auburn hair lay like a halo in the paintings at church. To the extent he could see the face, most it was gone, as were the buttocks, upper legs, and lower torso.

The scene pushed on Wayne until he wanted to vomit, but another shriek from Joey stopped him.

He got up and turned to Joey: "Take it easy."

As he spoke, a flash like a diamond's sparkle came from beyond the trees.

The boys followed the glimmer to the edge of the woods and across a field to a road ditch. There they found the source of the shine—the sun's reflection in the broken windshield of an olive two-door Pontiac. Obscured by tall raspberry bushes, the car apparently crashed into the ditch, because, besides the smashed windshield, the front bumper was dented. No one was in the vehicle. The driver-side door was open, a leather purse had sprayed identification and credit cards around the front seat and floor, and all the identification belonged to someone named Rose Molloy, whose driver's license showed her to be the dead girl in the woods.

Timothy pulled out his phone and called his father's work number.

CHAPTER 28

* * *

Waiting for Timothy's father to arrive, the boys shuffled for a minute along the steamy asphalt and reached the shade of a big maple. They sat in the road ditch's undergrowth, which was cooler than the road, and fanned themselves with their baseball caps. Joey, frantic for street cred, always wore his cap backwards or sideways. His showing-off riled Wayne: why go looking for trouble, whether with the police or with toughs like Luke Daveneau, who—Joey said—had gang connections?

Joey spit onto the ground, gravel mixed into its mud spattered grass. "Way to go, Waynie. Now we're stuck with Tim's father, head of the occupation force."

Even with the shade and the breeze under the maple branches, sweat slithered down Wayne's back. Heat pulsing, the sun climbed.

"Shut up," Timothy said. "And yes, for the umpteenth time, my dad's a cop. It's his *job*. Get over it."

Cicadas droned, giving a bass line to the calls of cardinals and blue jays.

Joey laughed. "He's an 'Indian scout,' waiting for the real cops to show up."

A car, a police cruiser, rumbled into view. Timothy climbed out of the ditch to signal his father.

As Mr. Wilson got out and approached, Wayne noticed how big and black the letters were on the side of the car—*Coyote River Police*. Wasn't using black for police uniforms scary enough? But Wayne figured that you wanted to look pretty scary when you pulled over a couple of Hells Angels choppers.

Stupid Joey, the wannabe gangster, daring him to bust through the backyard fence. If they'd just played Crime Scene, nothing would've happened.

They scrambled out of the ditch.

Mr. Wilson had stopped where the Pontiac's back end stuck out of the shrubs. He took off his sunglasses and stared at the field beyond. "Those sets of footprints coming toward the car—they yours?"

Timothy nodded.

"What about those?" Mr. Wilson said, pointing at the far end of the Pontiac to another trail, left by somebody with big feet. The track actually showed two lines of shoeprints—one leading to the woodlot, and one coming from it.

"Nope," Joey said. "Ain't ours."

"Guess we were too freaked out to notice them," Wayne said.

Though Mr. Wilson limped a bit, he was a bear, but not fat like Joey, who always supersized his fries order at the McDonald's in Ewing. He let out a long breath and scratched his forehead. "OK, boys, now just relax and tell me what happened, from the start. Tim, you go first."

Wayne and Joey standing beside him on the gravel, Timothy was telling how they'd jumped through the rotted fence boards.

Joey stretched his arms and yawned like a bored cat, as though his crying and screaming in the woodlot never happened. He shuffled toward the Molloy girl's Pontiac.

"Stay away from that car," Mr. Wilson said as he spun to face Joey. "It's a crime scene."

The irony struck Wayne.

Chapter 29

The memorial service started at ten a.m. in Tsorahsa. Director Collier had announced on Friday that any upper-school students who wanted to go to Pam Renard's funeral could sign up and be bussed in to the reserve. Faculty and staff could drive out there if they wanted to. First thing in the morning, Sol had dropped Tash off at her lab and taken her car to Woodmore. He planned to leave for Tsorahsa at nine o'clock. But, over the weekend, some boys scrawled graffiti in a washroom; Peacock made him stay until he'd painted over all the permanent-marker penises, breasts, and cuss words.

So, at ten, instead of being parked somewhere at Coyote River, the Tashmobile was only passing through the western margin of Hamilton, which meant Sol would be late for Pam's memorial service, if he saw it at all. He sped by commuters along the 403 and merged onto Highway 22. Fifteen minutes later, the road jogged onto the Ewing Bypass, skirting north of the town, the rooftops of a suburban housing tract flashing through gaps in the woodland off the bypass. Soon a concrete bridge carried the car over the Coyote River, which stretched below, wide and brownish-green and unhurriedly moving, low ripples on its surface obscuring what lay underneath.

Past the river, the highway curved, and Sol slowed. Two

OPP cruisers sat on the gravel shoulder, and someone in a white spacesuit and booties stepped from a van, marked *OPP Forensic Identification Services*, and into the road ditch. Two uniformed cops, one talking on a phone, stood on the gravel. Behind them, lines of yellow tape enclosed a clump of tall raspberry bushes in the ditch, ran through a field, and disappeared into a woodlot.

One of the cops gestured to move along, so Sol hit the gas pedal, and Highway 22 straightened out. After two or three kilometres he slowed again, this time because a steel truss—a hydro tower lying on its side—was blocking the road. Half a dozen flags of different colours and symbols flapped from the barricade's top rails, but one grabbed his attention—on a white background, two purple stripes ran straight across. Two rows, as in, the Two Row Exchange?

From the bunch of guys standing around the barricade, a hulk approached. A baseball cap shadowed his face, and a bandana revealed only his eyes. "Another hot day."

"You can say that again."

"Another hot day." Even with the bandana, the man's eyes revealed his smile. "Sorry, road's closed. Part of a land reclamation we're carrying out. Coyote River, I mean. You'll have to turn around, find an alternate route."

Looking up—way up—Sol tried to avoid the man's left arm, which was missing its forearm and hand, replaced by a steel hook. "I'm from Woodmore Academy, Oakville, and I need to get to Pamela Renard's funeral." He handed his work ID tag to the man. "The school's director said anyone from Woodmore could—"

"Yes, we know about that," the man said and passed back the ID. "Take the first right, that's 9th Line. Keep straight a good ten minutes, till the sign for Tsorahsa." He turned, and the looped chain of his pocket watch jingled. With his hook, he signaled to two men standing on the road's shoulder beside the blockade. They shuffled out of the way.

With his good hand, the man pointed to his artificial arm. "I'm a sculptor. Occupational hazard—got it caught in machinery."

Sol winced and nodded. He squeezed the car through the shoulder and back onto Highway 22. Taking the right turn, he looked back and saw three eastbound cars stopped, waiting in a line on the other side of the barricade. The sculptor was walking toward the first car.

Ahead on 9th Line, a sign announced the reserve. Gravel driveways with post-mounted mailboxes dotted the road. Beside its ditches, a wall of maples, pines, and oaks masked the houses beyond. A couple of hundred metres later, businesses appeared by the road. Craft shops, including one with teepees on its lot, sprinkled themselves in groups, their driveways leading to gravel parking lots surrounded by open fields. And beyond, green woodlands. So much open space, so much nature.

He wanted to pull over and wander into the woods, forget about the world that killed promising kids like Pam. He sighed and focused on the road.

A dozen cigarette kiosks zipped by the window. Touting the brands it sold, each booth flew banners along the roadside. He passed Rockpoint Methodist Church and minutes later a Salvation Army building.

The sign VILLAGE OF TSORAHSA appeared, and he turned right onto Greenwood Road, apparently the main street. At the only traffic light, a Bank of Montreal branch occupied a corner. Moveable plastic letters on a signboard glinted from the parking lot:

> *COYOTE RIVER*
> *MINOR HOCKEY REGISTRATION*
> *STARTS JULY 22*

Then Sol passed Veterans Park—a manicured green with a stone cenotaph and flagpoles that flew American, British, Canadian, and Iroquois flags. He'd have to read up sometime on Coyote River.

A passing car honked, and Sol swerved right. With his gawking, he'd drifted into the middle of the roadway, so he pulled over and reached for the map to the cemetery.

* * *

Sol parked. As he walked to the crowd gathered at the graveyard's far end, a farm tractor clattered behind him along the road. Looking for Bobby, he slipped past mourners and found the boy standing with Amy Ling.

Near them at the graveside, a bespectacled woman with a long silver mane was speaking to the gathering.

"... so as Coyote River's chief, let me conclude by wishing everyone comfort, most of all Pamela's parents, in the days ahead. Remember our belief when you think of Pamela: In nature, nothing truly ends."

Sol approached Bobby and touched his shoulder. The boy nodded.

Across Pam's plot, a middle-aged couple cried quietly. At the chief's invitation, some funeral-goers took turns

CHAPTER 29

shovelling dirt into the grave. Sol participated. He returned to Bobby and Amy as mourners received packets of yogurt-covered raisins, Pam's favourite snack. When earth filled the grave to capacity, a local musician led people in singing the Cranberries' "Zombie," a song Pam loved.

Two mascara-smeared girls sniffled beside Amy, and Sol recognized some Woodmore teachers among the crowd. Judging by the numerous navy blazers and plaid skirts, he guessed that Woodmore kids made up 50 percent of the crowd, which dispersed when the song of honour finished.

People drifted across the field of headstones, some tilted and illegible from two centuries of weather, toward the parking lot. Pam's folks lived close by, and the orders from Collier were for Bobby, Amy, and the two other floormates to join the reception at the parents' house. His face battling stubble, dried tear-streaks, and red blotches, Bobby walked with Amy and the Pilkington House girls.

As the kids passed Sol, he asked if he could speak alone to Bobby. He led the boy to a copse of maples and beeches and into cool shade.

"I'm so sorry about Pam," he said. "Have you spoken here to her folks?"

Literally looking down on Sol, Bobby loosened his school tie. "I never met them before she . . . you know. We'd talked about me visiting this summer, but I don't think she told them about me. At the church service, her father like walked away when I introduced myself. As her boyfriend, I mean."

Sol patted Bobby's shoulder. "Being here today, it'll help. I'm sure it will."

Bobby jerked and spun away. "You don't know anything about it."

"Fuck. Some thanks I get for trying—"

"Hey," Amy said from the edge of the street. Compared to the two dorm girls standing beside her, she was as short as a garden gnome, a skinny one. "Bobby, come on. Let's go."

Bobby stayed silent, his face still turned away from Sol. His shoulders heaved and he waved to Amy. "Go without me."

Sol felt like a jerk for matching Bobby's frostiness with his own. With grief weighing on the kid, Sol promised himself to cut Bobby some slack. "Come on, rock star. Tell me what—"

"She was pregnant. Like two or three weeks. I'm—I was—the father. And then, she goes and dumps me. A day or two before she died. She didn't want the kid, or she didn't want me. Maybe both."

"Jesus Christ."

"Pam always stonewalled me when I begged her to keep the baby." The boy's bulky frame slumped forward. "She never gave me like a clear answer—never a firm *yes* or *no*." He hid his face with his hands.

Sol took Bobby by the shoulders and tried to nudge him toward the three girls.

Bobby shook himself free. "I'm not going to the reception. Her father hates my guts, I already know that. So why bother?" he said, loudly enough that the girls heard.

Into the hush that followed, a tinny pop tune jingled from Amy's phone. She pressed a couple of buttons and scanned the screen. "Oh my God, you guys. Oh my God."

Amy stepped back and swayed on her feet.

"What's wrong?" Sol asked.

One of the girls approached Amy. "*What* already?"

"Director Collier, she's sent out a Woodmore-wide email. It's Rose Molloy. She . . . she's dead."

Chapter 30

April 1992

St. James Town, Toronto

"Grade Eight Conservatory exam is next month. Really got to push, if you want more than just Honors."

Sitting on the piano bench, Sol swung his legs back and forth above the worn wood floor. "This Brahms is real hard. My fingers are too short."

"Don't worry," Danny said, his forehead wrinkled. "We'll fix it, change the fingering for those big stretches in the left hand."

Don't worry. Whenever his big cousin spoke those two words, Sol worried. To Danny, "pretty good" wasn't good enough, because if Sol flubbed a couple of notes in a piece, Danny would throw his hands up the air, then take off his glasses and rub the reddened sides of his nose. So Sol's legs kept swinging, swinging, the arcs growing wider and wider and wider.

Without any warning, Danny slapped him, slapped his thigh

so hard Sol winced from the sting.

His face darkening, Danny said, "The bench is *already* rickety, and my folks slaved to buy me this piece-of-junk piano."

"Where's Aunt Noreen?"

During every lesson, Sol's aunt would busy herself somewhere in the background: baking in the kitchen or cleaning the bedrooms. But not today. No Aunt Noreen.

Danny looked down from his chair beside the piano. His face had changed from beet red back to freckled white. "Dad playing organ and conducting the choirs at St. Mary's isn't enough anymore. Mom got another part-time job."

The living room was open to the kitchen, and Sol missed the smell of Aunt Noreen's baking, which usually filled the space during his lessons. Today, with nothing to mask it, the stink of cigarette smoke oozed from the yellowed wallpaper.

Leaning over the keyboard, Danny opened the Grade Eight exam book to the Brahms *Waltz in A-Flat*. "Have the place to ourselves now. To really make progress, me and you need privacy."

The faces of Bach and Beethoven, Daniel Barenboim and Glenn Gould stared down from wall posters above the piano. Stared.

"OK. Before we work through this great piece, play through it. Start to finish."

Sol stumbled along the notes like how his father, last week, had staggered in late, bumped against the hallway walls, and woke Sol and his brother and sister. They stayed in their beds and said nothing. Mom's harsh whispers soon escaped from the parents' bedroom.

Danny snapped his fingers. "You seem to be daydreaming,

CHAPTER 30

kid. You've got to focus. And you're stiff as a board—I can help you relax." Danny got up and rubbed Sol's shoulders.

He'd never done that before, and Sol flinched.

"Hey, relax. I'm going to help you tame this waltz, but you've got to help me first."

"You said we'd change the left-hand fingering."

"Help your cousin out, like this." Danny's hand slid down from Sol's shoulders to the top button of his shirt. Danny's fingers, as big as cucumbers, undid the button. And the next one.

The walls closed in on Sol. "Where I can't make those big stretches between the third and fourth fingers."

Fingers moved lower again, and Sol shoved them away, banging Danny's left hand against the keyboard. Sol ducked and crisscrossed his arms over his face, but the blow failed to come.

Danny returned to his chair. "Well, what're we going to do here? I know. I'll go first." He took off his T-shirt and draped it over the chair back. "Hot in here, don't you think? Anyway, your turn. We'll both be more comfortable, so we can focus." He squeezed his right hand into a fist.

Sol took off his shirt and slapped it down on the piano bench. He laid his finger on the sheet music. "The first tricky part is here, where the third finger has to cross over—Danny!"

Danny's jeans button and fly were open, and he stood pulling the pants down. "We're family. Nothing wrong with love among family."

With the speed of a shoplifter, Sol grabbed his shirt and exam book and ran for the door, but fingers bit like steel vices around his ankle and he crashed on his elbow to the floor. Then, his cousin was dragging him across the living room floor. Sol reached out but found nothing to grasp and tried to stop the burning in his back and shoulders, but the scraping stopped only after they'd gone into Danny's bedroom.

The door slammed shut.

"Get up."

As Sol stood, his elbow stiff and aching, he lost his struggle not to cry.

"This is going to be so much fun," Danny said. "You'll see." Then he undid the fly of Sol's jeans.

***

"You can't tell anyone. Not your mother, not your father. Nobody. *Ever*. This is our special secret, and if you even think about squealing, I'll kill you. Don't think I won't know."

Sol's throat tightened.

"Let's get back to the piano," Danny said. "Make those changes to the left-hand fingering."

"OK," Sol said, his mind a blank wall.

Chapter 31

June 2007

Coyote River First Nation

"Mind-blowing," Amy said, looking down at her phone. "I don't believe it."

"Me neither," said one of her floormates, peering over Amy's shoulder at the screen. "Rose Molloy? She's a hater, a bitch, but . . ."

Amy raised her hand. "It goes on." She read from the email:

The spring term is virtually over, and exams are in process. Therefore, to finish the year on time and to permit students to focus on studying, Woodmore Academy will not be holding a memorial for either victim. However, we will have a joint service to remember Rose and Pamela sometime in the autumn term. In the spirit of the Two Row Exchange, we will encourage people from the Coyote River First Nation to attend.

"The tools. They can't do that," Bobby said. "A memorial for Pam and Rose together? Tactless."

"Don't you think it might help things?" Sol said. "Between Coyote River and Ewing?"

Amy pocketed her phone. "Right now, we don't have time to freak out about it. Bobby—it's the last time I'll ask—are you coming with us to Pam's place or not?"

Bobby gestured a thumbs-down. "I'll wait here by the buses."

Sol wondered if Amy had anything more to say about Pam, and he didn't want Bobby moping alone. He gestured to Amy. "Could you join Bobby and me? For a coffee, maybe?"

"What?" Amy said, arching an eyebrow. "When?"

"Now." Sol put his hand on Bobby's shoulder and looked across the graveyard. "I see a restaurant on Greenwood Road. A three-minute walk, tops." He glanced at Amy and with his free arm motioned to the boy.

She nodded but raised her finger. "The buses leave at four o'clock."

"We'll be back here long before then," Sol said. He started walking, and Amy and Bobby followed.

They passed by a recently-built strip mall that held a dozen businesses, including RBC Royal Bank, Ancient Echoes Salon-Spa, CKBR 88.9 FM, Coyote River Electronics, Eagle Eye Care, Jiggy's Variety & Groceries, Dreamcatcher Jewelry, and Robertson's Restaurant. If Sol had time later, he'd go to the jewelry shop and, assuming he could afford anything there, get something for Tash.

"You two are missing the reception, so get something to eat," he said as they entered Robertson's, bells tinkling on the door. "I'll pay."

CHAPTER 31

Amy looked up at him. "Thanks, Mr. Fitzgerald."
"Sol."

Robertson's seated about thirty, and noontime diners occupied three-quarters of the black-lacquered tables. As Sol and the kids sat down at a window booth, the beige blankness of the walls struck him. But beside the kitchen's pass-through a single picture hung: a Norval Morrisseau reproduction. Sol remembered the artist's name from a high school trip to the Art Gallery of Ontario. Hard to forget. Animal spirits (was that what they were?) painted in hot blue, green, red, and ochre—each shape walled in by black lines, like stained glass. He'd gone to church as a kid, only because his mother dragged him there, and the clerestory windows' stories gave escape from the boredom. At thirteen, though, he stopped going. He didn't care how much his parents yelled. He'd stopped doing a lot of things that year. And started up with others.

Bobby waved his hand in Sol's face. "Hey, maestro, over here."

Beside their table, a petite black-haired waitress stood holding a pen and order pad. Mid-forties. The name *Pauline* stamped on her white plastic nametag.

"What would yous like?" she said. As they ordered, a turtle tattoo peeked from beneath the sleeve of Pauline's navy-blue polyester uniform.

Voices came from the next booth. Two young women and a man chatted as they fiddled with their food and phones.

The man, wearing his baseball cap backwards, said, "It's payback. Somebody here had had enough. Over a year now, all the bullshit at the barricades. The OPP arresting people, and we're getting nowhere. Then the Renard girl . . ." With the back of his hand, he wiped his eye. "No wonder this Ewing chick's been found dead."

"We don't know yet where she was from," said one of the women.

"Come on, Greg," said the other, laying her knife and fork on her plate. "You honestly think somebody'd be that sick or stupid? Tit for tat never works. And even worse, if the Ewing folks start thinking like you do, the first fights are going to turn into gun battles."

"Oh, and you're a negotiation expert now," Greg said, as he used his napkin.

He got up, and the women followed him to the cash register.

Sol and his charges had all ordered the vegetarian omelette special, and plates of it now steamed, along with coffees, on the table. He looked from Bobby to Amy and back again. "Even with all we know about Rose Molloy, it's still a blow. Whole thing makes me sad."

Bobby pushed a bit of green pepper around on his plate. "It's creeping me out."

"Has anything," Sol said, "come to mind about Pam—or now Rose—since we talked in your room?"

"In her *dorm* room?" Bobby's eyes widened.

"Calm down," Amy said, her eyes rolling behind her glasses. She raised her arm and made a fist. "If you blab, this is going to get well acquainted with your face."

Bobby snorted. Amy's eyes were stone.

"Well?" Sol said. "Anything, Amy?"

"Nothing new, but . . ." She shifted her weight and knotted her fingers. "Um, there's one thing I didn't mention. A secret. I promised Pam I wouldn't—"

"Looks like you're spilling the beans anyway," Sol said.

Amy glared at him. "*Only* to help you find out what

happened!"

Sol grabbed a paper napkin and fished a pen out of his pocket. "Calm down. I get it."

Amy straightened out her fingers and sighed. "OK. The year before Pam came to Woodmore, she hooked up with a Coyote River boy, Luke Daveneau. He got involved with a gang that sold drugs on the reserve. Anyway, his bad-boy lifestyle attracted Pam awhile. She said she was sick of always being a 'mommy's girl' A-student, and she liked the novelty of smoking weed."

Bobby put his mug down, almost spilling the java. "What? I tried to get her to try it. She wouldn't. Went all prissy on me."

"Well, anyway," Amy said, "Pam's father—he's like a band councillor here—told her the Coyote River Police brought in the OPP and arrested two Mohawks on drug charges. Luke wasn't one of them, but Pam knew they were high up in his gang. Of course, even before that happened, she kept her fling with Luke on the down-low. Her father warned her to be wary around the reserve, because the local gang was tight with drug-smuggling Mohawks from Upstate New York. And the Hells Angels. That's crazy scary."

"Anything else?" Sol said.

"Hmm. Last August—"

"It's quarter to four," Bobby said. "We've got to get back."

Amy raised her finger. "Last August, Pam broke up with Luke before she left for Woodmore. From what she told me, she still had feelings for him, but she was so not going to follow him as he spiralled down. When she tried to end it, he goes, 'You stuck-up apple. You're ditching us for your prep school.' That tore Pam apart."

***

They walked back to the waiting buses, and Sol got into the Tashmobile and waved as he drove by Bobby and Amy. He wanted to see the reserve's country stretches. Knowing Tash wouldn't be home for two and a half hours, he steered the Jetta further into Coyote River, starting where Greenwood Road met 9th Line, then crisscrossing south and west, south and west. As he moved along the side roads, the sun flashed into his eyes from the car's front hood, and he scolded himself for forgetting his sunglasses.

The car zipped by a couple of lots with trailer homes, some of them rundown, rusty, and abandoned, but most of the properties suggested self-sufficiency, if not affluence. Farms with their tractors, cows, and rolled hay bales. A little boy riding his bicycle in the driveway of a new house, which could have been in any suburb in North America. Occasional "estate" lots with expansive two-and-a-half-storey brick houses, probably with lavish interiors.

Sol reversed his checkerboard route and drove through Tsorahsa from its opposite side and past the cigarette stores, Melody Mansion, and the bridge over the Coyote River, the last landmark bringing an old Simon & Garfunkel song to his mind—"Bridge Over Troubled Waters." At the barricade, the hulking sculptor recognised him, waved him on, and Sol sped along Highway 22.

He scanned through some crackly radio stations until a strong signal came in, playing country, but seconds later Conway Twitty's "I Couldn't See You Leavin'" faded out, and a newscaster gave the call sign, CKBR 88.9 FM in Tsorahsa.

CHAPTER 31

Our lead story: Earlier today, east of the Ewing Bypass, three boys discovered a body in a woodlot at the Coyote River-Ewing border. Coyote River Police responded, but they later turned the investigation over to the OPP because the victim, believed to be a teenage girl, was found off-reserve at a Ewing rural-route address. Foul play is suspected.

Sol straightened his shoulders and exhaled. "What the fuck is going on?"

Nearing the spot where he'd seen the OPP crew, he passed a showy house on a vast property, with helmeted kids on horses in a paddy near the road, a couple of trainers coaching the young riders. Hadn't Amy and her lunch buddies nattered about Rose Molloy's parents owning a horse ranch? Has to be a fluke, he thought.

But Rose *was dead*. Collier's email said so.

Past the paddy, the OPP cars and van still sat beside the road, cops milling around as a couple of white-suited crime scene techs emerged from a woodlot and onto a field beyond the overgrown road ditch.

The car met Highway 22 and Sol headed for Hamilton. He put the CKBR news out of his mind and focused on what he knew: before Woodmore, Bobby'd said, Pam had a boyfriend named Luke Daveneau on the rez, and he'd got her into smoking dope. Not surprising, because Luke was in a gang that dealt drugs the reserve. What if he'd found out about Bobby and Pam, and killed her out of revenge? Then Ray Havers had to die too—his bad luck, a hapless witness. But how could Luke have been on the library roof with them? Maybe because the guy *was* in a drug gang and kept Pam in ganja and Bobby's father in coke, because after all, a baggie of coke was found in Ray Havers's pocket. The Halton detective, Downey, said so herself. So, maybe Luke and his gang's enforcers killed the man, probably saying something like, "Sorry, it's just business, Ray," as they'd tossed him off the roof and then got rid of the only witness.

But Ray Havers was a banker, sending his kid to Woodmore, even donating money for renovations to the library. If he was in hock to a dealer, couldn't he have just fleeced money from the bank? A numbers whiz like him? Of course he could have. Havers wasn't the kind of guy to have trouble paying his dealer.

Fluttering his lips as he exhaled, Sol glanced to his right. South of the 403, the steel-mill smokestacks on Hamilton's waterfront belched dark exhaust. It obscured the foundries. Sol concentrated on the road and was soon approaching Burlington.

Chapter 32

November 2006

Oakville

After her latest encounter with Rose in the cafeteria, Pamela has dropped any pity she might have felt for the girl, any shred of compassion for her, because Rose, knowing who'd foiled the gang rape, still virtually blamed Pamela for the attack. So, there isn't going to be a SlutWalk in honour of Rose. Pamela doesn't have the time for it anyway.

She's trying now to ignore Rose, to not waste any more energy on her, so when Bobby asks if she'd like to meet his parents for dinner at their house, Pamela is keen. Getting off Woodmore's grounds will put her literally further away, for a few hours at least, from her nemesis, whose capacity for gratitude fills a thimble.

* * *

At a quarter to six p.m. on the agreed-upon day, she and Bobby drive out of Woodmore's student parking lot and head for the Clayton Hill neighbourhood. She's jittery, anticipating—and ready to point out—any stereotypes his parents may let slip. On the other hand, she wants to like them. Why? she asks herself. Do I consider this guy to be husband material, and why would I, not even out of high school yet, be in such a rush? Pamela tries but fails to answer the questions. She gazes absently out the window. Once they're within Bobby's quarter, Pamela loses all sense of direction, the car passing big houses on generous lots that front broadly curving streets.

"OK. We're here," Bobby says.

They park at the curb, and Pamela chuckles at the contrasting cars in the driveway. "A BMW, I'd expected that. But what's with the Smart car?"

"My father's," Bobby says. "Trying to be all eco-friendly."

Pamela's starting to like Mr. Havers already. From what she's seen, the man's not only environmentally aware but bighearted, friendly. He could keep all his money to himself, but Bobby says he's donated fifty thousand to Woodmore. If Mr. Havers were a jerk, she thinks, he would be bigheaded around Mr. Flynn and Director Collier. He does the opposite. Pamela remembers from a few days ago, she was studying in the library late into the afternoon. When she walked out the entrance, Trevena Way was empty of kids, but behind her, Pamela heard that sing-song voice and looked back. Mr. Havers stood outside the Admin building's entrance, talking to Assistant Director Flynn, who stood holding the door open. As Mr. Havers walked through the doorway, he touched Mr. Flynn on the shoulder, like they were old friends. That showed humility and respect.

Linking arms now, Pamela and Bobby walk up the

interlocking-brick driveway and he ushers her through the front door. Its deep reveal forms a nook that half a dozen people could stand in. Inside, the foyer is two storeys high. The sound of Queen's "Bohemian Rhapsody" wafts from an archway to the living room and echoes in the cavernous space. Over the music, they hear Mr. Havers's voice.

"You two have arrived. Welcome."

Before they walk in, Bobby dances with mock enthusiasm to the music, and Pamela can't stop giggling as he pulls her into the living room. Stark but expensive-looking decor. A decorating magazine would be happy to feature the design.

Nipping at a cracker, Mr. Havers perches on a white leather sofa. He motions to plates and napkins on the coffee table, and Bobby and Pamela sit down on chrome-and-leather seats, which stand on either side of a crackling fireplace. The outdoorsy smell of wood smoke is out of place against the pop music, which is too loud for easy conversation.

As if sensing her discomfort, Mr. Havers rises and turns down the volume by half. "So Pamela," he says, adjusting the shoulders of his V-neck sweater. "I hear you're on a student exchange. Have you picked up any financial mathematics at Woodmore, by any chance? As a banker, I fear kids aren't learning the basics."

"Um, I guess so." she says.

Mr. Havers merely smiles. Behind him, built-in shelves hold the stereo system, hundreds of books, as many CDs, and two-dozen vinyl LPs with frayed covers.

"You mean like formulae?" Pamela says. But she's thinking, what is this supposed to be—a midterm exam? She dislikes his expecting an academic show as much as she begrudges the same desire in her own father and in Coyote River High's teachers. Beside being called "apple," Pamela also heard "show-off" as a slur from her high school rivals, but she'd only been responding to the demands of adults, not trying to brag.

Mr. Havers nods. "Sure. How about the formula for, oh, the future value of a single sum. That's an easy one."

She gives him what he wants: "A single sum's future value equals its present value times one-plus-the-interest-rate to the power of the number of compounding periods. How's that?"

"Very impressive. I hope your intelligence rubs off on Robert here, because he is barely surviving in math and chemistry. Help him if you can. I have given up."

"Ha ha, Dad," Bobby says. He stares at his father, and red crawls up his neck and spreads across his face.

Mr. Havers meets Bobby's glare and doesn't recoil. His lips press into a thin smile and he shakes his head.

As a new song plays on the hi-fi system, Bobby sprawls in his chair. "Please, not 'We are the Champions' again. You're playing Queen like every day lately. Got anything easier on the ears?"

Mr. Havers rises, strolls behind the sofa, and pushes a button on the CD player. "Happy now?"

The quiet sucks the air out of the room. Pamela sighs with relief when Bobby's mother, in jeans and a T-shirt, strolls into the room and shakes her hand.

"Pardon my nosiness, Pamela, but your last name—it's French?"

"*Oui*—well, not really. There was tons of intermarriage going way back, and my family doesn't know who our first male Renard was. But my mother *is* French Canadian."

"Oh . . . *Je parle un petit peu de français*," Mrs. Havers says, but she's being modest. Still in French, she asks how Pamela likes Woodmore. The two of two of them chat for a minute.

Pamela figured the family would carefully avoid the subject of Ewing, but as everyone moves to the dinner table, Mrs. Havers launches into it. "It's happening just south of Brantford, right? I simply don't understand what started the clash," she says, and gestures with an upturned palm. "I'd like to know."

For the umpteenth time since arriving in Oakville, Pamela explains the Haldimand Proclamation and the drastic shrinking of the Haldimand Tract.

Mrs. Havers's hand goes to her mouth. "Wow, ten kilometres. On each side of the river. My high school history courses never mentioned it, but surely, the original area can't be returned after all this time? I mean, Brantford, Kitchener-Waterloo—*they* must lie within that area. Half a million people would have to move!"

Pamela laughs at the irony. The British and then Canadian governments, not too long ago, had no qualms moving *indigenous* groups off ancestral lands. "Don't worry, nobody has to move. But some sort of payback for the 950,000 acres would be nice. Here's the problem: the British were, and the Canadian government still is, 'on Indian time' when it comes to honouring treaties." She notices Bobby's parents' stunned expressions. "*On Indian time*—it's a slur meaning 'late.' But we've taken it back, like how, among themselves, blacks use *nigger* or Jews use *kike*."

Uneasy pause.

"This salmon is great," Bobby says. "So, Mom, how are things in the exciting world of accounting? Is that one partner still hogging the limelight for work you've done?"

Mrs. Havers's stories of office politics make us hoot, but her sketch of her sociopathic manager is chilling.

"I think the world's full of egomaniacs," Pamela says. "My father's on Coyote River band council. You want dysfunctional politics? Just go to one of the council meetings."

Everybody laughs, especially Mrs. Havers.

Bobby's folks, Pamela thinks, are OK. She's glad she came.

Mr. Havers clears the dishes off the table. As Mr. Havers picks up his wife's plate, he bends and kisses her. A dry, sexless peck on the cheek. Pamela gets the feeling they both want it that way.

Chapter 33

June 2007

Sol couldn't let what he knew stay locked away. If that ranch on the fringe of Ewing belonged to the Molloys, if the dead teen *was* Rose Molloy, he had to tell Detective Downey. During the drive back from Coyote River, the thought arose, but he'd forced it down again and again. Now he didn't care how crazy it might sound. Not at the apartment yet, he was cruising east on Lakeshore Road, through the downtown strip, but he pulled over and parked in front of Impasto, an art gallery. In his wallet, he found Downey's business card. He called her number.

"Downey."

"It's Sol Fitzgerald, from Woodmore Academy. You asked me to phone if I thought of anything else."

"Yes?"

"Something you should look into at Coyote River. Well, it happened outside the reserve, but just on the other side of the border with Ewing. This girl named Rose Molloy, she's missing from Woodmore but also from her parents' horse ranch. She may be lying dead in some woods."

"And you know this *how*?"

Sol wished the cop would just shut up and listen. "Along with the rest of Woodmore, I drove out to Coyote River today for Pam Renard's funeral, and I was talking to some of the students. Anyway, Pam's roommate was looking at an email from the Director. The message—it was sent to everyone at Woodmore—said that Rose Molloy was dead."

"You're sure about that?"

Glaring at no one, Sol shook his head. "Check with *anyone* at Woodmore. They can forward you the email if you want. But there's more. On my way back here, I heard a Coyote River radio newscast saying a teenager's body had turned up on a ranch just outside the reserve. Then, on 9th Line, I happened to drive by a Ewing horse ranch, and the OPP had yellow tape up in the ditch and running across a field into some woods. Guys in white coveralls and plastic booties were poking around. All of that can't be chance."

"Well, actually, it could be chance. If there *is* a relationship between the Molloy girl's death and the investigation you saw taking place, it could influence the Woodmore case, but that Ewing ranch enquiry—it's in the OPP's jurisdiction, not mine. I'll follow up with them."

You're welcome, Sol thought. "You know, myself, I used to think Rose might have killed Pam. Now I'm not so sure."

"Thanks for the information," Downey said, "but it's not your task to unravel the truth of what happened to Mr. Havers and Pamela. On the contrary, you're implicated by evidence found at Woodmore. So, just go about your job, and please, don't do anything foolish."

"*What* evidence?"

CHAPTER 33

"Goodbye, Mr. Fitzgerald."

Sol flung the phone on the passenger seat, pulled onto Lakeshore Road, and sped toward his apartment.

Chapter 34

Sitting at his desk, Ruvinsky grunted and returned Alison's nod. "What up," he said, leaning back in his chair to brush coconut crumbs from his paunch, a crumpled Tim Hortons bag lying on his desktop.

Walking toward her desk, Alison looked over her shoulder at him. "Good doughnut, John? Does it meet the approval of Homicide's junk-food connoisseur?"

Even over the ceiling grilles' hum, she heard a wave of giggles.

"Fuck off," Ruvinsky said as he turned to his files. "All of you."

Alison sank into her chair and stuck her tongue out at the back of Ruvinsky's balding head. But she'd seen his red-rimmed eyes, grey half-moons hanging beneath them. From Ed Loams, she'd learned that Ruvinsky's wife had ovarian cancer. Months, maybe weeks, to live.

In contrast to that dismal story, Homicide buzzed with light and chatter. After so much humidity, the morning's fresh air invigorated everybody.

Alison was thankful for the din. It gave privacy as she called Glenna Eastwood, an OPP constable in Cayuga, twenty-five kilometres south of Ewing. The two women were best friends

CHAPTER 34

in university, and they'd kept in touch for more years than Alison wanted to count. Was it really sixteen? U of T seemed like two years ago.

"So, your detachment working a fresh murder?" Alison said. "Is it, by any chance, a teenager named Rose Molloy?"

Glenna hooted. "How do *you* know, Parkdale Princess? Ident's barely finished up at the scene. Victim's name's not released yet."

Fitzgerald, Alison thought. An amateur, but a capable one. Of course, if *he* killed the Molloy girl, his "detecting" was one more lie.

The words "Parkdale Princess" pushed Fitzgerald from Alison's mind. She hadn't heard that epithet in years. In her first year at U of T, a clique of three Forest Hill girls gave her the nickname, and Glenna overheard the slur and befriended Alison. Glenna's action angered the in-group's members, so when they found out she was from Huntsville, they christened her "Backwoods." Their conduct only cemented the bond between the two outsiders.

Alison shook her head to oust the memory. "Long story. I'm on a double murder in Oakville, and, if I can believe one of my suspects, your Molloy case may be linked to it." She described the connections: at Woodmore Academy, the Ewing girl played racist pranks on a Coyote River exchange student; as the school year was closing, the bodies of Pamela Renard and Havers showed up beside the library; and then Rose Molloy vanished. "Now, it's a week later, and you guys just found the girl's body on a Ewing rural route."

"Holy cow."

"Do I have the last bit—crime-scene location—right?"

"Show-off."

"So can we share case information?"

"Have to ask the brass here. Get back to you. In the meantime, here's a tidbit: we found the body lying face down in her parent's woodlot. Two arrows were sticking out of her back."

"What?"

"Too tidy. It's like a setup for anyone who bow hunts on Coyote River. Else it's some psycho's twisted joke: Indians, bows and arrows. You know?"

"I get it. OK, I should really be—"

"Not even necessarily murder. Ever seen an aerial photo of Coyote River First Nation? Lots of humongous woodlands, so hunters love it. The hunting isn't regulated by the province."

Footsteps sounded above the office hubbub: Ed Loams, carrying a folder, was approaching Alison's desk. "I've got to hang up."

"A few years back on Coyote River, a man was shot and killed—with a bullet, in that case—by a stray shot from a hunter more than three hundred metres away. But people bow hunt there too, so the Molloy kid's death may be another accident."

"I have to *go*, Glenna—"

"Coyote River Police are questioning hunters and outfitters on the rez. Could have been an off-reserve hunter, though."

Loams laid the folder on Alison's desk. "Some forms that HR forgot to give you the first week."

"Thanks, Ed," she said as he walked away. And, lowering her voice, to Glenna: "My staff sergeant just came by. I didn't want him to—never mind. Call as soon as you can."

Alison ended the call. She hadn't wanted Loams to overhear her nosing around—out of jurisdiction. On the Toronto force,

CHAPTER 34

she'd gotten a reputation for doing that, and, in general, for being a go-getter and troublemaker. She was going to tread lightly at Halton Region, though. She was.

* * *

At ten to five, she answered a call from Glenna Eastwood: the Cayuga OPP detachment agreed to coordinate the exchange of case files, and the Halton Regional Police would keep its jurisdiction over the Woodmore investigation.

"When will I have access?" Alison said.

"Probably tomorrow afternoon. The IT folks'll courier you a SecurID fob. Then you can sign on to our VPN."

"Got it. Thanks, but you should add more abbreviations. I counted only three."

"You're a comedian. Should do lunch some weekend. One of those patios along Queen's Quay. Walk around, see if you can still turn the boys' heads."

* * *

Driving home, Alison looked forward to reading after dinner, but as she approached the traffic light at Francis Street and the bridge over Oakville Harbour, her musing ceased. The BMW in front of her squealed its tires as it swerved around the car ahead of it. The Beemer snarled through the intersection and bounded across the bridge.

She checked for cars and pedestrians. All clear. But should she—a detective, not a traffic cop—do this? Darn it, Marcia, or *any* kid, wasn't going to get run over by this reckless driver.

Following a couple of car lengths behind, she flipped on the emergency flashers. The speedometer read eighty kilometres per hour for the length of the bridge, but then the speeder slowed and pulled over past its far end, where dollar stores and burger joints fronted Lakeshore Road.

She radioed her location and the man's plate number, scrawled the speed in her notebook, and walked up to the driver's window. She flashed her badge. "Detective Alison Downey, Halton Regional Police Service."

The motorist, a white man in his early forties, wore a suit and cologne.

"Dangerous driving and speeding," she said. "Thirty kilometres an hour over the limit. If you hadn't noticed, I was right behind you at that intersection." Alison pointed across bridge.

"There's no defence for my tearing around that fellow at the light. But I swear, officer, he was distracted—talking on his phone—and crawling along at twenty kilometres an hour. I'm sorry, I just lost my cool. You see, I'm late picking up my wife."

He wasn't going to sweet-talk her, not this guy. "Driver's licence."

The plastic card reflected the streetlamp into her eyes, and Alison made out the man's name, Michael White.

She walked back to her car and relayed the licence number. When the record came back, it was clean. White possessed a spotless driving record and no arrests, but after she wrote the speeding ticket, Alison sat for ten more minutes in her car, so the guy's wife would be extra angry when he showed up.

Back at the BMW, she handed back the driver's licence. "Get out of the car, please."

White obeyed. "But, officer, I don't see how—"

CHAPTER 34

"I'm obliged to search you."

"On what grounds?"

"Spread your legs."

White sighed, and his head dropped between his shoulders.

She patted him at the usual hiding spots, including his crotch. Nothing. She handed him the ticket. "There you go. Get in."

White said nothing and drove away.

Confused by her overwhelming anger, Alison sat in the unmarked car and forced herself to loosen her grip on the steering wheel and breathe deeply. She'd never thought of herself as a cop who would abuse her authority, playing power games with ordinary citizens. Especially citizens who were male and white.

* * *

Alison's daughter led her through the kitchen and into the laundry room, where lemony sunlight fell across the ironing board.

"The window's a bit small, and it should be facing north, but at least I'll be able to paint by natural light," Marcia said. "So, what do you think? You must be sick of cursing this washer. If you buy a stacked set, I'll have room in here for a studio, and you'll get a dependable washer-dryer. Win-win."

"Hey, not so fast." Alison approached the two machines, their 1970s ochre enamel chipped at the corners. Until last year, they'd always been reliable. She thought of Director Collier at Woodmore, how the woman quarrelled with Ray Havers over funding the library's upgrades and repairs. Yes, everything did eventually fall apart, but Alison cringed as she imagined the cost of a new washer-dryer set.

She leaned over the dryer and peered into the space between it and the wall. "There's a grungy mess back here. Could be even worse underneath these old contraptions. And anyway, I'm not made of money."

Marcia pouted but soon brightened. She volunteered to clean the walls and floor once the worn-out machines were removed. Alison countered that an oil-painting studio would likely create a *new* mess and definitely reek of turpentine fumes.

Marcia raised her hand and said, "I'll tidy up after each session, and nowadays there's odourless mineral spirits. They have no smell, Mom, and they're way less toxic than turpentine. Anyway, when it's warm enough I can open the window."

The girl's knowledge was impressive, and her passion for painting was obvious. Yes, Alison thought, I'd rather have her more interested in art than in boys.

"Alright," she said. "But before you set up your easel or anything else, you're going to need a pair of heavy-duty rubber gloves and a dust mask for your cleaning duty. First I'm going to call the junk-removal people."

"Yes!" Marcia said, punching the air.

Alison pointed to the dryer. "A load just finished. So, before you get too excited, could you open that and fold the laundry?"

Marcia's shoulders slumped.

Chapter 35

In the Clayton Hill neighbourhood, sprinklers doused yards sporting grass as green and uniform as Astroturf. Bobby stepped off the bus. He turned slowly and shuffled toward home, exhaustion from working all day in the sun sapping his energy. Bobby waved weakly at Mr. Davies, a retiree who wore a frown and a Tilley hat everywhere, who was jiggling past on a lawn tractor.

At his parents' house, Bob2by closed the oak entrance door behind him and took off his grass-stained running shoes. His vitality improved as he considered that the job with Green Works was at least helping him save money for the tour. He could feel it—Burden Magic was going to *rock* the province. So, his life was good. He didn't care if Nathan and half his floor were going off to McGill, Waterloo, or wherever—getting ready for their hotshot business careers. No, thanks.

His forearms goose-bumped in the air conditioned foyer. On his daily slog of mowing, pruning, and digging, he was soaked in sweat by ten a.m. By the closet doors, a pair of Dad's shoes still lay on the vestibule floor, but another pair Bobby didn't recognize had appeared since he left for work that morning.

"I'm home, Mom. Someone else here too?" Chicken curry

and the CBC evening news wafted from the kitchen.

"Dinner's in twenty minutes." His mother peeked around the kitchen doorway and smiled. Blotches flowered on her cheeks and crimson edged her eyes.

"Smells awesome in here. Unlike me." He pulled off his drenched T-shirt and grimaced. "Disgusting. I'll shower and be down in ten minutes—oh," he said, turning and pointing to the mystery shoes, "are those Dad's?"

"Um . . . yes. Yes." She clasped her hands behind her. "I'm starting to collect his things for the Salvation Army, and I found them in the basement."

"But they're like size nine—way too small for Dad's giant flippers."

"Oh? That's right. That pair never did fit, so we shoved them out of sight. I'd forgotten."

Bobby shrugged and bounded up the stairs to his room. From the second-floor landing, he noticed an old tennis racket leaning against the door to his parents' bedroom: the racket belonged to his mother. She hadn't played in years, and she'd confided to Bobby that she hated the competitiveness of people at the country club.

So what's it doing out, he thought. It's not one of Dad's things for the Salvation Army.

At dinner, he ate with gusto. The tikka masala was just hot enough, the basmati rice perfect in texture, and the peas crunchy-soft and flavourful. His mother nibbled a few bites. Bobby hated to see her so down. Numb. What to say eluded him. Black was colouring his own thoughts too, but his landscaping job was a drug, cutting the gloom for eight hours a day.

"So," he said in desperation, "have you taken up tennis again?

CHAPTER 35

That's a good thing. Get some physical activity."

"I don't understand," his mother said, looking more scared than perplexed.

"Tennis. I just saw your old racket leaning against your bedroom door.

"You did? Oh . . . right." She shifted in her chair to face the kitchen window. And then blubbered. "No, no." Her hands covered her face. "I would've eventually told you—I would. I guess I can't protect you any longer. This afternoon I played tennis with a man, Carlos Perez, and he forgot his dress shoes." She stood and pulled two tissues from a Kleenex box on the fridge.

"Carlos *who*?" Bobby said, his whole body tightening.

"A business partner of your father's."

"Yeah, the waterfront condos. Old-English something."

His mother sat down and blew her nose. "They called it Tudor Gardens, but the site's in an old industrial area, and the charges for soil reclamation—or whatever it's called—skyrocketed above the estimates. Your father and Carlos were responsible for paying them. Not only that. Cost overruns on the building itself have been ridiculous. Well, the contractor stopped work, walked away from the project, and your father and Carlos were left in debt. Half a million dollars. On a half-completed building! Carlos blamed your father . . . couldn't sleep."

"Boohoo for Carlos."

"Please, stop. You don't know the whole story yet. About your father and me." With her fork, she pushed some peas around her plate. "I never stopped loving him, you must know that."

"Not sure what you mean."

"I won't keep the truth from you. Carlos—" Her voice broke and she retrieved a tissue from her pocket and dabbed at her eyes. "Carlos and I, with your dad's blessing, have decided to get married next year. You see, your father—"

Bobby thumped the table with the heel of his hand. "You can't be serious. Two weeks after Dad dies, and you're planning to marry his bloody business partner!"

"Don't." His mother brought another tissue to her eyes. "It's not like that. But you apparently don't want to listen."

Bobby got up and slammed his chair against the table and stormed out of the kitchen and ran upstairs. *You don't know the whole story yet*, she'd said. *About your father and me.* His mother was about to continue, so why did he rush away from her? Maybe, he admitted, because he'd feared he already knew too much of it.

Chapter 36

Chestnuts, oaks, and maples rose above Sol, their leaves fluttering largo, sounding like waves lapping a shore on a calm day. He felt the boulder's chill against his thighs, and then a different, welcome coldness met his lips as he tipped back the beer bottle. The drink was a last rite, his final taste before he cleaned out the cache. Tomorrow. He'd do it tomorrow.

"You're starting early," Bobby said.

Sol wiped his forehead on his shirtsleeve. "Cleaning windows in full sun, on a stinking hot day. Fuck, what do you expect?"

"You should try trimming hedges, and I had to walk ten minutes to get here. Round trip, that's . . . a third of my lunch hour. Lucky that Green Works is in this neighbourhood these days. Most of the summer, I'll be working across town. No lunch dates then."

"So let's talk already." Sol took another swig and unwrapped his sandwich: avocado, tomato, and Havarti on multigrain bread.

Munching on a chicken wrap, Bobby stretched out on his boulder. "I like being back here. The smell of the woods."

"What happened at your mother's last night?"

"She wanted to see me."

"And?"

"She always tells me to be honest," Bobby said. "But she wasn't with *me*." He rolled a stone in his hand and pitched it into the woods. "She's been banging my father's business partner for the last year. Not only that. Tudor Gardens, a condo project that Dad and this prick were building, went belly up. Left them with a mountain of debt. And get this—Perez blames my father." Bobby looked up to the trees and sky. He groaned. "Anyway, Mom must have said the same to the cops."

"You sure about that?"

"The police detective, Downey, talked to her yesterday."

"This guy Perez had two reasons to off your father: his interest in your mother, and being pissed off about the condo project. Who knows? He might have started the affair as part of a plan. Latch on to your mother, kill your father, and then, the final revenge, live happily ever after on the life insurance." Sol walked around the boulder and pushed his beer can into the booze-holding cell. "Depending on what your mother said—or didn't say—to Downey, the cop may know nothing about the affair with Perez. So we have to check the guy out. See what he was doing—"

"I want out of all this. I want some peace," Bobby said, sliding off his boulder. He lifted his backpack. "Me and Mom can't take it anymore."

"Your father and Perez, the guy's affair with your mother—"

"Why would Perez want to kill Pam? They were strangers. They'd never met." Bobby glanced down at his phone. "I'm going to be late getting back."

Sol followed Bobby, swishing through wood ferns and baneberry. "No idea about Perez and Pam either. Have to

CHAPTER 36

go with what we've got." Hidden under the edge of the lake woods, he halted, three metres from the Janitor Can's parking lot. "We're doing this for Pam, remember. For your father. So how can we look into Perez, find out what he was doing on the night . . . ?"

"My mother. We'd have to go through her, if you're so stoked about spying on Lover Boy. She can't take any more upset, so forget it."

"You really want to leave it to the fucking cops? What if they miss something? Just talk to your mother one more time."

Bobby folded his arms tightly. "Fine. But only because it's for Pam and my father."

"So we can see all the angles, ask your mother where she was when it happened—evening of June seventeenth."

"Hey, you're talking about my mother here."

Sol put his hand on the kid's shoulder. "The more we know, including where she was that night, the better."

"After work," Bobby said. "I'll call her."

* * *

Sol had eaten almost nothing at dinner, though Tash chided him. Now, as they drove into Toronto, she gave him a pre-exam talk, which he valued, and when she finished, he felt a bit calmer. They neared the U of T campus. As Tash turned right at Spadina Avenue onto Bloor Street, Sol remembered Imogen Frey's stabs at tutoring him. He'd met the minister at Ecosphere, an independent café, on Saturday. Stoked with caffeine, they'd spent a couple of hours on "everything you ever wanted to know about punctuation but were afraid to ask," as she put it. On the previous two nights, he'd studied the punctuation chapter in her grammar book. But he still had trouble, so she made him write real-life exercises. Still he struggled. The *comma*—that mark held a million uses, and he remembered three of them. He'd thanked Imogen, but he held no illusions about his chances on the final exam.

Tash parked in a drop-off zone in front of Hart House. Sol had been in the building once before, at an orientation lunch the week before Academic Bridging started. With its pointed stone arches and leaded-glass windows, Hart House looked like a set design from the *Harry Potter* films, which Tash loved (she'd read the novels). Young men and women, shouldering backpacks and chatting, sauntered along a broad walkway before the building.

"These coddled kids," Sol said. "Not a care in the world to crease their brows."

Tash turned off the engine and yanked out the key. "Don't be ridiculous. Yes, for some kids, 'mommy and daddy' pay for the whole thing, but believe me, earning a degree takes work—a lot of it. Ever heard of the word *all-nighter*? Students invented it. If you're accepted for next year, you'll find out soon enough. And despite appearances, some of these people are under a lot of pressure. University students have a higher-than-normal rate of suicide."

Sol shrugged. He got out of the car and waved to Tash, who flashed him a thumbs-up and an enormous grin as the car pulled away. Inside Hart House's foyer, taped-up sheets of paper gave directions to the exam rooms, and when Sol walked into his, a dozen people were sitting at sparse writing desks, the exam monitor gazing through the diamond-shaped pattern in the window to three Ultimate Frisbee games being played on a green as big as three football fields.

CHAPTER 36

During the exam, muffled shouts and laughter floated sporadically from the green, while Sol strove to apply Minister Frey's tips. But as he worked on an essay question worth 50 percent of the exam, what had happened to Imogen now happened to *him*. He tried to flesh out his thesis—the Windsor Strike of 1945, and Mr. Justice Ivan Rand's role in resolving it—but the damned grammar blocked his thoughts. He wrote as slowly as a wet-mopped floor dries. Seven minutes left . . . three minutes . . . one minute. Sol didn't finish, but if he'd got the easier questions right, he could still pass, couldn't he? No, he was fooling himself. Screwing up the final exam and somehow passing the course was impossible.

The thought unleashed an energy, an unstoppable force like water gushing from a burst dam. Waiting at the top of Hart House's entrance stairs, he was leaning against the ivy-covered wall, but he spun around and ripped two patches of ivy, one in each hand, from the stonework, and then a dozen more. The spurt of action left him panting.

The clunk of a car door closing.

"What in the world was *that*, Sol?" Tash glared at him, her arms resting on the hood of the Jetta. "What's wrong? Get in, before a campus cop comes after you."

In the car, after they'd both stayed silent for minutes, Sol finally spoke as Tash was changing lanes, leaving the Gardiner Expressway and merging onto the 401. "The damn test. I didn't even finish it."

Tash, her fingers clenching the steering wheel, shook her head. "You scared me. Sometimes I wonder if we should . . . you know, take a break?"

"Code for you want to dump me."

"That's not what I meant," Tash said, looking over her

shoulder as she steered out of the fast lane. "Maybe if you got a place of your own. . . ."

"I've had this problem a long time."

"What problem?"

Sol felt the colour leaving his face, the blood escaping to hide somewhere else in his body. "I learned piano from my cousin."

"And you switched to another instructor in your early teens. I know already."

"When I started, Danny was eighteen. I was nine. My parents loved the idea, because my lessons cost half the going rate. With two other kids to raise, they couldn't have afforded it without Danny."

"Finding an apartment is a hassle. I'll help. Spot you for first and last month's rent."

"Danny wasn't just a lot older than me. He was big—six feet, three inches. Built like a brick shit-house."

"How about this weekend or next? Check out the rentals online, drive around to the buildings."

"Back then, I was a skinny kid. Didn't have a choice. When Danny . . . started, I fought back. He half strangled me, just so I knew he could do it. Said he'd kill me if I told anyone."

Tash spun her face from the road and looked at him. "Told what?"

Blood rushed back into Sol's face. "He assaulted me . . . raped me. It stopped when I was thirteen. I liked girls, and I couldn't take it anymore. When I told my parents—this part's funny—they wouldn't even press charges. 'Bad for the family name blah blah blah.' But they never spoke to Danny or his parents again."

The Jetta swerved onto the highway's shoulder, a droning

tremor going through the car, but a second later Tash regained control. "Sol. Oh my God, I had no idea."

"Most of the time, fuck, I can rein myself in. But not always."

Tash's eyes bore into him. The eyes of a doe in an old Walt Disney film. He'd seen the look before, in former girlfriends—the surprise and sadness and pity, then, weeks or months later, the sorry-but-I'm-dumping-you chat. Those breakups were routine, and he'd gradually come to accept each new one with less and less hurt. No one could hurt him now, maybe not even Tash.

Chapter 37

The next day at noon, a dozen beer bottles stared out at Sol from their hideaway. It was a waste to empty them, but he had to do it, so he laid his lunch bag on a fallen tree trunk and grabbed two Sleeman Cream Ale, his sweaty fingers slipping on the glass as light flickered through maples and oaks whispering in the gusts that were blowing through the lake woods. Even with the wind, the morning was a furnace, and from washing windows in the sun, Sol had soaked his shirt and crotch. A twig snapped, then another, and Bobby's bulk entered the sanctuary.

"Starting early again?" Bobby said.

Sol tipped the pair of bottles, and beer splashed onto the ground.

Bobby's eyes bulged. "What do you think you're—"

"Call your mother yesterday?"

"Yup." Bobby opened his lunch: a chicken salad sandwich, carrot sticks, and a granola bar. "That Sunday night," he said, "she had dinner downtown with a couple of friends. Some place called Umbria."

"Been there."

"Her new beau, jerk-ass Perez, was off playing golf in a charity tournament at Clayton Hill Country club. And Dad

CHAPTER 37

had to work at the bank—some financial emergency. He'd been there since mid-afternoon."

"On a Sunday?"

Bobby wiped his brow with his forearm, then swigged from his water bottle. "Mom and her two friends left the restaurant around 9:30. She went straight home, tried to chill in front of the TV. But she felt tired and went to bed at 10:30."

"So, if anyone could actually back up her story—"

"You think she's lying to her own son?" Bobby crumpled his empty plastic water bottle and smacked it against the boulder.

"The cops may be thinking your mother drove from Umbria and got to Woodmore well before ten o'clock. I'm just saying."

"Whatever." Bobby leaned back on his rock. "She said Perez had been angry at my father, but that Carlos was a 'good man.' Supposedly, when the shit hit the fan on the Tudor Gardens thing, the guy had offered to find more investors and even to dig deeper into his own pocket. He told Mom his plan, but she didn't want him to. The messed-up project had already drained most of the money she'd inherited from her parents, so Mom wouldn't allow him or my father to waste another dollar on it."

"We need to find out if Perez could have been at Woodmore that night."

"He was pissed off with my father, OK. But if he was game to put more money into Tudor Gardens, why would he kill his only partner in the project?"

"If he can't prove he was elsewhere, then he's not free and clear. He's still a suspect."

"Just the other day, you said it yourself. We're not sure Mom even told the cops about Tudor Gardens or her affair with Perez. Maybe he's off their radar."

Through an opening in the trees, Sol stared at the distant playing fields, kids running after a soccer ball. "If detective what's-her-name isn't smart enough to know about Perez, that's her problem."

"We should tell her. Have a professional covering all the angles. This isn't a game, you know? You're a suspect."

"Didn't you say you worked a few summers at Clayton Hill Country Club?" Sol asked. "You know anyone there who might have worked the charity event?"

Bobby bit his lip. "Tony Laws. He's a drummer—into post-punk, not my thing. Anyway, he manages the clubhouse bar."

"Any Saturday or Sunday. Set something up, for this weekend, if it's doable."

"Left on pretty bad terms with the boss there."

"I don't care. We've got to look into Perez. So don't call the boss. Just go straight to Tony Laws."

"I'll *call* already." The kid looked away and crunched on a carrot stick.

"Help me dump these fucking bottles. I joined AA, promised Tash. And I'm committed to it." Sol picked up more beers, shimmering gold in a ray of sunlight. He felt—what?—nostalgia for getting plastered? He remembered the counsellors in high school and the Milton Hilton. *Sol*, they'd said, *don't blame yourself. Many, many survivors of . . . abuse can't control their anger. And self-medication is a normal response.* Smug bastards, those psych people.

A grin on his face, Bobby jumped forward, and his bear paw pulled at one of the bottles in Sol's hands.

Sol yanked the beer back.

"You need to chill."

Sol released his grip. Deep breaths. The mossy scent of the

boulders and groundcover. "Nobody gets that close to me, that fast. Nobody."

Bobby raised his hand. "I just wanted to save it for me and Nathan. Since Pam and my father were . . . we've come out here a couple of times at night. Nate says he wants to blow off steam, but I know he's just trying to help me. Spill my guts and all that. Should've told you—we've already taken four beers."

"You know what I said about drugs. And alcohol is worse than a lot of them."

"Party pooper."

Sol reached in, taking two more bottles from their dark fridge. "You're not getting any of these." Before the first cap was off, Sol's phone chirped—a new email. He upended the beers and waited for them to drain.

"Aren't you going to check that out?" Bobby said.

"Empty the rest of these."

Bobby crouched to reach the stash, as Sol scanned the email, a message from Academic Bridging:

> *SUBJECT: COURSE RESULTS, ABP100Y1 CANADIAN HISTORY*
> *Dear Mr. Fitzgerald,*
> *Congratulations on successfully completing the course named above. However, we regret to inform you that your average grade in that course does not meet the minimum requirement for advancement to . . .*

The message went on, listing Sol's grades for each of the assignments and exams. His weighted average was 71 percent, two percent below the cutoff for full time undergrad next year.

Two percent. He grabbed the empties at his feet and smashed them against the boulder.

Bobby slid out from the hiding place and backed away.

"It's over," Sol said between heaving breaths. "I'm not going to U of T. Average too low. I *knew* I'd screwed up on the fucking final."

"That sucks. . . . We should switch places. You want to get into school, I want to get out of it." He chuckled and punched Sol on the shoulder. "Take the course over, pump up your grade."

"Two stinking percent below the cutoff. Take the whole thing over again? Screw it."

Bobby looked at his watch. "I've got to munch this down. The foreman will mow off my dick if I'm a minute late."

Sol possessed no appetite and sat staring ahead.

Bobby left, and Sol checked the cache. The lazy kid hadn't finished. Four Sleeman lay untouched and inviting. He picked one up, opened it, and cold streamed into him.

It's not your fault. The psychotherapists had said that to him six years ago in rehab. Damn right, he thought. It's not your fault you can't control your anger. He raised his beer in a toast: that's true, Mr. Psychologist. So I'm going back to my golden drug. He finished the bottle and grabbed another.

When that was done, only one remained. He took his first swig from it and thought of the first time he'd ever seen Tash, his first day working in the Kelsey's restaurant, when she'd been whistling sadly that old Roberta Flack song. Soon they were spending Sundays together, hiking at the Mount Nemo Conservation Area, where no drone of traffic lurked, ready to spoil the illusion of wilderness. One day, they picnicked there, and after eating they lay on their backs on a blanket.

CHAPTER 37

Tash breathed deeply and exhaled. "The future is as open as this sky," she said. Sol doubted that, but he hid his fear like always. He needed to savour every moment with her, and he'd rolled over and kissed her, and Tash had put her arms around him, her scent mixed with the smell of cedar and pine needles.

* * *

Sol was twenty minutes late getting back from the lake woods to the Janitor Can.

Heat pulsed from Peacock's words: "Between your staggering around drunk, being late half the time, and your beer breath, you're a disgrace to the job. You're off for the afternoon. Get out of here."

Peacock took off his half-moon glasses and laid them on his desk. "And Sol. Jesus, get some help. You need it. I'll cover for you this afternoon, but there's no 'next time.' No second chance on this."

Chubby forearms tensing, he pushed himself up from the desk. "I'll fill in for you at Edwards Common."

* * *

Sol's memory of the bus ride home from Woodmore was a fog. He stumbled into the apartment, but he was awake enough to recall one hiding spot he'd missed during his everything-down-the-sink display to Tash. Reaching under the TV cabinet, he released a flask of Crown Royal from its duct-tape tether.

Metchnikoff purred and rubbed against Sol's shin as the

Crown Royal emerged. She tried to sniff the bottle.

"Not for you, Metch." Sol unscrewed the cap and took a swig. "This is your daddy's *other* best friend."

Metchnikoff's eyes said *screw you*, and she sauntered away. The vertical blinds hung half open, and the living room windows threw sunlight between bars of shadow, making Sol's drowsiness worse. He plopped onto the sofa, drank another mouthful, and thought: Tash won't be home for a few hours, so why not? The Crown Royal tingled inside him. Warm and comfortable. But soon, as he lay thinking, his ease became fury. Until then, he'd managed to block Peacock's scolding voice, his ultimatum. The nerve of the guy, a glorified janitor who didn't do much beyond ordering paper towels and guarding his whiteboard.

Before Peacock, the guards were hassling him. Before them, the police. Before the cops, his high school teachers. And next in line, Dr. Harishandra. All of them thought he was lazy, a loser, and they were right. He looked across the room. Against the wall stood an oak bookcase, its top hovering only a hand's width below the ceiling, ceramic figurines—Hindu gods and monsters—perched on the highest shelf. Tash treasured them, gifts from her grandmother. Sol hated them. He had to stand on a kitchen chair to dust them, and the silly things teetered, threatening to fall over, staring down at him in judgement, just like the teachers and shrinks and cops and jail guards and Peacock and Dr. Farooq Harishandra. Rage coursed through his body. But instead of knocking him down, that current pushed him toward the bookcase, which he shook blindly, his eyes scrunched shut, his teeth bared like an angry Pitbull's, as if the piece of furniture were cousin Danny. The Hindu dust catchers toppled from the top, followed by a couple of hundred books from the shelves.

Only shards remained of the statuettes, but they and the heap of books on the floor weren't enough to satisfy Sol's ire. With veins near bursting, he pushed over the bookcase.

* * *

A key clicked in the front door's lock, and Sol heard Tash's yawn and the thud of her bag hitting the vestibule table. His stomach fell. Bent forward on the sofa, he stared at the floor.

Tash gasped and her purse thudded against the floor. "What *is* this . . . ? What the hell happened?"

"Academic Bridging. I flunked, or close enough. Didn't get into U of T."

"And that warrants exploding an atom bomb in the living room?"

"I tilted the bookcase back up. Wasn't even scratched."

Tash raised her voice over the whine of the air conditioner. "Well, that's wonderful. Makes it all better."

Sol turned away from her, and the windows' glare ricocheted off the multi-gym's chrome struts, blinding him. He blinked and shook his head. "I'll put the books back, but I have to—"

"Sober up first?"

Even pissed off, Tash possessed poise—a straight back, with ease in her shoulders and neck. And she'd taken a risk when they started dating, Sol being a screwed-up ex-con, and her not dumping him after the first date showed her kindness. "Forgive me."

"You joined AA. You promised yourself, and you promised me."

"The figurines. From your grandmother."

He swallowed hard as she looked up at the empty top shelf of the bookcase.

"Where are they?" she said.

"Four out of the five. They're shattered."

Her mouth opened, but Tash said nothing. She sat down on the far end of the sofa, her back as straight and stiff as a broom handle.

"I'll pay for a new set," Sol said. He'd seen her angry before but never this quiet.

"Don't," she said. "It wouldn't be the same as having Nani's."

Claws ticked across the floor. Metchnikoff had scampered away when the figurines and books hit the floor. Now she appeared from around the sofa and sat in front of her staff members. Sol scratched the top of her head and wished life were as simple as petting your cat, but his life was messy, and lately, he created the messes, like the mountain of books on the floor.

Tash went to the windows. She stood staring out over the parking lot, her back to Sol. "You're a hard person to love. At least, it's hard on me."

Sol ached to say something.

"I'm scared," Tash said, gesturing to the scruffy heap of books around which satellite tomes, thrown by impact with the floor, dotted the living room. "This makes me scared."

"I came so close to making the damned cut-off grade. It killed me."

She turned from the windows to face him, wetness glinting on her cheeks. "I so wanted it—us—to work, but it just doesn't. I want you to move out by the end of July."

Chapter 38

Alison slammed the alarm clock's sleep button and stumbled out of bed, the red digits blinking *6:30 a.m.* When, she wondered, had the buzzer changed from a welcome to a bother? She was thirty-nine. That wasn't old, so why did she feel so tired? The chaos of the move from Toronto had sapped her energy. That was the answer, Alison hoped. Could it be an iron deficiency? The word *depression* flashed through her mind. No way, not me. She'd give it a few weeks and see her doctor if necessary.

What about Ray Havers's mental health? From what Director Collier said about the banker's financial worries, possibly Ray's anger during Woodmore's board meetings was masking his true mood, a dark one, black enough for him to consider suicide. But, even if Pamela Renard fought to thwart his jumping, in the struggle, *he* certainly didn't push her off the roof.

Sometimes I feel dead already, Alison thought. She donned her bathrobe and tiptoed along the upstairs hallway. Marcia and her mother wouldn't be up for another thirty minutes. For a senior citizen, Shirley Downey liked her beauty sleep, and the obsession with appearance ran in the family, so maybe Alison needed an extra hour of sleep each night. More rest might stop her crow's feet from getting any deeper. After showering, she dressed and put on the discreet makeup required of her job. Leaning close to the mirror, she noticed a grey hair behind her ear. No, half a dozen.

Alison stepped back. The white pinstripes on her suit jacket looked good where they were. She didn't need any on her head.

She strode to the kitchen and made toast. Pouring orange juice into a glass, Alison remembered the previous afternoon, when she'd sipped tea at the Havers's house with Ray's wife. With her pink hair styled punk, Debra was an odd fit as a Chartered Accountant. The widow had answered all questions calmly, even the one about her alibi. As she sat barefoot in scruffy jeans, her face drained of colour, Debra stared at her teacup and spoke in a monotone. "I had dinner with two friends that evening. We left at 9:30 or so, and I think they saw me getting into my car."

When Alison asked if Ray had any enemies, Debra volunteered two names. First, Ray told his wife about the spat with Gwen Collier, Director, over the library renovations.

"But," Debra said, "I can't see that tiff being something she'd harm Ray over."

The second name was Carlos Perez. Debra admitted to a year-long affair but insisted, without being specific, that she and Ray had reconciled. She offered useful details about the business relationship between the two men and about a real estate development, one that went bad and left the partnership in debt.

With the interview over, Debra said, "I'm exhausted. Mind letting yourself out?"

After leaving the kitchen, Alison had looked back from the

CHAPTER 38

roomy vestibule to see Debra still seated, scrutinizing her teacup.

Alison tipped back the juice glass and sucked at the last drops. If Debra, she thought, had had an affair and admitted it to Ray, he may have retaliated by starting a fling too. Middle-aged men, in Alison's experience, were drawn to affairs like smugglers to police stings, and what if Pamela had wanted to make the naughty banker pay for his fun? Being blackmailed could have made him act foolishly, violently.

* * *

"Downey, get in here." His face purple, Ed Loams was peering at Alison's desk.

She'd worked at Halton Region for a month, and during that time, Loams always called his officers by their first names. Until now. She got up from her desk.

Ruvinsky eyeballed her and chortled. "Deep doo-doo awaits you."

She shook her head as she passed by him.

In Ed Loams's office, two plastic chairs guarded his L-shaped desk. He pointed to one. "Take a seat."

Framed photographs and children's drawings plastered the beige walls. Crayon masterpieces by his two boys. Pictures of their peewee soccer and baseball teams, of Loams and the kids blowing out birthday candles, and of the whole family on a beach. A folded card with the words *Thank you Officer Ed* pencilled in shaky letters by a Grade Three student. A red-and-green paper wreath, curled and desiccated, from last December. A snapshot of him and a friend holding up some trout, a sunset flaring over the lake behind them.

"Had a call from a lawyer friend of mine," Loams said. "Michael White. Heard of him?"

The Detective Sergeant's elbow rested on the desk, along with a laptop, laser printer, stapler, and overburdened in-out box. Ceiling lights reflected off of his shaved head.

Michael White. Alison knew the name from the previous evening and her impromptu traffic stop. Maybe it was a coincidence and Loams was referring to someone else entirely. She prayed, let that be it. "Sorry, I don't—"

"You pulled him over for speeding last night. And apparently"—Loams smirked—"we're looking for a car matching White's BMW in a drug investigation, which is the reason you gave to search him."

Of course, Alison thought. White just *had* to be a friend of his. What was the probability?

Loams continued, "You, a peace officer entrusted to enforce the law, lied to a civilian in order to what—humiliate him? I've known Michael White for twenty years. A crown prosecutor, a damn good one. He volunteers on Oakville's race relations committee, and, because it would've made the whole force look bad, I've sweet-talked him out of pressing charges."

Alison was rubbing her hands back and forth on her thighs, her head down, her gaze unfocused. She sighed.

"I'm saving your ass," Loams said, "only because Norm Miller's leg isn't healed yet. Rock climbing—I *told* him it was a stupid idea." He leaned back and spread the palm of his hand across his forehead. "You're the only cop here who really knows the Woodmore case. Look, just solve this thing—before the August first long weekend. It ends up a cold case, you may get a shiny new desk job, because if you can't prove you're a first-rate investigator, you're not worth

CHAPTER 38

the risk."

***

The traffic crawled, but Alison wasn't going to let the glut of cars ruin her good mood. She turned up the alt rock on CBC Radio 2 and let her shoulders fall. On the steering wheel, she tapped her fingers to Blue Rodeo's "Bad Timing."

In the morning—after Ed Loams had performed his own Spanish Inquisition—she'd followed up with Debra Havers's two dinner companions on the night of Ray's killing, and one of the women confirmed seeing Debra get into her car around 9:30 p.m.

Downtown, ten minutes ago, Umbria's manager Antonio had recognized Debra from a photo that Alison showed him; he confirmed that the trio dined in the restaurant that night. He remembered Debra's high-pitched laugh.

All that was fact. But Debra had no one to vouch for her whereabouts after she left Umbria at 9:30.

A Hummer cut Alison off, but she only braked and whistled louder to the music.

After lunch, she'd hooked into Cayuga OPP's network and viewed the case file on Rose Molloy's death. She'd wondered all morning about it. A connection to the Woodmore murders called out to be made, but the *modus operandi* was different, as were the likely motives.

But her gut feeling proved correct. Besides casting the size-twelve footprints going from the road to the girl's body and back again, Cayuga's Ident staff had pulled fingerprints from the plastic vanes on the arrows in Rose's back. Alison got the prints to Don Gatti. He found eleven points of similarity between them and the set from the Woodmore crime scene, specifically the prints on the wineglass and the cocaine bag—prints with no match to CPIC or any suspect.

Chapter 39

November 2006

The stairwell's door clangs shut behind Pamela, who is panting from running up three flights to her floor of Pilkington House. The hallway returns to silence, a tinge of some girl's perfume hanging in the air. For fitness, Pamela's made a habit of using the stairs wherever possible, but she wonders if a deeper reason lies beneath her inclination. She loves learning. So, climbing ever higher, physically, reflects what she tries to do with mind. Nah, she thinks, that's so pretentious, Pam. But the truth is she gets a rush from either activity. At Coyote River High, she used to sneak into the janitor's room and climb the wall-mounted ladder to the roof; last year, she had a midafternoon spare and often sat on the rooftop gravel and looked up at the sky.

Whimpering interrupts her thoughts. The sound is coming from the corridor's far end, where light pours from a half-open doorway. Rose's door. Pamela tiptoes to the bright rectangle and peers cautiously around it.

Rose, with tears streaming down her face, sits at her desk

and grips an open textbook. She faces a wall, her profile visible to Pamela.

The last time they met in Edwards Common, Pamela made an effort—not that she had much reason—to help the redhead recover from the Halloween-party incident. The rumour, from one of Rose's clique, is that her archenemy broke up the assault before any of the boys "consummated" the attack in penetration. Her conscience is clear. She withdrew, momentarily, from her well-earned hate of Rose and offered her sympathy. Rose refused it. But the girl *must* want help, or she would've closed the door to cry in private.

Standing stock-still, Pamela takes a closer look. Except for Rose's buff cowboy hat centred atop her neatly made bed, the scene is chaotic. Her hair is a tangled mess, and her eyes are dark red holes. Candy wrappers and Coke bottles lie strewn over her desk. As she turns a page, her shoulders convulse.

Too bad, Pamela thinks. You had your chance, Rose. But as she spins away from the door, her elbow bangs loudly against it. She sprints for her own door, but Rose is quick, stepping into the corridor before Pamela can escape it.

"Was that *you* screwing with my door?" Rose says. "Spying on me?"

"I was closing it. We don't all want to hear your bawling."

"You got that right." Rose wipes her wet cheeks with the back of her hand. "Nobody's spoken more than two words to me since, like I'm some kind of leper. Thanks for your 'concern.'"

Bitch, Pamela thinks, you're basically nasty, besides being racist. But Rose's words are too close to Jane Taylor's, when Jane had blamed herself for getting raped. Not long after, Jane's father found her unconscious sitting in his car, its windows up and engine running, with the garage door closed. The doctor said she would have died with fifteen minutes more exposure. Jane's action shocked Pamela, because Jane was "only" violated sexually. She was alive after the ordeal, unlike Lily, whose murderer was never found. Jane could get on with her life. Lillian lost hers.

Pamela's eye twitches, heat creeps from her neck into her face and scalp. "A high-school friend of mine and my cousin . . . they were both raped, and cousin Lillian—"

"Got to study for this calculus final," Rose says, waving the textbook she's still holding, "so tell your story to someone else."

But like Rose's words at the lunch table a few days ago, her speech contradicts the reddened eyes, hunched neck and shoulders. She's weak, Pamela thinks, and I'm going to be strong, but only for you, Grandma Becky.

"I'm sorry for whacking you in archery class," she says, "but you gave me no choice. I couldn't just stand there and let you stereotype and put down Mohawks." Pamela wants to say, *You bloody well deserved it*, but restrains herself.

Rose gestures again with the thick text she's holding. "Calculus final. Understand? So please leave, and close the door."

Pamela wants to smack Rose, but she sees a way forward. "The studying—how's it going?"

"Close. The. Door," Rose says and slams the book on her desk. But a moment later, she moans and collapses, her head resting on the desktop, her arms splayed out in front of her. "I'm sorry. I keep thinking about—I can't concentrate. I can't study!"

"Rose, as I was saying, a good friend of mine was raped. It

happened a couple of years ago, and she took months to even begin to recover. So go easy on yourself." Pamela knows the advice is trite, but it's all she can say.

"Come in," Rose says, sitting up and gesturing, "and close the door." She blows her nose, then turns the chair to face Pamela. "No, I can't 'go easy' on myself. Not yet. I—I have to say something. See, my dad organized a group of business owners on Ewing's west side, and they're mad as hell with Coyote River's demonstration. Near the town border, the blockades mean businesses there have been shit since it started. I saw the effect on my dad. He's a nervous wreck!" Rose squeezes her fists. "He took it out on my mom—who can't sleep now, between worrying about the ranch and hearing the Mohawk warriors' ATVs 'patrolling' the Peaceful Meadows site at three o'clock in the morning—so I guess I wanted *you* to suffer a bit."

On the wall, a lemon patch of sunlight shines above Rose's bed. Gauzy curtains flutter on a warm breeze, carrying the scent of lavender.

"You succeeded," Pamela says. She's leaning against the door, her arms crossed over her chest.

"But I'd never heard about that old British governor . . . Haldimand?"

Pamela nods. "Sir Frederick Haldimand.

"Yeah, his land grant to Coyote River. The humongous size of it. I was just so angry that you were here, on your la-di-da Two Row Exchange, while my parents and the ranch were going down the toilet. So I'm sorry . . . for all the slurs, all the shit I put you through." Rose winces. "Like your door. Infantile and nasty of me. But I came by it naturally. With *my* dad, I grew up hearing more Native putdowns that you can imagine."

Pamela uncrosses her arms. "The protest, the blockades—I had no idea they'd damage your folks' business. And ATVs, they're buzzing around your ranch in the middle of the night?"

"Well, 'buzzing' is putting it mildly. My mom's become a zombie," Rose says. She stands up and turns to the window.

Rose's eyes are swollen, and the resignation in them reminds Pamela of Jane Taylor. "Look, you and me," Pamela says, "can—can we move in a different direction now?"

Rose nods but then winces. She gazes out the window without focusing on anything. "There's something else. Something I've never admitted."

"About the protest?"

"When those boys attacked me," Rose says, "dragged me into that barn, they didn't know I'm . . ." She sits down, picks up a pen and twirls it slowly in her fingers. "I'm not like most girls, and that makes it worse."

"Not like other girls?"

"Think of Joan," Rose says. Miming a vain weightlifter, she raises her arms and bends her elbows, her fists balled. "But not the butch type like her. I'm femme. . . . Anyway, I like *girls*. Not boys."

"Oh. I see. Well, that's OK, it's not—"

"I want to murder every single one of those boys. It's all I can think about—certainly not *this*," Rose says, holding up a sheet of paper with a long equation on it.

"None of it's your fault, Rose. Study to the extent you can now, or ask for a rewrite. Surely the school will understand."

Rose shrugs, then motions to her bed.

Sitting down on a corner of the bedspread, Pamela is closer to the window. Robins and Baltimore orioles sing their songs, and she realizes they've been chirping since she entered the room, but only now do the sounds reach her consciousness, like echoes in a dream. And she wonders whether this whole conversation is a fantasy, not real.

"Oh, I can *ask*," Rose says, "but I doubt it'll make any difference." She opens the textbook and rolls her eyes. She stands, than approaches Pamela. "You have to promise me two things. First, don't broadcast that I'm . . . you know. And don't even *hint* we've reached a peace agreement. My dad finds out I'm friendly with the enemy, he'll disown me."

"Understood." Pamela reaches for the door handle. "I'll leave you to study. Good luck on—"

"Wait! Open it slowly and scout the hallway first. No one you can see you leaving this room. No one."

Chapter 40

June 2007

Sol rode the elevator down and trudged out of the apartment building's lobby. After calling ahead, he walked for forty-five minutes to Miroslav's building: three storeys of dirty brick looming over a yard scattered with kids' bikes, toys, and cigarette butts.

Tash had kicked him out. Though she gave him until the end of the month, he couldn't stay for a second longer. Couldn't face her.

He slept on Miroslav's couch. At dawn, damned Miroslav shook him awake and made bacon and eggs. "You are all day running around Woodmore. You need a virtuous breakfast."

"I never get up this early."

Miroslav smiled and invited him to stay a few weeks, until Sol found a place. If he wants *me* around, Sol thought, the guy's desperate for company. The next evening, Sol went back to Tash's to gather his shaving kit and some clothes, and as he moved around the apartment, the air between them sizzled.

***

The Woodmore routine was a relief, like a drug pushing down his shock, his gloom at what the bookcase rampage cost him—his life with Tash.

In the evenings, he collapsed on Miroslav's sofa and stared at the TV. He had no drive to get up and go for a walk. To get up for anything.

***

Quitting time on Friday came, and, as they walked to the bus stop, Miroslav invited him to have dinner and a drink at the Blue Lion, which was on their bus route. By "a drink," Miroslav meant pop or juice—not booze. Sol didn't feel like eating, but his friend said the people and some talk and laughs would cheer him up.

Sol grinned. "You've been to the Blue Lion? Aren't there pubs that—"

Miroslav raised his palm. "Are catering to bohunks? Yes, them I go also. But I am getting feeling for Canada. If you hide in old country, you erection walls around yourself."

"You 'erect' walls." Sol grinned and pointed to his crotch. "An *erection* is something else."

Miroslav shrugged.

Once they'd taken a bus to the pub, Sol ordered fish and chips, and Miroslav a veggie burger. The smell of beer wafting as strongly as ammonia at Woodmore. "I'm pathetic," Sol said.

"Get distraction and carry on AA. Thinking on breakup will make you crazy man. I know from divorce."

"Distraction. . . . Well, I would have weight training,

CHAPTER 40

but now there's nowhere to put my equipment, other than a storage locker."

"What about this 'mellowing out.' Like yoga?"

"I could go up to Mount Nemo, hike around. But I don't have a car now."

"Community centre. Just beginner class. I go and feel better."

In the amber light and the hullabaloo around their table, Sol thought about the yoga DVDs under Tash's TV stand, including the one, still wrapped in cellophane, that she'd bought him. She'd said he needed to relax. Maybe she was dead-on. Better learn, he thought, to my anger, or she'll be right to stay away from me. And showing up at her place for the DVD will show her I'm trying.

He realized, though, there was more to the problem. In the bookcase rage, he'd lashed out at Danny, not at blowing the Canadian history course. He lashed out at fifteen years of feeling weak and guilty, at what his cousin did to him, at how the wound still ruled his nightmares and actions. Danny, who was now a church organist like his father and grandfather. The Fitzgerald music gene gave Sol his talent, but it also threw Danny at him.

For Sol, his parents' refusal to go to the police had hurt almost as much Danny's assaults. It all stopped twelve years ago, but the pain stayed fresh. So when Tash told him that yoga wasn't a fad, that it began more than five thousand years ago, he'd tried it. But, so far, downward-facing dog, and the other yoga moves he'd sampled, failed to help.

With dinner finished, he and Miroslav got on another bus. Heading toward Miroslav's, the sardine can was packed with silent workers and noisy teenagers. Sol, out of habit, checked his pocket for his keys when the bus approached his old stop outside the apartment in White Tail.

He pulled the bell chord and jumped up. "See you later at your place."

"But we are at building in few more minutes."

"Detour."

Sol hoped Tash was at home. He'd saunter to the TV stand, and she'd see him leaving with the yoga DVD. He'd say, "See, I'm making an effort to relax." But he knew that his display of willpower would be too late.

Chapter 41

It was a bright Saturday, 11:00 a.m., and Sol wished he was jogging in White Tail Park. Tony Laws sported a thatch of gelled hair standing at attention, trying to add height to his five-foot-five frame. "Bobby said you might come by. You in his band?"

As far as Sol could see, the two of them were alone in the barroom, Tony polishing wine glasses and raising them one at a time onto a rack. A half empty glass of beer stood on the bar, and Tony took a swig from it.

"I know him from work," Sol said and looked around the empty room. He hoped they could speak in private.

Tony followed his gaze. "The golfers don't begin drifting in here till mid-afternoon. I start earlier," he said, pointing to his beer mug. He winked and handed Sol a glass. "On the house."

Sol put up his hand. "It wasn't easy for me to get here, and I need information, not a drink." To get to the Clayton Hill Country Club, Sol had trudged for fifteen minutes from the closest bus stop, and as he'd walked through the parking lot, mock-Tudor timbers cast thin shadows on the clubhouse's white stucco. Now, the barroom, with its mahogany panelling supporting hammered copper plates, also carried a nostalgic mood.

"Suit yourself."

Sol turned from the window. "Carlos Perez. You know him?"

"He's in here a lot. Him and Bobby's father golfed together, then they'd drink in here and chat. Business stuff."

Sol nodded and scanned the paintings hanging above the booths' wine-red upholstery—pictures of horses and stables, and of mounted hunters riding with hounds. "Bobby tells me a fundraising tournament went on here three weeks back, on a Sunday. You happen to be working then?"

"'Putting for Parkinson's' . . . yeah. From noon till late." Tony drained his beer glass and poured a fresh one. "Sure you don't want one?"

"How late?"

"Eleven, eleven fifteen."

"See Carlos Perez? He was here."

"He stayed right through the shindig after dinner." Grimacing, Tony leaned on the bar and looked out the windows to the greens beyond. "Man's a loudmouth. And a lech. I know a girl, Brooke, works weekends here, and she launched a sexual harassment suit, but the prick has friends in high places. It didn't go anywhere. Brooke won't say, but I'm sure Perez paid her to stay quiet."

"Nice guy. That night, you see Perez leave?"

Tony turned back from the windows. "When I left, he was walking out too. Saw him get into his car, a bit after eleven."

Sol wondered where Perez had been headed. Home to bed, maybe, or to find Ray Havers and settle a score. Or . . . to have sex with Pam Renard? Sol knew of no link between the man and Woodmore, but according to Tony, Perez was a lecher, so

CHAPTER 41

Havers may've been trying to shield Pam before they died.

* * *

Volunteers in white T-shirts with the red maple leaf hammered and sawed and painted. Amid workers' voices and construction noise, the festival stage stood in the centre of Lakeside Park. Tomorrow—Sol had forgotten—was July first, Canada Day. He remembered going last year to the fireworks with Tash. As booms and flashes filled the sky, he'd wrapped himself around her against the night air. They'd lain on a blanket-covered boulder at the water's edge, Hamilton twinkling on the west horizon.

No matter how "fun" tomorrow night might be, he doubted he would come downtown again without Tash, just to see the show. He might as well settle in to the bachelor's life with Miroslav. The dynamic duo. Losers consoling each other, slurping coffee from paper cups, on the same waterfront bench every weekend. I need a beer, Sol thought.

Miroslav yawned. "Not used to waking early on weekend. To make breakfast."

Sol slapped the top rail of the bench. "Didn't ask you to, and I don't need bacon and eggs. Toast's enough, and I can butter bread all by myself."

"When Branca and children were still with me, I like to cook. Makes me relaxed, happy."

Sol shrugged. A dark sky hung over the lake, and though the banging of the construction went on, quiet haunted the air. Spellbound by ripples on the lake, he shaded his eyes with his hand. "Been thinking. Tash was right to throw me out. Who wants an alcoholic for a partner—oh, I'm sorry."

Miroslav waved his hand. "No need for."

"It was hard on Tash. She didn't need that crap. I mean, look at her and me, we're just too different. I couldn't care less where anyone came from, but Indian Hindu and Irish Catholic, that's a clunky combo, don't you think? Especially if we ever had kids."

"You are the demented man."

"How'd you get so wise, all of a sudden?" Sol said. "Divorced. And a drunk like me."

"Sorry for trying to help, friend."

Below a sky turned pewter, thunder growled off the lake, and Sol scanned the horizon for lightning. But the rumbling faded away.

"Age and sufferings. Someday you will understand these."

Sol's eyes stayed pointed to the horizon. "I can't do it to Tash. How do I know if I'll ever get sober? Stay sober? If we'd made a good life, had kids, and then I 'fall down' again . . . I couldn't forgive myself. She deserves better."

"There is no better—just people."

"I've clipped some rental ads. Got appointments with three landlords, and I'll be gone most of tomorrow checking out the places."

A teenage couple walked by the bench and climbed down over rocks to the water's edge. On a flat-topped boulder, the pair sat and hugged. Kissed. They kissed some more, keenly. He smiled, thinking, they should get a hotel room, and he fought a memory of Tash and him necking by the lake.

***

"Get much out of Tony?" Bobby said.

CHAPTER 41

Sol pointed to the Smart car outside on the asphalt. "Nice set of wheels you're driving. Wish I still had access to one."

"Try not to think about Tash. You know, she'd probably still let you borrow her car if you asked."

"The bus is OK."

They were sitting in a strip mall coffee shop. From the air conditioning, Bobby's forearms goose-bumped. He shivered, blew on his coffee and took a sip.

"Bus it is, then," Bobby said. "What about your talk with Tony?"

"Looks alright for Carlos Perez."

"Alright?"

Sol leaned forward with his elbows on the plastic laminate. He squinted and pushed his baseball cap lower to fight the fluorescent glare. "He and Tony Laws left Clayton Hill's clubhouse at the same time, about a quarter after eleven, so Perez couldn't have done it. The cop, Downey, said Pam and your father died around ten o'clock. If Perez had left at 11:15 for Woodmore, he wouldn't have arrived there until at least 11:30. By the time he got to the library roof—*how*, we don't know—he would've been two hours late."

"Maybe the coroner, or whoever, got the timing wrong. Did Ms. Downey say that ten o'clock was like set in stone?"

"No, I guess not."

"Good," Bobby said. "On TV cop shows, the coroners never know exactly. They give a few hours range, plus or minus." He rapped the tabletop hard with his knuckles. "Perez is a prick. We can't totally rule him out.

"But your mother's alibi. It's as fuzzy as his."

"Thanks for that vote of confidence. But this is like electronica, when one track fades out as another riff is fading in—no common key or time signature, just confusing."

Sol stared past his reflection in the windows. Beyond the metal roof overhang, fat raindrops polka-dotted the asphalt, and across the parking lot, a pair of headlights pulled in beneath the glow of a 7-ELEVEN sign. "Can't go any further with Perez. How about I talk to your mother face to face. Maybe I could pick up on things that you don't see. You're her kid, and it's hard to be even-handed about someone so close, right?"

Bobby folded his arms across his chest and looked away.

"It can't hurt."

Bobby stood up. "Better *not* hurt—my mother."

Sol caught a lift with Bobby back to Miroslav's. During the trip, they agreed. Bobby would ask his mother about Sol coming over to the house. The ruse was to say that Sol could barely sleep since discovering the bodies—which was true—and that her talking to Sol about Ray might calm the janitor's nerves. Not the smoothest plan, but it would have to do.

An hour after Bobby dropped Sol off, he phoned. "You've got the gig. Be here tomorrow morning, 10:30. Late notice, I know, but Mom volunteers with a drop-in centre, and past noon, tomorrow, she's on shift for a big chunk of the weekend."

"Tell me the address again?"

Chapter 42

Sitting on her bed, Alison reached for her credit card. Again. She smiled, because the purchase was a present for Marcia—a painting course at Oakville Galleries. The class ran indoors on Wednesdays, outdoors on Sundays. Elly had already registered, and Alison hoped the course would cement the new friendship. And keep both girls out of trouble.

Trouble. Alison thought of Pamela Renard and her Coyote River beau Luke. The young man had exposed her to drugs and potentially a lot more, like violence from his gang and trouble with the reserve's police. Given enough time, Luke could have gotten Pamela into a major mess, although not as dire a jam as the one awaiting her at Woodmore. She'd come to Oakville on the scholarship, and a few months later another young man, Bobby Havers, got her pregnant. And possibly killed.

***

In response to Alison's "come in," Marcia popped her head around the bedroom door. She informed her mother that she and Elly—and two boys they'd met in the Oakville Galleries course—were going to the Canada Day celebrations at Lakeside Park the next day.

"Uh-huh." Alison sighed, too loudly. "You can go, but be back for six o'clock. It's a Sunday, and your Gran's making dinner."

"We're staying for the evening. I've already promised Elly and the boys."

Alison knew that if Marcia stayed after the fireworks, anything could and would happen. She remembered another celebration, a U of T frosh party one night, a decade back. How she'd stood in uniform on the roof of Trinity College and talked to poor Rebecca, raped at the party. At an "innocent" frosh party. Well, Marcia was not going to be raped or otherwise abused on Alison's watch.

"Then say goodbye to your painting studio," Alison said. "If you want to go to the fireworks tomorrow, you'll be dismantling that studio. Tonight."

Marcia was a granite statue. "Fine, my studio's coming down. Why did you let me have it in the first place?" She ran out the room and slammed the door behind her.

Alison loved Marcia's studio space, its mellow scent of linseed oil. She loved seeing the canvases as they took shape on the easel, but if her daughter was going to lose something, she herself would have to live without it too.

Chapter 43

July 2007

At the Canada Day party, Marcia, Elly, and the two boys indeed stayed after the fireworks. At 11:30 pm, Alison drove to Lakeside Park and marched around until she found them, by the lakeshore path, where the kids were lounging on blankets Garry had brought. When Alison pulled her aside, Marcia refused to leave. Rather than making a spectacle of her daughter, who was already fuming, Alison told Marcia that the girl was responsible for her own safety overnight. And Alison drove away.

In the morning, Elly phoned her own mother, who took the teens out for breakfast and chauffeured them back to Alison's townhouse. Tamara Lawton, bespectacled and strawberry blond like her daughter, apologized. Alison wanted to slog the woman as well as Marcia.

But Marcia did lower herself to say, "I'm sorry, mother," as she and her friends climbed the stairs from the driveway. "But it was such an awesome night. The air stayed warm, and we talked until three in the morning." She gestured with a can of lemonade. "We'll be out back."

Shy about strangling her daughter in front of another parent, Alison forced a smile and wondered whether she really could take the art studio away from Marcia.

* * *

The four kids talked and laughed on the balcony.

From the kitchen, Shirley glanced at them and turned to her daughter sitting at the table. "Well, she came back in one piece. I still worry every day when you go out, but girl—I swear to God—last night you came close to a nervous breakdown."

"This butter tart is wonderful," Alison said and took another bite.

She looked at the issue of *Canadian Living* on the kitchen table. She wanted to throw the magazine across the room, but not because she felt angry. The emotion was fear. Seeing how Tamara Lawton reacted—breakfasting with the kids and then driving them back to the neighbourhood, as if nothing bad had happened—gave Alison a mirror on her own behaviour. She was uncertain she could bear the reflection.

"Don't repeat the mistakes I made with you," Shirley said.

"Marcia's not me, and the world's nastier now." As she pondered what to do, Alison took a napkin off the tabletop and wiped butter-tart filling from her chin. *Prepare for the worst but hope for the best.* Wasn't that a rule back in Girl Guides? It couldn't hurt to try, after what she'd gone through last night. She hardened herself to give Marcia "the talk," not just about safe sex and birth control, but date rape, with or without alcohol or Roofies.

For now, at least, Marcia was back and unharmed. That fact

CHAPTER 43

was a source of comfort. It failed, however, to ease Alison's nervousness about her job. Loams's deadline loomed.

Chapter 44

"Is pretty day, no? Blue sky, and not wet in the air." Miroslav raised his water bottle. "To this country."

Sol lifted his orange juice, and they drank.

The afternoon was dry but blistering at 35° C. A rock band set up on the stage and started playing. A musical magnet, pulling people toward the stage. Young couples walked hand in hand. Parents tugged their toddlers' forearms or gave up and carried the kids.

Miroslav elbowed Sol. "Stop staring at beer tent."

"You're not?"

They turned and walked toward the lake, the band booming and a medley of smells—from hot dogs to candy floss to sunscreen—assaulting Sol's nostrils. No escape from it all. No escape. Danny doing it, doing it, doing it to him. He shrugged. He'd always have that burden showing up in his nightmares. More yapping with mental health professionals wasn't going to cure him.

Along the waterfront trail, booths from a dozen charities and service groups faced the park.

"Let's go and take a see." Sweat had dripped down Miroslav's chest and soaked his T-shirt where its cotton stretched over his basketball paunch. "You have volunteered?"

CHAPTER 44

Sol shook his head.

A middle-aged woman minding the SPCA booth waved at them and smiled. "Hey, Miro, good to see you out here."

Miroslav leaned over the pamphlets on the display table and hugged her. "Me also, Diane. See you at next meeting."

Sol slapped his friend's back. "Had no idea."

"You should think about. Is part of the AA, you know. *Be of assistance*."

At the Kids Helpline booth, a guy and girl, both no older than Sol, sat on stools. The guy took a stack of brochures from a cardboard box and lay them on the tabletop. "I'm Ralph. Thinking of joining us?"

"Just browsing," Sol said and flipped through the material.

Sporting gelled green hair and a nose ring, Ralph took a paper form off the table and held it up. "You can really, really help kids here. The ones in dire straits. Filling in this form is all you have to do to apply. Security check comes later, but you don't need to bother with that now. We're looking for people who are good listeners. Who enjoy conversation."

Conversation. Well, talking over and over and over to himself hadn't killed Sol's demons, and neither had his long discussions with Tash. Talking with kids, trying to help them, maybe . . . but that assumed he'd pass the security check. What did he have to lose? He picked up an application form and filled it in, and when he was finished, he joined Miroslav, and they rambled along the trail. Waves lapped at the shoreline rocks, which gradually faded from view beneath the lake's rippled surface. Far-off boats and their masts glinted as Sol glanced west toward Oakville Harbour.

In that direction, three silhouetted figures shared a bench. He shook his head and took another look. With difficulty.

The crowd—including families, gathered at picnic tables or on blankets; cyclists; and sauntering couples—was a flowing obstacle. But there they were on the bench: Tash and her parents.

Her folks were talking, but their daughter slouched, her legs spread out. With eyes like stone, she looked out at the lake.

"Quick," Sol whispered. "Got to turn around."

* * *

Sitting on a leather sofa in the Havers's living room, Sol sipped the coffee Debra had offered. Sunlight strained through the sheer curtains of a bay window, which stood sandwiched between built-in shelving units. From what he'd just seen and heard, Sol wondered whether he and Bobby were wasting their time with Debra Havers. Maybe they should stop playing gumshoe, step back, and let Detective Downey do her job.

Thirty minutes before, Bobby had introduced his mother to Sol and—being a "live-in slave now," as the boy said to Debra—left to tidy the garage.

Debra—she'd insisted Sol call her that—stood five feet tall. Immediately, he wondered how could she have pushed her hulking husband off the library roof. It didn't seem possible, so Sol grasped for other possibilities. Maybe her fingerprints were on the handle of the mop the police found on the roof, but he couldn't exactly grill Downey about the evidence. Whatever the truth was about the mop, Debra couldn't have manhandled two people who both towered over her.

But the woman did have at least two possible reasons to want her husband dead. She'd been furious when the

CHAPTER 44

money Ray'd used to develop Tudor Gardens—her remaining inheritance money—vanished as the project went into a death spiral. In spite of the real estate mess, Debra was, according to Bobby, still in love with Carlos Perez. The two were even considering marriage. Maybe she'd hated Ray's guts for years. And besides, her alibi was fuzzy: two friends saw her leaving Umbria at 9:30 on the fateful night, but then she watched TV at home and went to bed early. With no one to back up her story.

Pam Renard's murder alongside Ray's suggested another spur. Debra could have discovered that he and the girl were banging. As simple as that. Or, worse, Ray could've confessed he was in love with Pam (how pathetic). *Hell hath no fury like a woman scorned.*

Sol knew not to suggest the Pam Renard angle, so his first question to Debra was about Ray's personality. What the man was like? After all, Sol was meeting with her because he supposedly had PTSD from discovering the bodies and needed "closure" to help his sleep. Debra's reply was frank: Ray was kind to her and others, was a snob sometimes, but was always an avid music fan, mostly of pop groups from the 1970s and 80s.

She led Sol down to a basement gym and gestured at the posters on its walls. David Bowie. Elton John. Queen. Glass and frames protected the images, yet time had yellowed their paper. Ray, she said, collected the pictures in his teens and twenties, spent thousands on concert tickets, and read the stars' biographies. He never stopped. Closely before his death, Ray was reading a new book on Elton John.

Debra circled her index finger around her ear. "A crazy fan. I loved that about Ray. Occasionally, he enjoyed a bit of classical too. Music gave him refuge from . . ." She looked down. "It's too bad, because we'd only just found peace with each other."

She'd motioned for Sol to follow her, flipped the light switch, and headed upstairs.

Now that she was fetching Bobby from the garage, Sol finished his coffee and put it on the glass-topped coffee table. He sat alone in the living room. The shelves on the front wall held books, CDs, a kick-ass stereo system, even some old vinyl LPs. Albums from the 1970s and 80s sat among hip-hop, alternative rock, and electronica. On a couple of shelves, classical albums peeked out: a lot of Schubert, Benjamin Britten, and Tchaikovsky. Ray's classical section. The books included fiction—some trashy, some not—and nonfiction—mostly business stuff, like *The Microsecond Manager*. All of this, Sol thought, is one big jumble. Maybe Bobby could help sort it.

Riding the bus downtown for Canada Day, Sol phoned the kid, and they agreed on another coffee meeting at the strip mall. Bobby would be away from his folks' house, free to talk with no chance of his mother eavesdropping. But whether he'd know his parents' secrets was doubtful.

Chapter 45

June 2007

Bobby believes her lie. Pamela asked him earlier in the week about having dinner again with his parents, and when he wondered why, she gave the excuse of wanting to get to know them better. Pamela knows she's being incredibly unfair, hiding her pregnancy from Bobby. She prides herself on meeting difficulties head-on, but this one is too big. Instead of first crushing Bobby and *then* provoking his parents, Pamela can't bear prolonging the matter: she needs everything to crumble at once.

As she and Bobby pull into the Havers's driveway, Pamela appreciates for the first time how huge the house is. The place must have at least one spare bedroom; maybe his folks will ready one for her and the baby. She laughs at the fantasy.

"What's so funny?" Bobby says as they enter the vestibule.

Pamela looks up into the double-storey space, a steel-and-glass staircase curving to her right. "Beautiful place you have here."

Minutes later, as everyone sits down at the dining table, the evening sun glows through a rear picture window. Rippling reflections from the backyard's swimming pool dance across the ceiling, and Pamela wishes she could jump into the water—for the splash of cold as much as for escape. After an Arctic winter and a cool wet spring, mid June is scorching. She returns her gaze to the spotless linen tablecloth, on which cut crystal and fine china glitter. She picks up her wine glass and turns it slowly in her hand.

Mr. Havers turns to her. "Fabulous, isn't it? The crystal's been in my family almost two hundred years."

Pamela nods absently. She wants to lose herself in the sparkling goblet, its facets like prisms, splitting the sunlight into rainbow spectrums. But she's not a child, and she can't escape into a daydream. Pamela is two weeks pregnant.

It seems wrong to spoil dinner with the news, so she waits until everyone has finished their strawberry pie. She takes a deep breath. "Not sure if this is the right time or place—well, there'll never be one—but I have to say this. I'm two weeks pregnant."

Colour drains from Bobby's face, and the room is as quiet as a still winter day.

Mr. Havers smiles stiffly. "Well, studying isn't all you two have been up to." He exchanges a glance with his wife. "I'm sorry, but the last thing Bobby needs right now is—"

"And what do you think *I* need right now?" Pamela says, surprized at how loud she's shouting, how tightly her fists are clenched. But the anger stems from the expectation that she's intent on capturing their son. She isn't. Pamela wants her baby, not Bobby and his family as well. It would be too complicated.

Mrs. Havers shakes her head. "Ray, we've been through this

a million times."

"Been though *what?*" Bobby says.

Mr. Havers puts down his napkin and leans back in his chair. "Sorry. Yes, you *both* have to think very carefully about this."

"A million, at least," his wife says, her chin in her hand. "And you were always as unmoveable as a mountain." She straightens her back and crosses her arms, elbows planted like bridge buttresses on the table. "Not anymore. It stops now."

"Debra."

"*What* stops, Mom?" Bobby says. "What are you talking about?"

"For years, I've thought you should know, but your father . . ."

Bobby's eyes are fixed on his mother's. Mr. Havers glances out the window, and Pamela follows his gaze. The pool's ripples mesmerize her, calm her, make her almost believe she's here purely on a social call.

Bobby's mother turns to him. "Alright. When I was eighteen—long before I met your father—I had an abortion, and—"

"Do you really think," Mr. Havers says, still staring out the window, "that this will help the boy?"

His wife slams the tabletop with her fist, rattling the dishes and glassware. "As you keep hearing, Bobby, your father wanted me to stay silent, thought it was better you didn't know." She wipes a tear from her cheek. "Well, now you *do*, and you should also understand that I regret it." Mrs. Havers looks to the other side of the table, to Pamela. "If you want my opinion, *have* the baby. You won't be sorry, won't be like me."

Thank you, Pamela thinks. You know my heart.

Mr. Havers picks up the dessert dishes. "They need to think rationally about this. And fast. Emotion has no place here."

"Emotion is everything here!" Debra says.

Bobby gets up and pushes in his chair. "We should go." He motions to Pamela.

"No, no," Mr. Havers say, still holding the dirty dishes in his hands. "We're going to sit down with you and discuss—"

"Come on, Pam, let's go."

As she gets up, Pamela's elbow hits Mr. Havers's glass on the edge of the dining table. The heirloom falls and smashes against the floor.

* * *

On the drive back to Woodmore, they talk and talk, resolving nothing. It's too soon, Pamela thinks. Bobby says it's too late. He wants to keep the child, but she has no answer for him. Or for herself.

Chapter 46

July 2007

The Group of Four, as Alison now called the troop, was meeting at Lakeside Park again to paint along the shore: they'd gotten excited about the landscape there during Canada Day. She pulled over to the curb on Front Street, and Marcia grabbed her *pochade* box and rucksack from the back seat. Standing around the gazebo in the park, the other three kids shouted and signalled, and Marcia—waving back to her mother—ran toward them. Alison took Navy Street to Lakeshore and turned north to fight the morning traffic on Trafalgar Road.

When she walked into Homicide, Loams was calling an impromptu meeting. Everyone gathered around him, and he reported that John Ruvinsky's wife had only days to live. He'd given John the week off. Ruvinsky, she thought, the poor bastard. Emphasis on *bastard*. Alison was going to Hell, she knew it. But she deserved pity too: sifting through her notes, she narrowed down the suspects to "only" five who scored highest on motive, opportunity, and means. Five of them.

How was Alison going to meet Loams's August time limit with that many suspects and no partner?

She took a deep breath and reviewed what she'd learned so far. First of all, the notion that Ray and Pamela were in fact murdered was speculation based on the green-fibre evidence—found both on the victims' clothes and in Havers's bank office—for which there could be innocent explanations. The pair may have fallen, by some weird accident, off the library roof; and, even if they were murdered, the green filaments hadn't necessarily come from the killer.

OK, Alison thought as she sipped her coffee, let's assume it was murder. It was obvious that Rose Molloy had lived at Woodmore and hated Pamela Renard. So, the redhead had motive and perhaps opportunity, because the question of how Rose could have accessed the roof garden remained. But none of those puzzle pieces mattered anymore. Rose was dead. Among the other people topping Alison's list, Debra Havers was livid that Ray gambled away her inheritance on developing Tudor Gardens, or trying to, and no one could vouch for her whereabouts after nine thirty on the night her husband and Pamela Renard were killed.

Unlike Debra, with her credible motive and weak alibi, the links from Woodmore's administration to Ray and Pamela yielded unlikely scenarios. Yes, during board meetings, Director Collier and Ray argued over school funding, but even if—counter to what Collier claimed—she and Havers never reconciled over the funding, such a disagreement wasn't a reason to kill someone.

Assistant Director Flynn, in his mid-thirties and fit, had physical bulk and quick access from his office to the roof garden. But what motive? Working with Coyote River, he'd

CHAPTER 46

helped to launch the Two Row Exchange, so he might've had influence on which students got picked. Perhaps Flynn was a predator, who'd chosen Pamela and eventually cajoled her into sex, only to have Ray Havers stumble upon them in the act. It was possible.

The only other staff suspect who had close contact with Pamela, if not with Rose, was Fitzgerald. When Alison first questioned him, he said he'd intervened for Pamela in the cafeteria when Rose spouted racist slurs, and he'd cleaned off the red paint from Pamela's dorm door. Bobby and Pamela were supposedly Fitzgerald's friends, but what if a love triangle developed?

The possibility suggested a trick to Alison: play the boy against the janitor—plop them in separate interrogation rooms, tell each one the other had confessed to the clash for Pamela's affections—and see what happened. Still, playing the trick might be unnecessary because Bobby, though he was tall and muscular, had a good alibi. Assuming the boy's roommate hadn't lied for him, he'd been back in Norton House by ten o'clock on June seventeenth. Unlike Bobby, Fitzgerald had no alibi beyond his own words—that he was downtown getting drunk when the double murder happened. Also, the janitor's "former" addiction to cocaine connected, maybe, to the baggie found on Havers's body, but Fitzgerald swore he'd come off coke in his late teens. On the other hand, although he was a Woodmore janitor, Fitzgerald's fingerprints weren't found on the ammonia-soaked mop on the roof garden, or on any other object at the scene. And, no ambiguity existed about Fitzgerald's conviction for aggravated assault. But that assault was against two would-be rapists: he'd saved a woman (Tashi Harishandra, his soon-to-be girlfriend at the time) from them, and his light sentence reflected his heroism. His conviction, however, showed he could overpower two opponents at once: he possessed the strength and savvy to throw a man larger than himself off a roof. Unfortunately, no proof existed that he'd been on the library roof that night, or that he had motive.

Alison put down her coffee cup and massaged her temples. So many contradictions, she thought, so much ambiguity. She grasped for any other hard evidence. Fingerprints—maybe they'd clear the fog. Although the set found on the mop, wine glass, and cocaine baggie matched nothing in the CPIC database, virtually identical prints were lifted from the arrows that killed Rose Molloy. Who in heaven had left those prints? They could belong to Luke Daveneau, drug-gang member and Pamela's former beau, but, in the preceding week, Alison twice called the reserve's Chief of Police, Zach Wilson, who'd had nothing to add to their first conversation, from when she and Ruvinsky drove to Coyote River. Daveneau was still absent from the reserve. For the young man's family—who didn't know, or wouldn't say, where he was—Luke's long absences were routine, and so, no missing-persons report had been filed.

Slouching in her chair, Alison sighed. If she couldn't interview Daveneau now, researching Mohawk gangs equalled a good use of time that would make her eventual interrogation of the hoodlum more informed. She entered the terms *gangs Mohawk cocaine* into her search engine and found a *Montreal Gazette* article titled "Mohawks, Gangs, and Tobacco." The story's details were worthy of a noir novel, but Alison skimmed and skipped, looking for the word "cocaine."

So vast are the profits and so poorly are the laws

CHAPTER 46

enforced that the contraband tobacco industry has attracted an unholy alliance of Mohawks . . . and members of organized crime. Outlaw bikers and Italian, Irish, Russian, and Asian mobs are involved in the manufacturing, distribution, and retailing of the illicit tobacco products, according to an investigation by the Gazette and the Center for Public Integrity in Washington, DC. . . .

Recent joint US-Canadian police investigations indicate that drug money has been used to finance the tobacco business. Tobacco products are then used to buy cocaine and marijuana, which are smuggled across the border using the same networks as the tobacco.

The result, Alison read, was that law abiding on-reserve Mohawks paid the price: increased crime in the community and threats to personal safety. She shook her head and thought, bad guys everywhere. It never ends.

The article focused on reserves near Montreal, 550 kilometres away, but Coyote River lay only an hour's drive from the Canada-U.S. border at Niagara Falls. If organized gangs had penetrated Coyote River—as they had in Akwasesne, near Montreal—then any cross-border smuggling from the reserve likely passed through Niagara Falls. So, if drug turf or money was the motive behind the Woodmore murders, the killer could be Luke, some other Coyote River criminal, or an American working with Luke's gang.

Alison snorted, thinking, well, that really shrinks the pool of suspects.

Resolving to try once more for news on Luke Daveneau's whereabouts, she called Zach Wilson.

"Finally, we know where he is," Wilson said, his voice as deep as an Oakville foghorn. "Sorry, I forgot to call you. My concentration is poor, I guess, because this community's hurting. You have to understand, Pamela Renard is one example of a thousand or more of our women, and I'm not just talking about this reserve or the Haudenosaunee. Missing or murdered, at much higher rates than nonindigenous females. I've dealt with it too many times *here*, and poverty's the common denominator. Or you hear about hitchhiking girls getting raped and killed along remote northern highways. But Pamela Renard went a measly hour off the reserve—to a posh private school, no less—and she *still* got murdered."

"Of course," Alison said. Without disrespecting Wilson, Pamela, or Coyote River, she needed to steer the conversation back to Daveneau. She winced before she spoke again. "On occasion, I have the same doubts. This won't make it any easier, but we have no proof it was murder. But assuming Pamela *was* slain, some evidence points toward Daveneau, so I need to interrogate—"

"Ah, Luke Daveneau," Wilson said. "I could've charged him in a minor assault last year, but I let him off with a warning. I played 'give the kid a chance,' but that was a mistake. Anyway, on June fifteenth, he—along with another local miscreant and two Hells Angels members—was arrested trying to cross the border at Niagara Falls, New York. Looks like they may have murdered a drug dealer in Lockport, northeast of Buffalo. Luke's charged as an accessory."

Alison whistled. "Is he back in Ontario?"

"Bail's too high."

"Whatever documentation you have on that arrest, can you attach it to an email?"

CHAPTER 46

"Sure, Detective Downey. And can you do *me* a favour?"

"I'll try."

"Find whoever killed Pamela Renard. Fast. Naming the killer, or killers, will release a lot of pressure."

"Pressure?"

"At the Peaceful Meadows site. A few hotheads on both sides created trouble from the start, but since the girls' murders, the general mood's approaching panic."

They ended the call, and Alison tossed her phone on the desk. She picked up her pen and rhythmically tapped it against her knee. *June fifteenth*. Whatever Luke Daveneau's role may have been in the American drug dealer's killing, he was arrested two days before the Woodmore murders. So, being behind iron bars in another country gave him a good alibi.

Chapter 47

The Nobles 330 polisher skipped over the gym floor as gracefully as a drunk, threatening to break Sol's wrists with its jerkiness, and it left behind an uneven gloss. A month back, he'd told Peacock the tri-nut threads were stripped, letting the tube and socket assembly vibrate about the switch box, but the replacement parts were still on order. Reaching a corner of the gym floor, he switched off the 330 outside the door to Equipment Storage. He wondered if he should bother going in. From all the kids running through and dropping equipment—lacrosse sticks, pommel horses, tennis rackets—the floor in there got scuffed within five minutes of him polishing it. But he remembered his father's words: *Always be honest in your work*. Sol unlocked and opened the door and recognized the weak but unmistakable smell of sweat and feet.

Inside the storage room, he scanned the shelves and wooden bins of basketballs, soccer balls, floor hockey sticks, and volleyballs. The folded trampolines and archery targets against a wall. The football helmets and lacrosse sticks. The bows and arrows. He remembered Amy Ling's story about Rose in archery class—the redhead's slur about Pamela's "natural" skills as an Indian. He snatched a handful of arrows

CHAPTER 47

off the rack and looked them over. The tail ends each held three orange rubber vanes, stamped *QuikSpin ST Speed Hunter*. He must have seen too many Robin Hood movies, because he'd expected to see feather vanes.

Clank clank. Sol lurched at the noise as, beyond the shelving, the exit door swung open. In the flash of daylight, Sol squinted as pre-teen girls shouted and bounced soccer balls through the doorway. Who were these kids? School was already over for the year. As they passed by, they tossed the balls into the correct bin, but one girl missed. Her ball slammed into Sol's chest and the arrows dropped from his hands and clattered on the floor.

As Sol rubbed his stinging chest, Ms. Steele came in behind the last girl.

"I don't get it," he said. "How's there a class going on?"

"Summer soccer camp. Brand new revenue stream for the school. Assistant Director Flynn came up with the idea." She ran her hand through her bristly hair. "Eh, saw that ball clock you. You alright?"

Ms. Steele approached, fingering the whistle attached to her keychain. Sol shrugged and bent to pick up the arrows.

The exit door opened again and a gaggle of boys came in, chucking soccer balls into the bin, as the girls had done. Flynn appeared and closed the door behind him. "Jane, I will see you in a few minutes at Edwards Common."

"Can we sit those kids down for lunch without them destroying the place?"

"I will have those children shipshape in ten seconds," Flynn said, treading past Sol. He looked down. "Speaking of shipshape—or not—why are those arrows on the floor? Someone could get hurt, you know."

Sol shrugged.

Flynn raised an eyebrow and walked away, into the gym.

"Going on a hunting trip?" Ms. Steele said, her burly arm pointing to the arrows. "You were studying those fletchings pretty carefully. Amazing how the technology's evolved, eh?"

"Yeah." Bending down to the floor, he picked the bolts up and rolled one between his fingertips. "Heard about your run-in with Rose Molloy on the archery field—last fall, I mean. She deserved the suspension."

"That kid was asking for everything she got. Everything."

Yeah, Sol thought, Rose was nasty. But she didn't *deserve* to die.

Ms. Steele strode past him toward the gym doorway. "One less bigot, eh? That's fine by me."

Wondering why Steele was so concerned with the arrows, and so full of hate for Rose, Sol placed the shafts on the rack. He refused the weight of Steele's words. If she herself had killed Rose, the woman wouldn't broadcast her guilt. And she wouldn't tell a suspect, someone with everything to gain by passing the confession to the cops.

He switched on the Nobles 330 and swore as it staggered and bumped across the floor.

* * *

Halfway through the morning, Bobby phoned. He begged Sol for a noon meeting at the lake woods. Green Works was tending lots in Old Oakville by the lakeshore. So, it was a bit of a jaunt, but Bobby could bike over to Woodmore for lunch.

"Too much of a hassle for you," Sol said. "Let's meet tonight."

"Dude, this can't wait."

Chapter 48

Sitting at a plastic table in a shopping-mall food court, Tamara Lawton and Alison wielded plastic knives and forks over plastic trays. On the morning after Canada Day, when Tamara had driven Marcia, her own daughter Elly, and the two boys home from Lakeside Park, Alison reacted angrily to the woman. But by the same evening, guilt and embarrassment followed, and she phoned Tamara to apologize. By the end of the conversation, Alison felt she had a new friend.

Now they were on their first lunch date. Alison's teriyaki chicken on rice swirled up trails of steam, and she felt the heat on her wrists. In the crowded food court at Mount Nemo Mall, a five-minute walk from 21 Division, she and Tamara talked amid the noon hour din.

"Why couldn't I see it?" Alison said, looking into Tamara's blue-grey eyes. "From the day Marcia got her first training bra. But the last few weeks, it's as if I'd built brick walls around us, and Marcia knocked them down with a wrecking ball."

"A what?" Tamara shouted, the food court reverberating with the beeping of chip fryers and the chatter of two hundred conversations.

"Wrecking ball. I'm afraid of losing her. That she'll run out of the house after one of our fights and never come back."

Pamela Renard never came back, that was for sure. Alison wondered what Pamela's relationship was like with her mother on the reserve. The girl broke up with troublemaker Luke. But did she do it willingly or because of an ultimatum from her parents? Her leaving for Woodmore had been, possibly, a way out of an emotional tug-of-war. . . .

Tamara nodded. "Teenage daughters can be so sweet, can't they? Whilst sneaking off doing God knows what with God knows whom. I just grin and bang my head against the stucco."

Alison scanned the nearby tables. Why was everyone so young? Clothing-store sales clerks with their gelled hair and wearing suits they couldn't afford. A twenty-something woman, her face smooth and glowing, the Barbie-doll type Tim was screwing to weather his midlife crisis. "I wanted Marcia to stay a child. If she wasn't getting any older, then *I* wasn't either."

On the way in, a chunk of chicken missed Tamara's mouth and plopped into her Styrofoam cup. "From the high board, a perfect dive." She clapped lightly. "But speaking of 'getting any,' are you?"

"Huh?"

"Getting any, full stop." Tamara's eyes widened and her lips puckered.

"As Johnny Nash sang it, 'I can see clearly now.' I'm thirty-nine. Energy is fading, along with my looks."

Tamara frowned, unaware of the orange sauce and rice grains stuck to one side of her mouth.

Alison gestured to the same spot on her own face.

"Oh." With a paper napkin, Tamara wiped her mouth. "I'm forty-three, and I've been there. Respect yourself. Accept that you're middle-aged. It happens to the best of us."

CHAPTER 48

Tamara put her knife and fork down and spread her soiled napkin over her Styrofoam plate. "Be a joiner. For instance, outdoors groups. You lace up your trainers, get some outdoor exercise, and meet people. If a gorgeous guy happens to be in the group—"

Alison failed to stop her eyes from rolling.

Tamara slapped Alison's forearm. "A lot of people like you and me out there. Life gets complicated, blah, blah, blah."

"I love cuddling up with a good book," Alison said. At least she could trust a hardcover not to dump her for a thin trade paperback. "Have you read Margaret Atwood's latest?"

"Date. Use the dating websites—I have—or not. But do something." On the back of her meal receipt, Tamara wrote something and passed the paper to Alison. Two web addresses: eMatch.ca and the URL for Tamara's hiking group.

"The time," Alison said and picked up her tray.

"Half-twelve. Must get back."

They rose from their chairs.

"I must be off," Tamara said as she turned and waved. "Don't have to join my outdoors group if you don't want to, but it'd be brilliant if you did. With eMatch, just use caution and common sense. But hey, you're the detective. You can smell a liar from a kilometre away."

Chapter 49

Bloodroot and sarsaparilla rustled as Bobby waded into the forest sanctuary, the spokes of his bicycle tires festooned with leaves and twigs. He waved to Sol. "Could we eat at the lakeshore?" he said. "I need to hear the water, and we need privacy."

Sol dropped his sandwich back into his lunch bag. "This isn't private enough?"

"Not today it isn't."

As they hiked through the woods, patches of sunlight swayed on the ground. The forest canopy murmured, male cardinals marking out territory with their clear whistled song: *wheet, wheet, cheer-cheer-cheer-cheer*. Arriving first at the thin strip of pebbled beach, Bobby looked out over the lake, light pounding from blurred white clouds, foot-high waves smacking against the rocks.

"I think my father . . . I think he was gay," Bobby said.

Sol wasn't sure he'd heard right.

"*Gay*, Sol," Bobby said. "Like homosexual, or bisexual, I guess. Last night, I picked through the stuff on his home computer. Mom wanted me to look it over, see what we should do with it, so I was looking at his web browser's history and all these pages from GayChoices.com came up."

CHAPTER 49

"Dot what?"

Bobby turned away from the lake. "A gay dating site. I couldn't log in. So, in Dad's desk drawers, I rifled around and found a sticky-note with a user name and password on it, which let me into GayChoices. Oh my God, he's been a member for years. I never had a clue. But anyway, lately Dad messaged only one user, *braveBoy*. Back and forth for three weeks. The last messages were about when and where to actually meet up. That was May 2005, virtually two years ago. After that, no more posts by Dad or braveBoy."

"Likely they met, then," Sol said. "And either their date sucked, or they clicked and didn't need the online chats anymore."

"I don't understand. And I don't care if Dad was gay. Sing your own song, live your life, whatever. It's not a no-no anymore. Like look at the TV sitcoms." Bobby stood up and paced over gravel alongside the shoreline rocks. He stopped and faced Sol. Wet streaks glistened on his cheeks. "Why couldn't he have just told us, Mom and me."

"Your father was older. Things were different back—"

"But to die without telling the . . ." Bobby's voice broke on the words. "And now I wonder if . . ." He turned and focused on the blue sweep of Lake Ontario.

"If *what*?"

"That website user, 'braveBoy.' Maybe he had something to do with Dad and Pam. It's possible. I looked at his profile on GayChoices.com, but he's got all the privacy settings turned on. You only see his name and the date he joined."

"Any good with computers?"

"I use email and the internet, type my own essays. That's about it. Math and computers aren't my forte."

Sol finished his cranberry juice and scrunched up his lunch bag. "So the guy stays a phantom. We're not going to yell, 'Hey, braveBoy,' from the top of Mount Nemo and hear someone holler back, 'Yeah, that's me. What do you want to know?'"

"Wait . . ." Bobby, his brow creased, gestured *stop* with an outstretched arm. "Yelling! I can't believe I forgot. Dad's bank branch, when I talked to Aunt Beth like two weeks ago."

"You've lost me. What are you talking about?"

"There's this janitor at the bank. Eun Kim, I think her name is. So tiny I don't know how she lifts a vacuum cleaner. She said my father had 'shouted with a man' lately, after hours on some of her night shifts. I could tell it alarmed her. So, who was the 'man'? Some RBC Bank client, pissed at my father over an investment or something?"

"Maybe. Carlos Perez, more likely. Or he might've been braveBoy."

"A big question mark. So what do we do now?"

Gesturing to Bobby, Sol got up and walked toward the lake woods. "The two of us can turn on a computer and not much more, so we've got to go to the dark side—Detective Downey and her pals. The cops must have an IT guru who can find out *something* from GayChoices.com."

"Fine, but *you're* the one who's going to phone her."

"She won't believe me. You're the witness for your dad's online chats *and* for what the janitor saw at the bank, so it's got to be you. Have her card?"

Bobby sighed and took his wallet from his back pocket.

"Phone her," Sol said. "Now."

Chapter 50

Alison flinched when her phone rang and almost spilled her coffee. She moved her mug away from the computer keyboard and answered the call. Bobby Havers's bass voice rumbled through the phone. Over the next ten minutes, the boy apprised her of a computer user name (braveBoy, from a gay dating website) and an RBC janitor's memory of Ray Havers quarrelling on several evenings with "a man." The latter statement was maddeningly vague, but the former surprised her.

As Bobby spoke about his father's apparent homosexuality—and how the banker had arranged to meet with braveBoy, a member of GayChoices.com—his voice cracked. "He never said anything about it to me."

"A man his age," Alison said, "may have been conflicted—afraid to tell you. Thanks for this, Bobby. We're going to need your father's computer, so we'll be calling your mom."

Eager to follow up on the boy's report, she ended the call.

The office for GayChoices.com was on the west end of Mississauga: a thirty-minute drive. She phoned and set up a meeting for three o'clock. With a call to Ray Havers's bank branch, she verified that security videos were available going back to Friday, June eighth.

She also made an appointment to see Woodmore's Director, whom she'd . . . forgotten about? Alison Downey, flawless professional. But the Havers and Fitzgerald angles had lately consumed her time. If Norm Miller would ever come back to work from his rock climbing injury, *he'd* be following up with Gwen Collier, the snowboarding headmistress, who'd made peace—so she'd said—with Ray Havers over their school-funding spats.

Alison found the staff contact list, addressed the envelope to Ruvinsky, and found a stamp for it. As she emerged from Regional Investigative Services and into the parking lot, she fanned her face with the packet.

* * *

On the Origin of Species. Bleak House. Tess of the d'Urbervilles. Das Kapital. Ulysses. Someday I'll read the Darwin, Alison thought as she glanced at the bookshelves in Director Collier's office.

"I hope your investigation is progressing." Collier said. "Woodmore needs closure on this tragedy—the sooner, the better." Her elbows on the desktop, she pressed her fingertips together and leaned back in her leather chair. "And you're here to tell me what?"

"Not tell. Ask." Alison took out her notebook and pen. "You were hiding something in our first interview, and I'm here to find out what it is."

"There is no time to lose. Woodmore's reputation is at stake. And you want to dither by harassing me?"

"The first time I was in this office, you dodged my gaze.

CHAPTER 50

Talking about your boardroom fights with Ray Havers, you looked away, to that painting." Alison pointed to the abstract on the wall. "And when you said your relationship with him was strictly professional, you looked down at your desktop. And you're now crossing your arms."

Collier looked down at her arms. She uncrossed them and shrugged. "This school—its people, its reputation—is all I care about."

"If you lied, now's the time to tell the truth."

Pushing a strand of hair from her brow, Collier looked out the window to the playing fields, her face sculpted by the light. Such perfect, wrinkleless skin, Alison thought. I should at least enquire about which Oakville doctors do chemical peels. She shivered, though, at the idea and found comfort in the used-bookstore tang coming from the wall-to-wall shelves.

Apparently spellbound by the window, the Director stayed silent.

"Ms. Collier? We can have this conversation elsewhere if—"

Collier got up and paced behind her desk. "Five years ago. A different school. I'd just gone through a divorce and . . . I don't know, it just started. You'll understand I wanted to keep this particular skeleton in my closet."

"You've lost me. What started?"

Collier returned to her desk chair and looked out the window again. "I had a fling."

"OK."

"But it was, well, unusual," Collier said, lowering her head and rubbing her brow. "I didn't plan it, it just sort of happened, as I said. . . . The affair was with a Grade Twelve boy. Totally unprofessional, I know."

"And illegal."

Collier turned back from the window. "I realized too late that it had to end. But the boy told his parents, and they let the school know. Luckily for me, my uncle was on the board, and the parents reached a settlement with the school. The police were never involved. Needless to say, I was dismissed, but due to my uncle's compassion and influence, the school gave me a respectable reference letter. Please—please don't make this public."

"You know I can't guarantee anything," Alison said. And she thought, With those dubious sexual boundaries, Gwen, you've now shot a few levels higher on my list.

* * *

The home of GayChoices.com was smaller than a jail cell. It hid on the second floor of an office complex in a Mississauga business "park." Walking from her car to the building, Alison thought of a better term for the landscape—"parking lot."

Inside, the office's décor was milk-crate minimalist, and the only plants—in a small vase, on one of the four desks—were white plastic trilliums.

She approached a green-haired woman sitting at the desk with the flower vase. "I'm Detective Downey, Halton Regional Police. I called a little while ago."

The woman pulled her gaze away from the twenty-four-inch monitor in front of her and motioned to a chair in front of her desk. "Right, the user info. I'm Rebecca Lang, one of the crazies who run this operation."

With no interruption in the clicking of keyboards, chuckles issued from the workers at the other desks. A set of double doors behind them led, Alison figured, to the server room,

CHAPTER 50

because a mechanical hum emanated from the wall.

She sat down and smiled, looking Rebecca in the eyes. "My name's Alison. That necklace is gorgeous, by the way. So, how'd you make out with the user record?"

"We want to weed out lurkers and other creeps, so every member has to provide full ID and a credit card with an address that matches their driver's licence. We've got the info for this user 'braveBoy,' but I've talked to my partners. . . ." She waved toward the occupants of the other three desks. "You need a warrant."

A bubble of chewing gum emerged from Rebecca's lips and grew to the size of a grapefruit. She deflated it before it burst.

"You familiar with the Woodmore murders in Oakville?" Alison summarized the case and how learning braveBoy's identity could be a critical breakthrough. "You have to understand, Rebecca, that as each hour passes, the trail gets colder. Checking your data is key."

"Everyone's talking about the erosion of privacy. We don't want to be one more company that violates the—"

"Please," Alison said, knowing she was about to lie but feeling too pressured not to. "I'll handle the user's record with discretion, and if the information isn't relevant, I won't record it at all as part of this investigation."

Rebecca raised one eyebrow and sighed, her lip ring glimmering in her screen's glow. Several mouse-clicks and flurries at the keyboard later, she printed braveBoy's personal information and passed the paper to Alison. "Don't tell my buddies," she whispered, jerking her thumb at the other desks.

Alison scanned the sheet, and at the first- and last-name line, she stopped. User braveBoy's real name was Grafton Flynn, Woodmore's Assistant Director.

Chapter 51

June 2007

Sluggish and heavy, air hangs in the grey morning, as Pamela and Amy trudge toward Edwards Common. Bobby and one of his housemates leave the entrance of Norton House, and when he sees the girls, he jogs up to them. Pulling Pamela aside, he waves Amy ahead to the dining hall. Dull smudges under his eyes suggest lack of sleep, and Pamela herself slept poorly last night. Why did she tell Bobby's parents she was pregnant? On the drive back to Woodmore, he was furious about it. She's glad that both Bobby and his folks know. Mrs. Havers's guilt over her own long-ago abortion was sobering to hear, but Pamela knows from chats with Mom and Grandma Becky that the choice should be hers alone. She's still undecided. The pressure of time, however, weighs more heavily on her with each hour.

She forces herself to meet Bobby's eyes and their expression of torment. "You look like you could really use some breakfast," she says.

He drops his chin to his chest. "What're we going to do?"

CHAPTER 51

"For the next week or so," Pamela says, laying her hand on his shoulder, "all we can do is grit our teeth and get on with studying. Then, when exams are—"

"You're insane!" Bobby twists her hand from his shoulder. One of his Norton House friends calls to him, and he stomps off.

"I'll tell you," she says, "as soon as . . ."

But Bobby's already too far away. Pamela realizes she's crying. Between the burden of choosing and the bouts of morning sickness, how can she possibly concentrate on finals? And a smaller problem niggles: whenever Amy asks, Pamela claims stomach flu is behind her vomiting, but that lie becomes more dubious with each passing day.

* * *

After breakfast, Amy leaves for the library. Pamela sits and fidgets at her dorm-room desk. Suddenly half an hour has passed, and she's accomplished nothing. Pamela thinks about Rose, about the unlikely peace they reached. Did that really happen, each respecting the other? Whatever the state of their association is, when they've since come across each other in Pilkington House and around the campus, Rose has looked healthier, if not exactly cheerful; Jane Taylor's struggle was a long one.

Pamela's books and class notes scold her from the desktop, but despite her uneasy stomach, she needs to get outdoors and clear her mind. Not by herself, though. Maybe, she thinks, it would help Rose too to be outside for a while. She gets up and walks down the corridor.

In answer to her knock, Rose opens her door by a crack.

"Oh, it's you."

"Do you have a few minutes to . . ." Pamela speaks to the crack, her voice trailing off as she ponders whether they're once more enemies.

But Rose pokes out her head and says, "Hallway clear?"

Pamela glances behind. "As far as I know."

"Then be quick!"

After Pamela is past the threshold and the door is closed, she notices a trace of light in Rose's eyes. "If you've got a few spare minutes," Pamela says, "I'm going for a walk. . . . Strength in numbers."

"You think I'm weak?"

"I need this walk—right now my concentration for exam prep is zero—and I could use some company. It doesn't matter to me where we go."

"Where's the nerd?" With thumbs and forefingers, Rose mimics glasses around her eyes.

"Amy's gone to the library. She spends most of her life there."

Rose shrugs. "OK, but nobody can see us together. How about the lakeshore? The woods make a thick curtain in front of it. But to get there, you walk down the west side of campus. I'll take the east."

Minutes later, Pamela enters the lake woods. Thirty metres in, she stops and looks up. Sun rays touch her face—Grandma Becky says they're the arms and hands of the Creator—then she sits down among the partridgeberry and yellow flowers of bellwort, closes her eyes, and focuses on her breathing. Slow deep breaths. In April, it often seemed like prayer during Ms. Steele's classes in yoga. The teacher said the word was Sanskrit for *union* and that yoga was about finding harmony with the universal spirit, so now Pamela takes in the woodland silence and scents. Maybe she's in that union right now. Although Pamela is unsure, a space seems to open, a room that may be large enough for her and her baby . . . but then a crow, as if it's contesting her thought, caws and flaps from a poplar's branches and sails past her head.

Sighing, she gets up, plods toward the far edge of the woods, and emerges onto a pebbly windswept beach where, high in the metallic blue, a silver sun burns, reflected like white sparks from Lake Ontario's expanse. Rose stands at the shore, waves slapping against groups of boulders, gulls crying as they hover and dive. She's picking up stones and throwing them into the lake, and as Pamela approaches, Rose glances momentarily to the east where, from this great distance, downtown Toronto looks like a fortress with skyscrapers for battlements.

"Rose!" Pamela says, but the pounding wind carries her voice away.

Rose continues tossing rocks, but each time her body moves faster, as if she's driven by mania. Even with the gusts, Pamela can her Rose grunting on each pitch. Finally, the girl turns on hearing Pamela's shoes crunching against the gravel.

"Took you long enough," Rose says and resumes chucking stones. Her grunt is now closer to being a shriek.

"I stayed for a bit in the woods." Pamela now sees the reddened face and damp eyes. "Look, Rose…"

"What!" The last throw causes Rose to stumble, and she falls to her knees and crouches. The gulls screech as they scatter. "What the hell am I supposed to do?"

Pamela considers the question. Time and a lot of talking may help. They did for Jane. She bends down, puts her hand on Rose's shoulder. "Respect yourself. That revolting pack of boys wanted the opposite. But that's *them*, not you. They're the ones who deserve shame, and I'm glad they're getting it. Publicly."

"Well, yeah," Rose says, still curled up on the pebbles. "It's been on the frigging TV news! How am I supposed to live with that?"

"It's *their* shame, their humiliation. Hold your self-esteem tight, Rose, because someone's always waiting to take it away." Pamela wants to say, *Like you, at the beginning of the year, were waiting to smash mine.* Rose has apologized, though, seems finally to understand the basics of Coyote River's history, and Pamela sympathizes with the Molloy ranch and other Ewing businesses near the Peaceful Meadows site. Rubbing Rose's shoulder, she aches to talk about her *own* problem.

Chapter 52

July 2007

Over spaghetti and a salad sprinkled with pecans and dried cranberries, Alison chatted with Shirley and Marcia at the dining room table, but her thoughts slid again and again to Tamara's advice, to join eMatch and the Halton Outdoor Group. Now Alison wondered how, at lunch, her new friend finally convinced her. She shook her head and looked at Shirley. "Mm, this sauce takes me to heaven. And the pasta is perfectly *al dente*."

Despite her chitchat, a buzzing tightness was creeping into Alison's chest. GayChoices.com. Grafton Flynn being *braveBoy*. On the website, he and Ray Havers had chatted intermittently for three weeks. They'd arranged to meet. . . .

Shirley cleared her throat. "You might be interested in what Marcia's just told me."

Alison turned to her daughter. "What's this?"

Marcia laid down her fork and picked up a DVD case lying beside her placemat. *"Jackson Pollock: His Life and Art*. I signed it out of the library. Going to watch it tonight at Rob's house."

"That's . . . great." Alison swallowed hard. "He seems like a nice boy."

Marcia sat with calculated cool. "Pollock is the guy who basically invented abstract expressionism."

Shirley frowned. "The fellow who dripped paint all over the place."

Marcia passed the DVD to Alison. The cardboard cover showed Pollock, paint can and wood stick in his hands, creating his signature look: a buildup of undulating lines in umber and cream and white and ochre and beige and green—a light green, which made her think of the lime-coloured threads found on both victims of the Woodmore murder.

Marcia looked down at her bowl. "I'll be back by ten."

"That's fine," Alison said, hoping she sounded calm.

After dinner, she took her laptop to her bedroom and filled in the eMatch.ca questionnaire, but as she clicked through the form's sections, Alison was still thinking of lime green.

* * *

As she walked into Homicide, Alison imagined striding into Loams's office and revealing her find at GayChoices, but she knew the wiser action was to search through the RBC security videos and try to locate footage of Havers with the mystery man. Then she could confidently approach her boss with the dating link and whatever the videos revealed.

She sat starting at her computer screen, her desktop stacked with the security DVDs. Sun blasted through the windows beside her desk. She yawned. To get though the videos, Alison would have to commandeer Homicide's coffeemaker, but

CHAPTER 52

Ruvinsky's desk sat empty, so he at least wouldn't be draining his usual twelve cups a day. She wondered how his wife was doing—likely not well, with a stage-four cancer.

During her visit yesterday to Havers's RBC branch, Alison had interviewed Eun Kim, the janitor Bobby mentioned. When she asked which night or nights Eun was referring to, the tiny woman couldn't remember: "It at least four, five weeks ago." About the green fibres Ident found on a fabric chair in Ray's office, the caretaker responded just as vaguely, saying that all furniture in the building was vacuumed weekly. She didn't remember seeing any such threads. Alison had thanked Eun and then obtained the security videos from the officer on duty.

Alison thumbed through the pile of DVDs on her desk. She decided to peruse first the disc, labelled *Sunday, June 17*: the Woodmore murder happened that night. If nothing showed up, Alison would work back through earlier videos. She skipped to 7:00 pm, because (if Eun Kim had remembered correctly) the arguments between Ray and the other man occurred in the evenings.

She sipped her coffee and sat up straight. The screen showed a grid of grainy views within the bank, and she soon focused on the top-right frame, which showed half the information kiosk and a hallway with office doors receding in perspective.

A thousand sips later, she sat slouched in her chair. Except for ten riveting minutes of Eun Kim vacuuming the hallway, nothing moved in the frame. To stay awake, she switched throughout the afternoon between watching the June 17 video, getting up for coffee, and doing paperwork. Alison considered giving up and viewing an earlier date's DVD, but before she could act on that thought, the video showed an office door opening and, emerging from behind it, Ray Havers. His posture was tense as he looked down the corridor, opened his door wide, and shuffled back into the office.

Alison wrote down the time stamp, 7:26 p.m. In the video, nothing happened after that. Ray's office door remained open. She was halfway up from her desk, on her way to refill her cup, when a movement in the video sparked Alison's peripheral vision: a light-haired man, in khakis and a lime green shirt, marched into the frame. His back to the camera, he stopped outside Havers's doorway. He said something and went in.

The time stamp read 7:34 p.m. Fifteen minutes later, both men emerged from the office, and, with matching frowns, they spoke to each other. Over each other.

She recognized the blond one. Grafton Flynn.

Havers grimaced, and his arms jerked about as if he were having a panic attack. He bent forward and covered his face with his hands. Flynn gently touched the banker's shoulder and spoke, but Havers shook and turned away.

After a moment, they walked together—their faces masks of tranquility—down the hallway and out of the frame.

No need for coffee now. Both pieces of evidence—the bank video and the GayChoices registration—were circumstantial, and the green shirt wouldn't necessarily match the fibres found on the bodies at Woodmore. But she had reasonable grounds to obtain the shirt and have Ident analyse it. Nevertheless, she'd wait to arrest Flynn. She'd simply get his alibi for after 6:34 p.m., June 17. And watch his body language as he spoke.

Something besides the new evidence itched her mind. She flipped back through her case notes and stopped at the June

CHAPTER 52

20 entry:

> *12:00 p.m. Interview with Grafton Flynn. "I didn't know Havers. He sat on Woodmore's board of directors."*

He didn't know Havers? Forget about a chat at Flynn's convenience, she thought, and dashed out of the building to her car.

* * *

At Flynn's downtown address, a block of upmarket condominiums on Robinson Street, she buzzed the building manager and flashed her badge.

Two minutes later, standing outside Flynn's unit on the fourth floor, she knocked and announced herself. No answer. She tried again, rapping louder, her voice rising to a shout. She tried the door handle. Unlocked.

"Mr. Flynn. Are you in there?"

She had no search warrant, but—she rationalized—Flynn could be inside lying hurt. Or dead. She swung open the door and again called out to Flynn, heard only silence, and stepped past the threshold.

Inside, she scanned each room. Everything looked undisturbed. Flynn never mentioned he was from the US, but the American flag hung over his bed. Overall, the suite suggested military-like order, as clean and crisp as an officer's dress uniform, so Flynn's leaving his front door unlocked seemed odd.

Whatever had happened, the condo's only "mess" appeared on the side table in the entry hall, where, in a ceramic tray, everyday items lay jumbled: a magnetic card with *RBC* scrawled on it in black marker, a key-ring, two tennis balls, take-out menus, gift cards to Starbucks and Indigo, and half a dozen issues of *Canadian Yachting*. Alison reasoned that the *RBC* card, given to Flynn by Havers, had allowed him into the bank on June 17. The security footage was filmed after-hours, so how else would he have gotten in?

She padded around on the living-room carpet, which was so white and spotless it seemed to glow. Trophies crowded the stone mantelpiece: awards for golf and tennis and judo and archery and triathlon and fencing and boxing. Framed photographs showed Flynn with family—in particular, an older man who was obviously his father—and among teammates on football and basketball teams. Two of the photos revealed, behind the smiling teenagers, a banner emblazoned with a crest and the words *St. Patrick's Catholic High School, Stamford, CT*. Grafton Flynn, an All-American boy. No wonder he taught phys. ed.

From the witness list, Alison called Flynn's work number. It was 5:20 p.m., so Flynn might still be at work. But the call went to his voicemail. She tried Woodmore's main administration number, and the receptionist replied that Flynn had already left.

"He ever mentioned a bar or café he goes to after work?" Alison said.

The receptionist chuckled. "That's easy—the Blue Lion. Usually a few times a week. I know because I've shared a pint there with him, a number of times."

The Blue Lion operated only one block north, on Lakeshore Road, so Alison walked to it. The clientele were young and old, office workers and road crews, but the Merrie England

CHAPTER 52

décor united them. Alison mentioned Flynn to the bartender, a middle-aged man who dressed dapperly. He knew Flynn as a regular but said the younger man hadn't come in yet today.

Alison stayed for a half an hour. Flynn never arrived, and the influx of after-work drinkers eventually ceased.

In the car, Alison closed her eyes and turned the ignition key. Dinner would consist of reheated lasagna (and scowls from Shirley). She drove. Commuters—doing their part for the country's greenhouse gas emissions—sat in stop-and-go traffic on the 403. Alison barely noticed them, her mind grasping for Flynn's location.

She remembered the magnetic card, hand-labelled "RBC," on his condo's foyer table and wondered if she'd misunderstood the security video. Perhaps Flynn killed Havers to *obtain* the pass card so that, days or weeks later, he could enter the bank alone. Flynn robbing a bank, in order to . . . buy a yacht? Alison couldn't imagine him robbing a bank for any reason.

Chapter 53

Heat and the smell of cinnamon wafted from the kitchen, and Miroslav waved.

Sol nodded to him and closed the front door. "Smells great. What are you baking?"

"The cinnamon muffins. You will like."

As Sol bent to take off his work boots, his phone dinged with a new text message. He checked the screen and saw that Tash was the sender, but the text itself was gibberish.

"help cum 2 my pl8c crazy arro"

What's this supposed to mean? he thought. She thinks I'm crazy and . . . *arro*. Arrogant?

But Tash wanted him over there anyway, she needed his help, and he could use the trip to give her back the key. On the keyboard, he poked her speed-dial number. He braced himself more with each ring, but finally only her voicemail greeted him. From the plastic tray on the kitchen counter, he pocketed his old apartment key and returned the gaze Miroslav was aiming at him.

"I'll get my own dinner," he said. "I have to—to go somewhere."

Miroslav tilted his head. "But you will desire warm muffins."

CHAPTER 53

"Got to go. I'll have one later."

***

It was late afternoon and stifling. Sol was hiking toward his old digs—Tash's building—and the slog would take forty-five minutes, but how drenched he got didn't matter. Rush hour traffic droned. As each car crawled by, its hood mirrored the sun into his eyes. He put on sunglasses.

Feeling woozy from the car exhaust, he kept walking and reached Tash's apartment block. From behind her building and beyond White Tail Park, clouds were moving forward, crisp and grey. He shivered as cool dry air broke through the wall of humidity.

***

The situation was screwed up, and Tash never screwed up. The security buzzer was broken. It had to be. Thinking she might be in the bathroom, Sol stabbed the button three more times, leaving ample time between each try. Strange. She wouldn't have gone out after just texting him to come over.

Waving at a tenant who seemed to remember him, Sol caught the entrance door before it closed. He took the elevator and, on the eleventh floor, strode past apartment doors, the hallway's air playing a medley of fish and chips, curry, and fried steak.

At Tash's unit, no answer to his knock. He tried again.

"Tash, it's Sol. You texted me. Sounded urgent."

Again, he knocked and waited, knocked, waited. He put his key in the door and twisted it.

"Tash?" He stepped in and closed the door behind him.

Bloody handprints and sweeps decorated the foyer wall. A copper tang wafted from it, and red splotches peppered the floor like some kid in Edwards Common had spilled ketchup. Nausea crept into Sol's guts.

Rustling. A muffled moan coming from the kitchen.

He stepped toward the sound. To his left, Tash, her back against the stove, sat on the parquet floor. Her mouth was gagged, her ankles and wrists bound with polyethylene rope. Blood coated her nostrils and had sprayed across her face. She grimaced as she looked up at him. Her eyes widening, she tilted her head toward the living room and mumbled something against the cloth in her mouth. Was she saying sorry?

"Be quiet, Ms. Harishandra." The voice came from the living room, directly behind Sol. "Mr. Fitzgerald and I have something to discuss. Solomon, please turn—very slowly—so we can face each other like gentlemen."

Chapter 54

June 2007

Pamela recoils at how Bobby looks, the two of them lingering outside Edwards Common after breakfast. His expression is a mixture of resignation and anger, as if he's read her mind.

With Bobby in that state, she has to think fast but carefully about their options (or lack of them), so she decides to pause her studying marathon. With Amy gone to the library, Pamela says goodbye to Bobby and walks, crunching over the already parched, yellowed grass, back to Pilkington House.

The sky presses its greyness upon the campus, and Pamela's mind is hazy. She likes Bobby. He's a good person and talented at music—not so much at academic subjects, as Mr. Havers cruelly loves to point out. Bobby needs time to get past his father's putdowns and the expectations behind them. He needs time to figure himself out, accept himself fully. Pamela can't help him with those tasks.

Unlike Bobby, Pamela knows who she is, and so finds that Mr. Havers is a bit too old-stock British for her comfort. If that attitude is bigoted, then she's guilty of building a wall between her and the man. Pamela admits, though, that *class* forms the barricade. She thinks of the Havers's tony neighbourhood, elegant, spacious house, and fine crystal. Her family will never be good enough for them. Mutual respect will be absent. And even if, she tells herself, those possibilities exist only in my too-sensitive imagination, my self-knowledge won't change how I feel.

As for Mrs. Havers and her hard-won advice at the dinner table, Pamela wasn't swayed by the woman's remorse about her decades-old abortion. Pamela has, instead, promised herself she'll finish at least an undergrad degree before starting a family. She cringes at the idea of aborting the fetus inside her, and she understands—she feels—Mrs. Havers's anguish. Besides, Pamela has often imagined the children that cousin Lillian will never have. Against the weight of that vision, those forever unborn children, how can she be so cavalier? But she has read and reread the medical websites. It's still early enough in her pregnancy to terminate it safely and, Pamela hopes, with some of her morality intact.

She worries how Bobby will react to her choice, but he deserves to know the truth. For the moment, cruel practicalities are working against her qualms. As soon as she's climbed to Pilkington House's third floor and is back in her room, Pamela opens her laptop and enters the search string *Oakville clinic abortion*.

Chapter 55

July 2007

Sunlight spilled through the windows and blinded Sol as he spun around, his eyes adjusting. He recognized the man standing at the far corner of Tash's living room. Grafton Flynn. The bowstring was straight, relaxed, but the arrow was loaded and ready in his grip. Although Flynn's hands were as big as baseball gloves, Sol had fought big guys before and won. After high school, when he came off the nose candy, he'd trounced guys, little and large, by training with free weights and doing a hundred sit-ups a night. He'd started each fight with words: Sol always waited for the other guy to throw the first punch.

The three-bladed arrowhead glinted. Trying not to focus on its razor-sharp edges, he glanced to his right: in Tash's poster from *The Ramayana*, Rama and Hanuman were still fighting Ravana, the devil king.

Sol looked at Flynn. "I'd watch where you point that thing, somebody could get hurt."

"I am merely practicing my stance."

"OK. Want me to pop into Woodmore and get a target for you?"

Flynn laughed. He was a jumble of opposites. Dress pants, shirt, and tie. But he stood holding a bow and arrow. Beside him on the floor, an unzipped hockey bag. His expression was calm, but, below his underarms, patches of sweat soaked his shirt. Opposites.

The air tasted sour, and Sol wondered whether the stink was drifting from the hockey bag or the man's armpits.

Flynn cast his eyes down for a second. "Employee data gave this building as your address. Tut-tut, you must keep your contact information up-to-date. I arrived here and your lady friend apprised me—after a little struggle in the vestibule—that you had moved out."

"Whatever the trouble is, I'm sure—"

"You know, if Ms. Renard hadn't taken a liking to you, I would not be here now. In Woodmore's hallways, I'd several times observed you conversing with her and the Havers boy, and I once saw the happy trio walking, like old friends, toward the 'Janitor Can.' Yes, I know that's what you custodians call it—how hilarious. But I digress. In my duties as Assistant Director of Woodmore Academy, I learned from Pamela that you had defended her against Rose Molloy's slurs and ugly pranks. And it is said, 'Chivalry is dead.'" Flynn relaxed the bowstring as he tittered.

Sol was about to jump at him but realized the distance was too great. Flynn would have time to react.

"So when I computed the sum of your relationship with those girls," Flynn said, "plus your enthralment with the target-point arrows in the gym, the answer gave me no choice."

"You're into fitness, Mr. Flynn." Sol pointed to the multi-gym. "It's a Cybex, semi-professional model. Go ahead and try it out."

"A conscientious worker. I've noticed that about you, Solomon, and you're not stupid. How can I know you have not relayed your suspicions to the Halton Regional Police Service? Such a shame. You were making a new start, getting on with your life. Unfortunately, you have to be the next victim of the 'Coyote River Killer.'" Flynn winked. "A reserve resident bent on revenge for Ms. Renard's death, and who has already slain Rose Molloy, the daughter of a prominent Ewing land owner."

"Come on," Sol said, "I helped Pamela survive Rose's shenanigans. And even if nobody at Coyote River knows that detail, then fuck, why would they take revenge on me, a nobody janitor? You're not going to fool anyone, definitely not the cops. Even I can see that."

"*Au contraire*. Never underestimate the stupidity of police organizations."

"Why do any of this?"

"You know, my ruse is shaky—I will admit that. What is the vernacular? I am 'making it up as I go along.' Luckily, I have your lady friend to accompany me, as a bargaining token."

Flynn drew the bowstring and aimed. "I am truly remorseful," he said, and released the arrow.

The pain knocked Sol down, and his key fell from his hand and tinkled against the floor. He stumbled to his feet but the burning stole his will, and he could focus on nothing but the agony and the smell of blood and the fiery flow down his back. Flynn reached into his hockey bag, grabbed another arrow. Twisting on the floor, Sol spotted him reloading and tried to relax. What was the point now? Sol was done. At least he'd tried to find restitution for Pamela, so it was a good way to go out.

Flynn pulled back the bowstring, but an ear-splitting bang burst from the kitchen, causing him to jerk as he released the shot. Sol craned his neck and saw the arrow had pierced the bow-wielding monster Ravana and lodged in the wall. The crash from the kitchen screwed up more than Flynn's aim: he'd stumbled onto his ass and was pushing himself up from the floor.

Seeing his chance, Sol ignored the red-hot coals in his shoulder and got up and leapt at Flynn, the pain vanishing as he arced through space and landed an uppercut to Flynn's jaw, the giant dropping his bow as he lurched backward and banged into an aluminum window mullion. But Flynn recovered. After barely ducking a jab, Sol reflexively kneed the prick in the nuts and Flynn doubled over, allowing a kick to the head that knocked the predator to the floor. Sol straddled the huge chest. He hit and hit and hit, and Flynn's bloodied eyes finally closed, his skull thudding against the parquet tiles.

Groaning, Sol struggled to his feet. "Like riding a bicycle." He fingered his shoulder where the arrow stuck out. "Fuck, that hurts."

Metchnikoff's claws clicked across the floor. Finding bravery—now that the danger was over—she hissed at Flynn's prone mass.

From the kitchen, Tash was speaking but the gag muffled and distorted her words. Gingerly, Sol went to her. With only one arm at full strength and flexibility, he struggled with the cloth and duct tape as Tash urged him on with grunts and groans. Finally he removed the gag.

CHAPTER 55

"Alright, can you untie me?" Tash said. "But first call 9-1-1 before that wacky creep wakes up."

Sol grunted, lashing Flynn's wrists to the multi-gym's struts with skipping rope. "Tying him up first."

He made the emergency call and phoned Detective Downey. Then, lumbering to the kitchen, he had to step over a large frying pan and Tash's phone to reach her. Tash looked at him, then down at the pan.

"It was on the stove. Used my chin." She wiggled her wrists as added explanation. "With that thing sticking out of you, I don't know how you're standing up, let alone walking around. The instant the paramedics get here, you're off to the hospital."

Chapter 56

As Alison was eating reheated goulash at the kitchen table, her cellphone rang. She took the call (it was Fitzgerald again) and avoided the reproachful glare from Shirley, leaning back against the fridge with her arms crossed in front. When Alison heard the tautness in Fitzgerald's voice and the content of his words, she dropped her fork.

"What's the matter?" Shirley said.

"I have to go." Alison used her napkin and got up from the table. "Don't wait up."

"I thought you were putting this all-hours work behind you—spending more time now with your daughter."

* * *

She drove east on Lakeshore and turned north onto Trafalgar Road toward Fitzgerald's address. Or was it his girlfriend's place? He'd been so incoherent on the phone that Alison wasn't sure. After a couple of seconds on Trafalgar, she groaned: 6:30 p.m., and the traffic was still bumper-to-bumper. She wished her daughter was right when, a week before the move from Toronto, Marcia had said, "Oakville's out in the sticks."

CHAPTER 56

***

Blood smears on the vestibule wall brought on Alison's gag response. But she squelched the reflex before she could embarrass herself in front of two uniformed constables who were untying Flynn from the steel bars of a home gym.

So, she admitted to herself, Fitzgerald was telling the truth.

She bent down to face Woodmore's Assistant Director. "Grafton Flynn, you're under arrest on suspicion of murder in the deaths of Ray Havers, Pamela Renard, and Rose Molloy." She gave him the talk about his rights.

His eyes half open, Flynn grunted.

"Cuff him."

Back at the kitchen, a young woman—apparently Fitzgerald's ex-girlfriend—sat with her back against the kitchen stove, while a medic shoved cotton batting into her nostrils and applied bandages to her nose. Fitzgerald stood shirtless and grimacing, hunched over a countertop. An arrow's tail protruded from his shoulder, a ring of bandages taped around the entry wound.

He turned and struggled to stand straight. "Am I still a suspect now?"

She ignored the quip and got the medics' OK for Fitzgerald to stay a couple of minutes. After borrowing some medical tape, she pressed it around a plastic bag she'd placed over the arrow's rubber vanes.

The attending constables recapped their notes for her. After the medics had revived Flynn, he gave his version of events—that he was the victim—but both Fitzgerald and Harishandra had denied his statement.

The medics interrupted the cop who was speaking. They

had to take the injured trio for more care, so Alison told the uniforms to accompany them, keep watch at the hospital, and bring each one to 21 Division if and when they got the doctors' go-ahead.

"And tell the docs we'll need that arrow," she said, pointing to Fitzgerald. "Ident will check the tail end for prints."

Standing in the kitchen, she noticed a colourful poster on a wall. A scene from an Eastern holy book? Whatever the image was, another arrow protruded from it. No one had mentioned the stray shaft. She approached the poster. The bolt had struck between two figures—a green-skinned man drawing a bow-and-arrow against a multi-armed blue monster, who also flexed a bow. There's coincidence, she thought, and there's *crazy* coincidence.

She shook her head and turned to the constables. "You guys missed this." She pointed to the arrow. "Notify Ident."

As everyone except her left for Oakville-Trafalgar Hospital, Alison considered the next hurdle—getting Flynn's confession. The circumstantial evidence *might* convince a jury, but the killer's own words would seal his future. And save Alison from a desk job.

* * *

The young woman's poise crumbled more with each sentence. Tashi Harishandra hadn't sat down with much composure anyway. Bandaged nose. Twin bruises like purple wings under her eyes.

In an interview room at Regional Investigative Services, Alison was questioning her, and Harishandra's story of the fight with Flynn matched Fitzgerald's. So, either the pair—or

CHAPTER 56

ex-pair, now—had colluded to tell the same story, or they were telling the truth. She prayed for the latter. One less loose end to steal the case's shrinking time.

Harishandra's version, however, did differ from Fitzgerald's in one logical way: it began earlier, before Fitzgerald arrived at the apartment. Flynn must have snuck behind a tenant into the building. Then, knocking on her door, he lied. He asked for Fitzgerald, and when Harishandra said the janitor had moved out, he said he had to speak with her anyway. He wouldn't stop knocking. Close to calling 9-1-1, she tried to humour him first. She checked that the security chain was in its slot and unlocked the door, but the awkward conversation she was expecting didn't happen.

Harishandra's supple brown hands were shaking now, but she continued. The door had swung into her face. Split her nose.

She'd fallen backwards and had no memory of the struggle, just of Flynn lashing her wrists and ankles. He dragged her behind a kitchen counter, brought in a huge hockey bag, and took it into the living room. As he jostled things around—she couldn't see fully past the cabinet, but she saw him raise a bow and put an arrow to it—she'd been able to free her phone from her pocket, twist to her side, and text a disjointed SOS to Fitzgerald.

"That's it," Harishandra said. "That's all I saw and all I know. Sol—" Her voice broke, and she sobbed. "He must be feeling even worse, but I'm exhausted. Can I leave now?"

✵ ✵ ✵

In her wanderings around 21 Division, Alison had several

times noticed Don Gatti working overtime, so she walked into the Ident lab. He wasn't there. She ran out to the parking lot, where he was walking to his car. Alison winced in disgust as she undid the top two buttons of her shirt, then she approached him. "Hey, Don, any luck with those prints?"

His eyes went where she'd figured they would. At least she'd stopped him from driving away.

He smiled. "Far as I'm concerned, Flynn's prints are a match to the arrow-vane impressions. Verification still has to be done by whoever, but my second-level comparison knocked it out of the park. Same zigzag scar in the left thumb's ridge formations."

"Excellent work." She punched him on the shoulder. "Mind giving me a print-out of the results? Before you leave, I mean?"

"I'm late for my daughter's soccer."

She gave him a pouty, open-eyed glance.

Gatti returned his car keys to his pocket. "Why not. It'll only take five minutes."

* * *

Fingers intertwined on the table, Flynn sat as composed as if he were at a Woodmore board meeting. Maybe the posture explained why he'd refused to have a lawyer present in the interview room. He held his back ramrod straight, but his face was a bruised, swollen tomato. He sniffled. The knuckle of his index finger kept wiping at his nostrils.

Standing in the doorway, Alison tried to remember whether he was sniffling when she'd first questioned him in Trevena Way. What sort of detective was she to have missed that giveaway? She shook her head and sat down at the table.

CHAPTER 56

"Mr. Flynn. May I call you Grafton?"

He ran his fingers through his hair. "You know, I have always abhorred that name."

"Alison." She pointed to two video cameras, each looking down from its corner of the ceiling. "You've declined a lawyer, and you're aware that you're not obliged to answer any questions."

"Yes."

She opened a folder of results from Ident. "I know you're a reliable person, a good person, who wants to do the right thing."

He nodded.

"Could you tell me what you think of some results from our crime lab?"

"Of course." The waver in his voice denied the words.

"This sheet shows two thumbprints." She passed him the paper. "The one on the left—we lifted it from a broken wineglass on Woodmore's roof patio."

Flynn shrugged, but she noticed his flitting eyes and sweaty forehead. Excitement shivered through her. She fought to tame it. "See the zigzag scar? On the right is your thumbprint, from the impressions we took earlier tonight. Same scar."

His brow furrowed, he glanced back and forth across the sheet. "I've dined up there on many occasions. Woodmore periodically entertains parent groups and VIPs on the roof garden, and some of the servers are as clumsy as bulls in a china shop. So your finding of similitude on a dropped wineglass is to be expected."

She thrust a new page across the table. "Here's another of your fingerprints, taken tonight. Beside it is an impression lifted from a baggie of cocaine—we found it in Havers's jacket at the crime scene. The prints are identical."

"Can you substantiate that Mr. Fitzgerald did not plant the drugs at the scene?"

"Clutching at straws, Grafton."

"I know what it is like to be an outsider, so I try to help outcasts who merit an opportunity. You know, I assisted Solomon in getting his job at Woodmore. I convinced the board to allow his hiring, despite his recent jail term."

"Good for you. Do you own a lime green button-down shirt? Cotton-linen blend?"

"That blend is the most comfortable."

"A man with high standards."

"Burberry Prorsum. Much of my casual attire is of that brand."

She showed him a colour photograph. "When the lab work is done, it'll show that these green fibres will be from a green cotton shirt—yours. The strands were picked off of Havers's suit and Pamela Renard's dress. You pushed both of them."

"This is all—what is the term?—circumstantial?"

"You're aware of the dating website GayChoices? I have proof that your username with that service is 'braveBoy,' and I've obtained all the posts between you and Ray Havers. They'll also be evidence at your trial."

"None of this attests that I killed Mr. Havers."

"One more thing."

She started a DVD player sitting on a rack beside the table. The grainy footage showed Flynn and Havers as they walked—arguing, gesticulating—from the banker's office, down the hallway, and out of the frame. She pressed Pause and tapped the screen with her finger. "Time stamp reads June 17, 7:49 p.m., about two hours before Havers and Renard died.

CHAPTER 56

Grafton, any jury with common sense will convict you. And the evidence keeps growing, like the analysis we're running right now on your saliva sample. That test will match your DNA to the skin we found under Pamela Renard's fingernails."

She leaned toward him and touched his shoulder. He flinched.

"So just tell me. What happened? Why'd you have to do this?"

"I have nothing to reveal."

"Fitzgerald and his ex-girlfriend told me that, during your attack on them, you confessed to the killings. To being the 'Coyote River Killer.'"

"A fairy tale. They concocted it." He touched a bruise on his forehead and winced. "Solomon beat me savagely, you know, and I have no memory of being at that apartment."

Alison sat back and shook her head.

Chapter 57

June 2007

At Sunday breakfast, in a variation on Pamela's inviting Rose the day before, Bobby asks *Pamela* if she's interested in taking a walk. She agrees, having hoped for a private moment to tell him the truth, and meets him a few minutes later at the entrance to Pilkington House. Cramming for finals, students must be nestled into their rooms or the library, because, despite fine weather, the Pilkington's vestibule and the walkway beyond it are deserted. Pamela sees her opportunity. With no words to soften the reality she's getting an abortion and wants to break up, Pamela instead dithers with a pathetic cliché: "We need to talk."

Bobby's laugh is acid. "No kidding, we do."

They walk to Taylor Green and sit on a bench by the ornamental pond. The scent of lilac fills the air, and Bobby looks south, past the student parking lot. Pamela follows his gaze, to where Sol's maintenance building lurks behind the maples along Service Lane.

"Supposed to be on a walk," Bobby says. "Not sitting around.

CHAPTER 57

So, what're we going to do? The baby."

"We'll walk soon, but not quite yet."

The tennis courts lie beyond the pond, and the slow *pock . . . pock . . .* of volleys echoes off Pilkington House. Who has time, Pamela wonders, to play tennis with exams on? Even her thoughts are a stalling tactic, because she knows Bobby won't respect her decision. Sitting rigidly on the bench, Pamela avoids his eyes.

"My abortion date is set," she says, "and I'm not changing my mind."

Bobby refuses her words. "Pretty certain I'm not going to finish Grade Twelve, at least this year, if ever. You think I can't take care of a baby, our baby, while you go to school." He smiles. "But I can. I've babysat for years. I love little kids."

Pamela chokes her impulse to tell Bobby he's insane—naïve, at best. She'll try a roundabout tactic instead. "What about touring with Burden Magic? You'll really throw all that away?"

"Lots of musicians bring their kids on the road." Bobby's still smiling, still buoyant about his fantasy of playing family.

Her veiled approach failing, Pamela changes her tone. "You're cracked!" She grips him by the shoulder. "You have to finish high school. You owe your parents—and yourself—at least that."

Bobby's brightness has faded. But he's determined to keep trying. She can see the hope in his eyes. He needs to understand that their relationship is over. "I'm off to university next year. I could be thousands of kilometres away. UBC and McGill have both accepted me, and UBC is offering me a two-year science scholarship. If I decide to go to either—"

"Long-distance relationships," Bobby says. "Lots of people

have them. But Toronto's accepted you too, right? Why not go there, stay close to your folks and Coyote River?"

"We're both so unsettled in our lives. It would be too complicated."

Bobby's pallor is a grey as limestone. "Are you saying what I *think* you're saying?"

Pamela crosses her legs and hunches. She is a fortress.

"Alright," he says, his voice cracking. "You want to be rid of me, you win."

"Bobby, please. I don't want to do any of this, but I've got to get on with my life. I'm sorry. Really."

Pamela puts her hand on Bobby's knee. He lurches away and stands up.

"Look," she says. "This weekend, can I help you with exam prep? The chemistry final's on Monday, right?"

"I don't need your charity." Along with Bobby's hard words, his stuttering on them shows the hurt beneath. "Nathan can help me."

Pamela fails to smother a laugh. "You can't be serious. Nathan's no better than you at math or chemistry. You said so yourself. If you're going to pass chemistry—and your year—you've got to do well on the final, right? Then let me help you. For starters, tonight. Meet me at the library. Our table. Seven o'clock. And bring all your chemistry stuff."

Bobby grunts dismissively. But he touches her shoulder and nods.

Chapter 58

July 2007

From Alison's dealings with Ed Loams, he seemed like a man who wasn't controlled by anger.

But he was fuming now, and his diction had changed accordingly: "You're fucking kidding, right? Did they allow this sort of thing back in Toronto?"

He sighed and ran his fingers across his skull. "Ruvinsky's helping you here and there, but you're almost solo on this case. Well, Norm Miller's due to leave hospital next week. He'll be back on the job by September, and believe me, when you work with him, you won't follow out-of-jurisdiction tangents. Not without first clearing it with me."

Pointing to his watch, he said, "Why can't you just focus on Woodmore? Do it, before any more parents call demanding we solve it and preserve the school's reputation for safety, blah blah blah." He eyed the wall calendar. "And here we are, toward mid-July."

"August first," Alison said. "No time to lose, sir."

She shifted in her seat, one of the plastic chairs in front of his desk. Comfort eluded her, but of course Alison couldn't relax, not with what she'd just asked of her boss.

Loams fingered the sagging skin under his jawline, as if he were willing it to stay taut like the bald casing of his head. "These photos from Flynn's condo may suggest a thing or two—yeah, the man may have gone to high school in Stamford—but they verify nothing. At best, we'd be doing Stamford's work for them. More likely, we'd just piss them off."

"I don't agree, but anyway, isn't that a small price to pay? To solve another murder—or several—that Flynn may have committed? Think of the victims' families."

Loams gazed at a framed photo on the wall: himself and two other fiftysomething men, holding up their day's catch, the surface of a small lake rippling behind them. "No time, no money, to go on a wild goose chase for a US jurisdiction."

"Dock my pay for the time involved."

"Forget the whole idea. Now. And get back to work. You haven't cracked Flynn yet."

"I need to liaison with Connecticut."

"It's your career," Loams said, shrugging. He gestured to the detectives' desks beyond his office. "Go ahead, but keep it on the down-low around here. And don't think you're getting a time extension because of this detour."

Chapter 59

The Kids Helpline office occupied unrented space in a north-end strip mall. Sitting at a desk, Sol felt jittery, as if he were taking a test, which he *was*, in a way.

He cleared his throat. "Kids Helpline. How can I help you?"

Over the last two weeks, he'd spent eighteen hours in training, but he still wondered if he could listen to people's burdens and reply without making things worse. He'd job-shadowed Ralph, the nose-ring guy who'd managed Helpline's booth on Canada Day. Ralph was sitting now at the next desk, in case Sol needed help. Which of course he would. Only because his workstation had a headset with a microphone, Sol could physically (if not mentally) handle the calls despite the sling that cradled his left arm. The arrow had damaged some muscle and nerves in his shoulder. A six-month recovery loomed.

With his good arm, he tapped his pen against the notepad. The time was past 9:30 p.m., and Sol had only handled two calls since eight o'clock. The first one was a teenage girl caught in the middle of a feud between two best friends. The second call was a prank by twelve-year-old boys, their voices cracking between high and low pitch as they'd guffawed. This *great way to help kids,* he thought, was going to be a waste of time. After all Sol went through to be there—his record popping up, Helpline's board denying his application, and finally Detective Downey speaking to the director for him—the work was a letdown. With air tasting of gypsum dust from the marred, unpainted walls, the office itself further lowered his spirits.

A new call, thank Jesus. The voice, a teenage girl, if Sol guessed right. He asked if she, or anyone she knew, was right now in danger.

"No. Like I guess not, but I need to talk to somebody."

"You can talk to me," Sol said and gave the spiel he'd memorized in training: that Helpline was anonymous, laidback, and focussed on pointing callers to handy community resources.

"I can't tell nobody. Don't know what to do. Well, I . . ."

Wait, he thought. Just wait, like they said in training. The voices of the other volunteers merged into a drone.

"My mother, she has this new boyfriend. Partner. Whatever. Moved in with us a month back. And he . . . does stuff to me."

"Do you want to say what kind of stuff?"

"Can't." Silence, followed by sniffling. "It ain't worth it no more. I want to kill myself. I'm *dying* to kill myself—hey, that's kind of funny."

Kids Helpline wasn't so lame anymore, and Sol's pulse sped up. "I can tell you're young, so things are hard enough already, but if someone's abusing, assaulting you—"

"Raping. That clear enough? Six feet three, a big pig. Says he'll kill me if I tell. . . . It's a sick joke, because my stupid mom thinks he's Mr. Wonderful."

The hammering in Sol's chest was reverberating, moving down into his stomach and up into his head, outward into his arms and legs, the sound ringing like church bells playing

CHAPTER 59

harmony but out of tune, turning music into a cacophony that boomed off the walls of a room with no door. He wanted to rip off the headset and cover his ears. Instead he slammed again and again the hand of his good arm on the desk.

"What was that noise?" the girl said. "Are you still there?"

Sol's voice was trapped in his chest.

Ralph tapped him hard on the shoulder. "Sol, buddy, what the . . ."

The girl's voice again: "Is anybody there?"

Sol ignored Ralph, he had to. "I'm going to help you. Just hold on for a minute."

He knew then, and accepted, that he'd never get over Danny's assaults, but the girl was young. If he could help to change her situation, the damage would stop years sooner than it did for him. Sol clicked off his microphone and turned to Ralph.

"Hey, sorry." He grabbed the sides of the desk and tried to shake it, and then, grinning, he said, "Well, it still feels pretty solid, it survived my pounding on it. I got a little excited there."

"Yes, you certainly *did*. OK, then . . ." Ralph said, his eyebrows hovering near the dusty ceiling tiles. He and the other volunteers cautiously turned away. Eventually, they returned to their own calls.

Sol switched his microphone on. "Real sorry about the wait. This is only my view—you don't have to act on it—but here goes. . . . First, *you're* the victim. No matter what you think you've done to deserve it. And second, no one, including your mother, is going to punish you if you file charges against the prick—"

"Language!" Ralph said, glaring.

"The man . . . who's been assaulting you."

"You don't know nothing."

Sol exhaled, rested his chin in his palm. "You at home right now?"

"A friend's place."

"Stay there. I've got phone numbers for the teen shelter in town and the cops." He read out the digits and waited as she wrote them down. "It's your choice, but I'd suggest you call the police and tell them what's been happening. Then stay somewhere safe—at your friend's place or the shelter."

"I don't know. . . . Maybe," the girl said, but her tone had brightened. "Got to go."

Sol took a breath and blew it out. He felt euphoria, but it was unlike his coke-fueled Superman hallucinations in high school. More like a runner's high, and he was a runner.

Ralph leaned toward him. "I was going to switch off your line. I was that scared, man."

"My life, I've had some real assholes to deal with. Call brought too much back."

"And you never told anyone here? Or on your application? People's lives are at stake in some of these calls, that's why we have the rules. Look, I won't say anything. But you can't go off the rails like that again."

Ralph is so right, Sol thought. If I was able to help that poor girl, I can help anyone—hopefully with more calm next time.

With that resolve, he answered the next call.

Chapter 60

Curled up like a frightened sow bug, Flynn covered his eyes with his hand. Ceiling lights droned, and the video cameras' LEDs glowed like green eyes.

"The longer you keep lying, the worse things will be for you," Alison said. "And I mean during your trial and at sentencing."

She was on her second coffee, although she didn't need the caffeine. She'd bounced out of bed like Marcia still did on Christmas Day. "Where did you and Ray Havers go after you left his RBC branch?"

"To a restaurant." He sniffed twice. A third time.

As he raised the back of his hand toward his nose, she slid a box of tissues across the table.

Careful not to press on his bruised cheek, he blew his nose. "Ray telephoned me. Another one of his hissy fits. He demanded a 'talk' over dinner. He had been, well, harassing me lately, although the prodding arose over a year ago. I didn't want another meltdown from him, so I obliged."

"Harassing you how?"

"Matrimony. Marriage. That was his desire."

"He put the question—proposed—to you at dinner?"

"He pirouetted around the issue. The evening was pleasant, and we have had evening drinks on Woodmore's roof garden before, so he suggested we go up there to enjoy the view as dusk came on. It was our 'special place'—at least to him. I stupidly fell for the ruse, because once we were sipping the *Romanée-Conti*, his mood turned by 180 degrees. He rolled out his hobbyhorse: 'Same-sex marriage has been legal since 2001. Why can't you see that it's OK?' Detective, I must have heard the sermon a hundred times before. I'll admit, Ray was a good man, but . . ."

"What went wrong?"

"Ray had become desperate. He was heading into his late forties, and he had thought I was going to discard him. For months, I tried to convince him otherwise, but he would not believe me. He must have thought a marriage certificate was the only way to hold onto me. I told him, again and again: 'I want *you*, not a public ceremony where I'd be ridiculed by my family.'"

"Ridiculed?"

"You wouldn't understand. . . . A couple of weeks ago, Ray told me his wife and he were beginning amicable divorce proceedings, but I had replied that that made no difference to me." Flynn wiped at his nostrils. "In any case, on the night in question, Ray stood up from his chair and shouted, 'It's now or never, ever, Graf.' I put my hand on his forearm and told him to relax, but he lashed out and my wineglass smashed on the patio stones. He ran to the roof's edge and climbed up on the parapet. When he announced he was going to leap, I tugged at his clothes to pull him back. From behind us, I heard her voice."

"Whose voice?"

"Why was she even *on* the roof then? I will never know. But, oh, the poor girl. The irony. You know, I had helped

CHAPTER 60

to establish The Two Row Exchange, and I facilitated the selection of both scholars—Woodmore's and also Coyote River's."

"Pamela Renard."

"She understood somehow that Ray was, you understand . . . like me. At any rate, she must have followed us—I don't know how—into the administration centre, because she stepped onto the patio and rushed up to us and pleaded with Ray not to jump. Something about having seen the 'old rock posters' in his basement, and that she 'understood.' I remember her naïve speech: 'It's great that gays and lesbians can get married now, but whether you and Mr. Flynn marry or not, everything will be fine. Please, come down.' But she could not comprehend the trials of being gay—to be continually swimming against the current, as it were. Always against the grain. That is why, for close to two decades, I have needed the temporary escape provided by drugs."

"Like cocaine, which you planted on Havers's body."

"I realized then: the poor girl knew about us. Knew about Ray and me. All I could think was that if my father found out, I would lose everything. You know? My job, my home . . ."

"I understand it's not easy, and homophobia isn't going away, but don't you think—well, this isn't the 1950s, or even the 1980s, is it? "

Flynn slammed his palm on the tabletop. "The beatings commenced when I was thirteen years old. My father thought he could whip the 'queer'—that was the term he always used—out of me."

"You threw them off the roof."

"I did not intend to, but I couldn't control myself. Ray went first, he yelped, vanishing below the parapet, and Pamela would not stop screaming. In any case, she knew about us." Flynn covered his face with his hands and moaned. "She knew. There was no other choice, I had to silence her."

* * *

Back from a thirty-minute break, Alison slid a photograph across the table. "Can you tell me what these are?"

Flynn had been to the washroom and seemed refreshed, calmed down from his confession to the double murder. He picked up the photo. "Arrow fletchings."

"The one on the left was taken from Fitzgerald's shoulder; the one on the right, from Rose Molloy's back."

Alison pulled another image from the case folder. "Fingerprints, taken respectively from those two arrows. All the prints are yours. That means we have enough evidence to charge you with the attempted murder of Solomon Fitzgerald and the killing of Rose Molloy. What I don't understand is . . . why? Why do any of this?"

Flynn's face crumbled. "After Pamela had been . . . I heard a different scream from below, and there, standing along the edge of Trevena Way was Rose, her mouth hanging open. Where Ray and Pamela had fallen was in shadow, you know, but the impudent little racist must have heard our struggle, approached, and discerned their bodies. She stepped back and looked up, and even from four stories above, I registered the shock in her eyes. She dropped her books and—suffice it to say—I pursued her. By the time I got down and onto Trevena Way, she was across Taylor Green. I figured she would attempt to flee by car, if she had one, so I took a shortcut to the faculty parking lot and waited."

CHAPTER 60

Alison leaned back. "Like a predator."

"Sure enough, her vehicle emerged from Brown Lane, drove past me, and turned left onto Lakeshore Drive. I followed at a safe distance."

"Tracking its prey."

Flynn wiped his bruised forehead with the back of his hand. "She drove west out of town, through Burlington, and into the countryside. Drove on and on and on. I always have a variety of sporting gear with me, and all I could think about was the hunting bow in the trunk. And that we were heading in a westerly direction."

"Toward Ewing and Coyote River."

Staring down at the table, Flynn nodded.

"The Molloy girl was running home. How convenient. You could kill her there and—with a tactless ploy about 'bows and arrows'—put the reserve under suspicion."

Flynn shrugged. "Her car traversed a bridge spanning the Coyote River, which I remembered from my trips to the reserve when we were planning the Two Row Exchange. Highway 22 soon curved, and I saw my chance. I forced her off the road and into the ditch. No alternative presented itself, because at Woodmore, she had seen the . . . victims, and she had seen me on the roof above them." With a tissue, he wiped at his eyes, one of them badly swollen. "You know, desperation fogs one's morality."

Alison snorted. "Just tell me happened next."

"The sky was clear and the moon full, so vision was not a problem. I think the poor girl was dazed from the collision, because she did not move for a minute or so. I used that interlude to open the trunk and arm myself, but before I could place an arrow in the bow, she crawled out of her vehicle.

Seeing the bow in my hands and the quiver on my shoulder, she bolted over the property fence, which ran beside the ditch. Looking to her right, she kept calling, 'Dad. Dad.' I still do not know why. The cry of a desperate child, I guess."

"She was home. You killed her on her parents' ranch."

Flynn leaned forward and rested his forehead in his hand. "I swear I did not know. I knew she lived near Coyote River, but . . . In any case, she was limping away—injured from the collision, I suppose—and I ran after her, across a field and into some woods. You know the conclusion of the story, I assume."

"Humour me."

"I did not act in cold blood," Flynn said, straightening his posture. He pulled his shoulders back, his chin up, into a regimentally rigid pose. "I am not a sociopath."

"How about psychopath?"

"I am simply a wounded man."

"And your personal troubles justify killing three innocent people?"

* * *

The Stamford lead lay waiting—demanding—to be explored. Again Alison interrupted the interview with Flynn and returned to her desk.

She felt like a telemarketer when she cold-called the Connecticut city's police, but her chutzpah paid off, because the force's captain of Criminal Investigations was interested in some Canuck cold-case help. They agreed. After receiving and decrypting Flynn's fingerprint files from Halton Region, Stamford would do a search for them against its unsolved murders.

Four hours later, Alison received an email from Stamford's Crimes Against Persons division. From the prints she'd emailed, the branch ran the test and found convincing likenesses with fingerprints from a 1998 unsolved murder, and a detective would follow up with her. She got up from her desk and walked toward the centre of Homicide's work space. About to jump in the air and hoot, she remembered Loams's warning. *Keep it on the down-low.* So she kept quiet. She also stayed away from Loams's office, though she hungered to lean into his doorway and say, *Case is virtually wrapped up, Ed*.

* * *

As the guard clanked the bars shut behind Alison, Flynn looked up from his seat on the holding cell's bench. "Again? What more information could you possibly need?" He touched his swollen cheek and winced. "You have my confession."

Shifting her weight from one leg to the other, Alison took out her notebook. "Ever heard of, or known, a woman named Claire Bonham?"

"Not that I recall. No."

"Sure of that? She was an American, from Stamford, Connecticut."

Twitching, Flynn averted his eyes and played with his hair, then fidgeted with a sleeve of his jumpsuit. Alison wondered if he'd be any calmer without the cocaine withdrawal, but his mental state didn't matter now, because, about the Bonham murder, Alison knew that he knew that she knew.

"Stamford is my hometown, yes, but Claire . . . Bonham,

is it? Hmm, it's vaguely familiar perhaps, but I'm really not sure."

"That's strange, because you killed her in 1998."

"You know, I do not feel well at all."

"I've been in touch with the Stamford Police Department, and they just matched your fingerprints to some lifted—a decade ago—from the Claire Bonham murder scene."

"That is a nonsensical statement," Flynn said. "Now I've considered it, though, there may have been a *Claire* in one of my Stamford English classes."

"You didn't know her?"

"Possibly we were in the same tutorial group together." Still fidgeting, Flynn's torso and arms and neck bent inward and he looked blankly at the tabletop. "But there is nothing more about her that I can recall."

Alison said nothing, merely crossed her arms in front of her. After a moment, Flynn looked up and she stared back. And waited.

"Claire," Flynn said, wiping his eyes, as though his emotional show excused his outright lying. "She was my 'girlfriend' during my last year at the University of Connecticut, when I was still trying to convince myself I was heterosexual. We studied together, went to a few dances and movies. I enjoyed her company, and the odd innocent kiss didn't bother me. I told her I didn't want to rush the relationship's development.

"But one evening, she discovered me . . . necking with a boy, in some shrubbery on campus. Poor Claire. She became entangled with the wrong fellow. She didn't get angry or laugh at me, as my father had. And, dear God, once she knew, she wanted me to come out. Silly girl. I couldn't trust her—as I couldn't trust Ray, or Pamela, or Rose—to keep a

CHAPTER 60

secret as dangerous as mine. Word would have spread all over Stamford. 'Graf Flynn. Star athlete and big faggot.'

"I graduated two months after the unfortunate incident with Claire. A string of—"

"You mean after you strangled her."

Flynn jerked and slid his arms across his chest like deadbolts. "A series of rapes had occurred on campus at the time. You know, the police talked to me about Claire, but they caught the campus rapist soon afterwards. They must have subsumed Claire's death under his deeds—I don't really know, frankly. I was a good student and got a scholarship to do an MA in English at UCLA. I 'jumped at the chance,' as the cliché goes, to travel to the other side of the country, get away from my father, and lie low."

"'Must have subsumed Claire's death,'" Alison said. "That's a good one. You mean the cops thought the rapist killed her, so *you* evaded justice. Is that your backhanded confession, Grafton?"

Flynn turned in his chair and yanked up his shirttail to reveal his bare back. Alison gasped at the scars, crosshatched like the pen strokes in Marcia's ink drawings.

"My father's method of behaviour modification," Flynn said. "It failed me, as I failed him."

Chapter 61

"I'm in big trouble with my mother," Bobby said.

Sol sipped coffee from a chipped mug. "About?"

"The tour. She hates the idea."

Sol already knew about the plan: Burden Magic's drummer drove an ancient Volkswagen van, and among the band's four members, they'd scrounged enough cash for a one-month tour of bars around the GTA and southwestern Ontario. They'd even gotten a spot in a small rock festival in Kitchener. But for Bobby, the support his mother usually gave him dropped to *pianissimo* when she'd heard about the tour.

Sol was sitting with the kid in a strip-mall coffee shop near Miroslav's apartment, their table bolted to the linoleum. They'd started an evening walk but, because of a gusty north wind, went into the café to warm up.

His eyes unfocussed, Bobby looked out the window. Silence for a couple of seconds. "I don't know what to do about my mother. She says she supports my music, but she freaks out about touring with the band."

"Speaking of music . . . At your folks' house, who collected the classical records?"

"Touring. That's what bands do to make money, especially now with all the illegal downloading. So what's her problem?"

CHAPTER 61

"I remember the living-room shelves, and a couple of them are full of classical CDs."

"Yes, but so what?"

"They belong to your father?"

Bobby nodded.

"He left us a clue. Couple of them."

"Like what?"

Not able to sleep one night last week, Sol had realized the link: Ray Havers collected records and posters of gay musicians—classical and pop. The albums included Schubert and Tchaikovsky, two composers that cousin Danny had raved about: *See? They loved men, so it's OK, Sol.* In Ray's basement, the posters were of Elton John and Freddie Mercury and George Michael—gay pioneers in 70s and 80s pop rock. Sol wished he'd figured it out earlier. But, before the clue from GayChoices.com surfaced, he couldn't have known.

"I shouldn't have eaten that doughnut," Bobby said, his eyelids drooping. "Let's get out of here."

"Your father's records . . ."

"Come on, I need that walk. Cold air will wake me up."

Sol zipped up his jacket against the wind and followed Bobby out of the coffee shop. He decided to bury the overlooked musical hints. Exposing them would be cruel. Why should Bobby, every time he looked at his father's CDs or posters, be reminded of Ray's murder?

Chapter 62

With a deadpan look at Alison, Loams said, "Congratulations, you get to keep your job."

Sitting in front of his desk, she stared at the floor.

"To be frank, I only set the deadline to see if you'd crack and prove, once and for all, you're a liability."

"When is Norm Miller back to work? What kind of partner can I expect?"

"You didn't go to the union, and you didn't break. First-rate detective, if a little headstrong, and that's not always a bad thing. But one more stunt like searching—without an ounce of reasonable grounds—drivers for drugs. . . . Michael White is still pissed off." Loams shook his head. "I can't cover your ass like this again."

"Is Norm a real rock-climbing geek? Weekend warrior like you, I bet." Alison pointed to a framed photo of Loams fishing from a speedboat.

"I don't understand. Why'd you search White when you pulled him over for speeding?"

She lowered her head and again scrutinized the carpet.

"Don't fret," Loams said. "Let's call it a rhetorical question."

He got up, opened the office door, and led her to the centre of Homicide's floor space. Loams must have emailed everyone

CHAPTER 62

except her about a pending announcement, because the staff gathered around the two of them. He then commended Alison on solving not one case but three.

Though heat crept up her neck and face, she silently cheered the cracks showing in the Wall of Silence. Perhaps someday it would collapse.

* * *

After Ruvinsky's wife succumbed to her disease, he was off for a fortnight, then a further week passed with everyone at Regional Investigative Services tiptoeing around him. Nobody knew what to say other than platitudes. Late one afternoon, as Alison was approaching her car in 21 Division's parking lot, Ruvinsky scurried toward her. Chilly gusts shoved the clouds. In his rush, he hadn't buttoned his overcoat, and it flailed behind him.

"Hey, great work on Woodmore," he said.

"Thanks. I'm late for an appointment."

"Sorry I was kinda icy when you'd transferred here from Toronto. Dealing with my wife's cancer was . . . I thought I was a strong son of a bitch. I'm not. Took it out on everybody in Homicide, especially you."

"Pas de problèm." She grabbed the car's door handle.

"Huh?"

"French for 'no problem.'"

"Ooh, fancy!" Ruvinsky said, but his smile was genuine.

* * *

Alison stood at the edge of a limestone cliff. She looked down,

down, and remembered her first time on the library roof, seeing the scrap of cotton printed in a poppy design, a girl with a ripped dress and smashed skull lying four storeys below.

. . .

"Oi, daredevil," Tamara said. "Don't be daft." She grunted as she laid her backpack on the ground, a carpet of red and yellow maple leaves. "Right, so you've met three wankers through eMatch—shite luck, yes. But don't give up so easily."

"How long is this hike?" Alison said. "Either I'm really out of shape or you hiking geeks are marathon racers." She wiped her brow. "'Mount' Nemo—ha. But it *is* quite a climb."

Following Tamara, she sat down on the leaves and waved for the others to go ahead. She braced herself with outstretched arms and leaned back. Cold against her palms. Fall had come early: the nights were cold for mid-September, and the tang of organic decay spiced the air.

"About eMatch," she said, "I'll keep paying my membership, but I'm staying clear of it for now. Too much time sitting on my rear in front of a computer screen."

Oak and maple leaves swirling around them, Tamara frowned. "You have to give the poor fellows a chance."

Poor fellows. Alison thought of Ray Havers and Flynn, and pitied the latter despite his brutal selfishness. If Flynn had grown up in a different family, with a different sort of father, he may never have destroyed five lives. Including his own.

Alison's mind returned to her own search for love. "The Halton Outdoor Group," she said. "Way less pressure than eMatch. And, assuming that climate change doesn't kill our winters, I'm looking forward to the cross-country skiing trips." Unlike on her eMatch dates, she wore no makeup today. If Alison's wrinkly-eyed face showed her age, at least

CHAPTER 62

she was telling the truth, not propping up a façade.

A north breeze cooled her sweaty T-shirt and Alison shivered.

Tamara gestured for them to get up. They joined the rest of the group at the lookout. Before the indigo horizon of Lake Ontario, Burlington's downtown ran along the shore, and suburbs spread like outstretched fingers into the countryside.

Tamara inhaled, lifting her face toward the sky. Strawberry blond hair flashed in the sunlight. "What a gorgeous view. I usually have to be rat-arsed to feel this good."

"Charming," Alison said.

But she was smiling. Oakville's rooftops, huddled along the sweep of Lake Ontario, glinted to the east. And somewhere in town, Marcia was out with her friends, perhaps painting a related subject, the lake reflecting quiet clouds.

Chapter 63

Rush hour in downtown Toronto, and the passengers crammed against each other amid a smell like the slop Sol had eaten in Maplehurst Correctional Centre. The bus, its windows fogged against the evening chill, crawled east along Bloor Street. He fingered the crimson medallion in his pocket. Weeks ago at AA he'd gotten the chip, a One Month Token. The colour of the anodized aluminum was supposed to show how hard it was staying sober, even for thirty days, but it made him think only of blood, the blood caked in Pamela's hair and splashed over the quadrangle's flagstones. Sol wondered how he could have prevented her death. Instead, he'd done the opposite. If he hadn't hardened her backbone to call out Rose's slurs, to mock them as nasty and vile, Pamela might have left Woodmore by last October and so never have met Ray Havers. But thinking about might-have-beens, he realized, accomplished nothing. He groaned, idly flipping his scarlet medal in the air.

Besides his getting the token, a lot had happened since the night he punched out Grafton Flynn. Detective Downey had thanked him, even said Sol would make a good cop. *If* he could learn to control his anger. Like that was ever going to happen. But the more kids he aided through Helpline, the

CHAPTER 63

better he felt.

On the other hand, a recent change was bugging him. When he'd told Miroslav he was moving out of the apartment, the guy had acted like a jilted lover. The move wasn't a matter of choice. Sol liked Miroslav's cooking, and splitting the rent was practical, but he felt he was mooching. Anyway, they both needed to move on, get a life. Growing old with an even older bachelor, that would be pathetic. He stopped fiddling with the one-month chip and pulled the bell cord for Saint George Street.

As the bus doors opened, chilly air hit Sol's nostrils, and he pulled up his collar. He didn't mind. The early cold snap gave him a jolt like caffeine, which he would need to stay extra alert; he jogged south toward the lecture hall. He felt less intimidated taking the course this time, with Minister Frey guiding and critiquing him through the written assignments. Tash had also phoned and offered to help with essay writing. Sol refused.

* * *

A couple of weeks later, at Tash's invitation, he met her for lunch. They talked about trivia. Sol couldn't read her eyes. When they said goodbye, she touched his arm.

Chapter 64

June 2007

Three taps on the dorm-room door.

"Anybody there?" It's Rose's voice, a gravelly whisper. She knocks again.

Pamela turns from her desk to the clock by her bed. Ten minutes to noon. Amy just left for the library, so, after listening for any other voices in the corridor, Pamela opens the door. Facing Rose, she worries, not for the first time, that the girl's assault and suffering have blurred her own judgement in offering kindness and accepting a tentative, if secret, friendship. Has Rose really changed? The racial slurs, the stereotyping, the defacement of the dorm-room door, which Rose is now standing before, are unforgettable.

"Hi, Rose," she says, and the girl nods.

How, Pamela asks herself, can I be friends with this person? But the redhead isn't last fall's prejudiced bully. In words and actions—whether during their chat in Rose's room or the clandestine walk to the shoreline—Rose does seem genuinely different, changed, and not only because of her Halloween-night trauma.

"Mind if I . . ." Rose says, gesturing to the foot of the bed.

"Go ahead."

Lilac wafts through the window, and Rose's colour looks improved, her posture more erect. She sits and, from behind her back, produces a greeting-card sized Two Row Wampum. Quality craftwork. Purple bead-rows glowing on a background of white.

Pamela shakes her head. "When—where did you get that?"

"Oh, years and years ago," Rose says, waving casually. "Alice, a friend of mine from Coyote River, gave it to me for my tenth birthday and—"

Like the shrill chirps of robins beyond the window, Pamela's laugh startles Rose. "You can't be serious."

"Dead serious. Alice and I—we were best buddies as kids, but ever since Dad shoved me into Woodmore, I haven't seen her much, maybe once or twice a summer—to watch a DVD with a bunch of other kids, or at the Coyote River Pow-wow."

"Oh, wait a second. This is a project for theatre arts. You're acting, right?"

"Then, this year, after the blockades went up, I started getting nasty Facebook posts, threatening ones. Posts from my 'friend' Alice."

Pamela hoots again. "Come on, you're acting!"

"But you know what?" Rose fingers the wampum belt. "These little beads still bring back good memories. Playing, exploring from morning till dusk, with Alice on the rez." She paused, a dreamy look in her eyes. "I almost threw this thing out when her brutal Facebook posts started. But I couldn't do it."

Rose sighs, then gets up from the bed. When she's opened

the door, Rose hesitates, spins back to Pamela and extends the wampum. "In a few days, we're all leaving this school forever. I've decided to head to Nova Scotia—theatre at Dalhousie—and you're off to, where is it? I'll probably never see you again. So, here, keep this." She grins. "Something to help you remember your best enemy."

* * *

After dinner, Pamela speed walks toward Woodmore Library, because tonight she needs time to tutor her ex. *Oh, Creator*, she thinks, *keep Bobby from flunking the chemistry final*. She's unsure whether her prayer is glib or sincere.

Whether Bobby passes the course or not, Pamela hopes he and his father develop a better, more respectful, relationship. But she won't prompt the change. Courting trouble is what Pamela must avoid, because she and Bobby have almost straightened out their mess. Once she has the abortion and leaves Oakville, the baby crisis will disappear. Not, according to Mrs. Havers's experience and Pamela's heart, that that will ever really be true.

She wonders if she'll be able to keep the secret from her family, especially Grandma Becky. But whether she does so or not, Pamela's elated knowing she'll spend the summer in her community. A tutoring job at Coyote River High's summer school awaits her. Tutoring. That's a welcome contrast to her summer jobs as a Public Works traffic signaller, and thinking of roads reminds her that blockades are still up at the Peaceful Meadows site. She wonders if she'll spot Rose there among other Ewing people. If that happens, they can wave to—or simply wink at—each other and hope no one notices.

CHAPTER 64

But now only the library looms. In the waning sunlight, its limestone glows peach against a pearl-blue sky, the day's heat fading, the traffic on Lakeshore Road calming, like the Coyote River's flow on a quiet evening. Compared to when this year began, the building's walls look smaller, less dangerous.

Author's Note

The ideas for this story came to me in 2011. I wanted to write a mystery novel, and I wanted it to reflect something of contemporary Canada. So, one of my concepts came from the Grand River land dispute (aka the Caledonia land dispute), a flare-up of which occurred in 2006–2007. Happening about 100 kilometres southwest of Toronto, the clash made headlines around the world.

In 2006, when I heard news coverage of the conflict, I didn't know how to interpret it. And I realized I knew nothing about Six Nations of the Grand River, the most populous First Nations reserve in the country—and only an hour's drive from my hometown. How many other white Canadians were similarly lacking in knowledge? I wondered. And could I fictionalize the land clash—a piece of the current Canadian scene—as part of a crime novel?

Recognizing my ignorance drove me to do some historical research about Six Nations. And two real bits of history appear in this book: the Two Row Wampum Treaty of 1613 and the Haldimand Proclamation of 1784. However, although the text echoes the Caledonia flare-up's years, 2006 and 2007, I've fictionalized both the land clash and the quarrelling groups—in name and substance. My aim was not to play journalist. Instead, I wanted to explore, as a storyteller, the challenges people in a similar situation might face.

Acknowledgements

Four sources provided key information in my research. First, thanks goes to Haudenosaunee elder Tom Porter and Invert Media, accessed at fourdirectionsteachings.com, for teachings about Mohawk numbers, culture, and religion—specifically Sky-Woman and her daughter's Twins, the matrilineal clan system, and the sun's light being "the hands and arms of the Creator."

Second, for the Mohawk numbers appearing in this book, thank you, Native Languages of the Americas, a non-profit organization in Minneapolis, Minnesota, accessed at www.native-languages.org/mohawk_words.htm.

Third, for permission to excerpt from the article "Mohawks, Guns, and Tobacco" by William Marsden (April 28, 2009), thanks to the Montreal Gazette, and specifically to Cheryl Minnis, Licensing Associate.

Fourth, the burial scene was a challenge, as I've never been to a Mohawk funeral service. From my own experience, though, I know that culturally mixed families often create a synthesis—of the old and the new, of one culture and the other—for memorial services. Aware of this reality, I drew creatively from two sources: "Death Rituals Among the Mohawk People," by Doug George-Kanentiio (https://www.indianz.com/News/2015/04/16/doug-georgekanentiio-death-rit-asp); and "Witness to a Native American Funeral," by Gail

Rubin, 3 April 2011 (https://agoodgoodbye.com/memorable-life-celebrations/witness-to-a-native-american-funeral).

To my manuscript readers, thank you for your time and thoughts. In rough sequential order, you are: Mary Anne Jacuzzi, Carol Campagnaro, Patrick Harkins, Ivano Stocco, Shaun Hedican, Jeanine Holland, Pamela Young, Kasia Jaronczyk, David Switzer, Jay Thornton, Luke Hill. Special thanks goes to novelist Adam Lindsay Honsinger and his partner Rain Bone. Your detailed critiques were invaluable.

Ashley Strosnider, my copy-editor (and currently Managing Editor of *Prairie Schooner*), deserves recognition for solid work. Beyond the limits of her contract, Ashley was able to catch small plot-holes that had escaped my awareness.

Finally, to my wife Jeanine, I owe a huge debt for supporting me through the years of writing this novel. Without her understanding, this book wouldn't exist.

About the Author

R. B. Young is a writer, visual artist, and author of the novel *Crimes of Disrespect*. He has published short stories in literary journals including *Postscripts to Darkness*, *Other Voices*, and *Great Lakes Review*. In 2017, the editors of the book *Polish(ed): Poland Rooted in Canadian Fiction* (Guernica Editions) included his short story "Paper Icon." He has worked as an architect, urban planner, and web designer. But he gave all that up to become a (very bad) amateur blues guitarist in Kingston, Ontario. His website is rbyoung.ca.

You can connect with me on:
- https://www.rbyoung.ca
- https://twitter.com/RBYoung6
- https://www.facebook.com/youngfiction

Subscribe to my newsletter:
- https://www.rbyoung.ca/get-newsletter.html

www.ingramcontent.com/pod-product-compliance
Lightning Source LLC
LaVergne TN
LVHW041619060526
838200LV00040B/1350